A Bitter Silence

Tony Packer, Volume 3

JT Viner

Published by HSB Publishing, 2024.

This is a work of fiction. Similarities to real people, places, or events are entirely coincidental.

A BITTER SILENCE

First edition. June 29, 2024.

Copyright © 2024 JT Viner.

Written by JT Viner.

Table of Contents

A Bitter Silence (Tony Packer, #3) 1
Chapter 1 2
Chapter 2 6
Chapter 3 15
Chapter 4 22
Chapter 5 29
Chapter 6 35
Chapter 7 40
Chapter 8 47
Chapter 9 54
Chapter 10 64
Chapter 11 70
Chapter 12 75
Chapter 13 82
Chapter 14 88
Chapter 15 94
Chapter 16 101
Chapter 17 108
Chapter 18 113
Chapter 19 122
Chapter 20 128
Chapter 21 135
Chapter 22 141
Chapter 23 148
Chapter 24 155
Chapter 25 163
Chapter 26 171
Chapter 27 179
Chapter 28 185
Chapter 29 191
Chapter 30 198
Chapter 31 204
Chapter 32 209

Chapter 33 214
Chapter 34 221
Chapter 35 226
Chapter 36 233
Chapter 37 239

ALSO AVAILABLE FROM JT VINER
A Bad Place Alone
An Absence So Cruel

To join my mailing list and receive news on work-in-progress and new releases, please e-mail me at james.viner.author@gmail.com. I will never provide your e-mail address to any third party.

Chapter 1

The twin glass doors at the front slid open with a faint whine, and a blast of cold air from outside hit Kasey. The dress was tight and rode high up on her naked thighs, with nothing but thin straps over her shoulders to hold the top up. It offered no protection from the chill at all.

But despite the cold outside, she wanted to be away from the hotel now that it was done.

She walked out onto the wide concrete steps at the front of the building which led down to the narrow space for cars. The large potted plants on either side offered little shelter from the cold.

The rain was much stronger now, and the wind from the Swan River was blowing it hard against her, making the chill even worse.

Kasey shivered fiercely, wishing that she had had the sense to bring a jacket.

She stood at the bottom of the steps, looking out into the night and knowing she would be soaked as soon as she stepped out into the downpour.

She felt him behind her.

He stepped down onto the ground beside her and put his hand on the small of her back.

She leaned against him, feeling the odd mixture of emotions that she always felt when he touched her.

"It's cold out here," he said, "Shall I call you a cab?"

Kasey turned to him and smiled, shaking her head.

"I'm fine," she said, "Don't worry about me."

For a moment, she thought he might insist, but he simply nodded instead.

She felt vaguely disappointed by this.

"God," he said, looking out into the rain, "It's really coming down."

"Where are you parked?" she asked.

"In a carpark up near the mall. At least it's underground. Still, it's going to be a fair hike to get there."

Kasey nodded. She always found the small talk afterwards awkward. She knew he did, too, and wondered why they had to do this every time.

He looked at her for a moment longer, a slight smile playing on his lips. "This was wonderful," he told her, "You were wonderful."

She smiled. "It was very good."

He let out a slow sigh. "But over much too soon."

He looked away from her and back out into the rain. It was starting to pick up, now, the wind blowing the freezing cold rain under the roof with a low hiss.

"Well," he said, "we'd better go before it gets any worse."

Kasey nodded. "Yeah. We should."

He leaned towards her, then stopped and glanced back towards the doors.

He put his hand on her upper arm and began to gently move her out of sight of the doors and towards one of the large stone pillars. His hand felt warm on her naked flesh, just like it had earlier.

He stopped at the end of the narrow space between the pillars. They were out of sight now, but were now so close to the outside that the wind and the rain were blowing against them much harder.

Turning Kasey to face him, he leaned down and kissed her. As she pushed against his chest, he held her upper arms in both hands, pulling her against him.

Again, she felt the odd mixture of emotions. Part of her never wanted the kiss to end; the other part of her couldn't get away from him fast enough.

Finally, after a long moment, he broke the kiss and let go of her.

The wind was pushing drops of rain against his face and he was squinting because of it.

"Right," he said, "I'd better go. I'll call you."

Kasey nodded. "Goodbye."

He gave her a last smile and then stepped out into the rain.

Out of the protection of the building, the wind immediately began to tear at his back, whipping his clothes forward as he hurried away. The pale grey material of his shirt instantly darkened as the rain saturated it.

Kasey stood there a moment longer, watching him disappear into the gloom.

She waited a few minutes more, trying to find the courage to leave, too. Looking around, she could see the spire of the Bell Tower twenty metres away and the wide expanse of paved ground leading away to the river. Riverside Drive continued on past the park, its bitumen slick with water that glistened beneath the streetlights.

She had left her car at the Convention Centre, which was a few blocks past the train station. At the time, the weather had looked gloomy, but she had decided to chance it. Since then, it had begun to pour and she cursed the decision to park there.

Kasey checked the zip on her handbag was closed and pulled it tighter against her side.

Knowing that she could not put it off any longer, she put her head down and hurried out into the rain.

The downpour hit her like a physical slap, icy-cold rain splattering over the naked skin of her arms and splashing up over her ankles.

Shivering in the cold, Kasey began to move hurriedly along the footpath.

She had worn the stiletto heels for him, knowing how much he enjoyed them. He had enjoyed them so much that he had told her to leave them on in bed.

But they were difficult to hurry in, and she was scared she might slip over on the wet concrete. She thought briefly about taking them off, but they had a high strap that did up around her ankles with two buckles on each foot. If she'd thought ahead, she would have taken them off before leaving the shelter of the overhanging roof, but it was too late now.

With the rain hammering against her back, Kasey rushed along the footpath, halfway between a walk and a run.

She shivered in the cold and gave a low groan.

When she reached The Esplanade, she turned the corner into the road across from the officer towers and the old building on the corner. The edge of the building beside her hung over the footpath here, giving her the slightest respite from the rain, and she paused. But the wind was still pushing it hard against her, and she would have to cross the road up ahead.

She could see the lights of the train station in the distance, offering a brief sanctuary.

There was little traffic at this time of night, but the occasional headlight flashed through the gloom. With the rain battering against her, she had her eyes squeezed shut and her face down, thin arms wrapped around her chest in a hopeless attempt to protect herself.

Lights behind her lit up the ground in front of her, her shadow suddenly expanding in the split second it took for the car to reach her.

She barely had time to gasp in surprise.

The car smashed into the back of her knees, her legs collapsing beneath her. She was dragged under the car and along the footpath.

There was a moment of indescribable pain, as the skin was flayed from her face.

One of her knees shattered beneath the car's wheel.

She tried to scream, but her breath was gone.

She was pressed flat to the ground, the engine screaming against her head.

Then, mercifully, the darkness took her.

<u>Sunday</u>

Chapter 2

The umbrella was useless.

The wind pushing the rain along Barrack Street from the river was so strong that the rain was almost horizontal. No matter how Packer angled the umbrella, it provided only the slightest amount of protection for his face and nothing at all for the rest of his body.

It was only a five-minute walk from his apartment, but the rain increased without warning on the way, and he was soaked through by the time he got there.

As he crossed the space behind the Supreme Court building, he could see the flashing lights casting a blue glow over the road in the darkness.

There was a patrol car parked across one end of the street and a uniformed officer in a black rain coat standing beside it with a torch to stop any car that might come past.

As Packer got closer, he could see a second police car at the other end of the street, doing the same.

Part way along the footpath, there was a small group of shadowy figures standing around in a group, torch beams pointing at the ground.

Packer crossed the road and walked closer to the patrol car.

The officer in the raincoat stepped towards him.

"Okay, mate," the officer said, "There's been an incident here, so the road's been closed off. You'll have to go around."

Packer was forced to put the umbrella down, as he fished in his pocket for his wallet. The rain battered against his face.

"Senior Sergeant Packer," he said, holding up his ID for the officer.

The officer lifted his torch up and shone it at the ID, so he could check it.

"Sorry, Sarge," he said, "Didn't know."

He looked past Packer along the street.

"Did you walk here?" he asked, frowning.

"I live nearby," Packer said.

"Even so, it's pissing down out here."

"You're wasted in a uniform, you know that?"

6

Packer walked past the car over towards the footpath as the uniformed officer muttered something under his breath.

As he got closer to the huddled group, he could see that there was an overhanging roof from the building behind them. The rain was still being blown in by the harsh wind behind it, but the area where the group was standing was sheltered from the worst of it. That was something at least.

One of the group turned as Packer drew closer and lifted his torch, shining it on Packer.

Packer raised one hand and held it out in front of his face to ward off the glare.

"It's alright," he heard Claire Perry say, "It's my sarge."

The torch was lowered back down to the ground.

Two uniformed officers holding torches were standing a couple of metres apart. Detective Senior Constable Perry was standing next to one of them.

Between them on the ground was the shape of a woman's body. There was street lighting here, but the closest was at the corner twenty or thirty metres away and its light was dulled by the heavily-falling rain.

"Hi, boss," Perry said, as Packer drew closer.

"Geez, Sarge," said one of the uniforms, "You look bloody soaked."

"Are you related to that prick standing over there?"

"What?"

"Doesn't matter."

He looked between the two uniformed officers. "Alright. What's the story?"

"Hit and run," one of them said, "There was a '000' call at 3:45am and we were called to respond. Got here five minutes later. When we got here, there was a guy here who saw it. He reckons it was deliberate."

"Why?"

"Says he heard the car accelerating before the impact, then took off again."

"Where is he, this witness?"

"We put him in the pack of the patrol car," the officer said.

The two officers exchanged glances.

Packer let it go for now.

He stuck his hand out towards one of them.

"Can I have your torch?"

"Yeah, sure," the officer said, holding it out, "It's pretty ugly, though."

Packer didn't reply, but took the torch. Shifting it in his grip, he held the powerful beam over the woman on the ground.

She was wearing a skimpy dress that left her shoulders and legs completely uncovered. The back had torn down, leaving her bare skin exposed and showing a dark-coloured mark running down across her shoulder blade. The bottom had ridden up, revealing a naked buttock with the narrow thread of a G-string concealing nothing. Her arms were splayed out at awkward angles. Her right leg was clearly broken, the thigh twisted at an angle and knee shattered. The nub of a broken bone pushed up below the skin. Blood pooled around her face and chest.

Packer moved the torch beam across the ground near the body.

About ten metres away, he could see the marks left from tyres that had tracked mud up off the street and onto the paving stones. From the edge of the tyre marks, a red trail of blood was scraped along the ground, finishing at the body about five metres away.

She had been dragged along the ground underneath the front of the car.

It was lucky she was lying on her back, because her front must have been a mess.

"Do we know who she is?" Packer asked.

"Nuh," said one of the uniforms, "No handbag and nothing on her body."

Packer looked up at him.

"Did one of you walk on the ground near her?" Packer asked, looking over at the two uniforms.

One of them glanced quickly at the other, then down at the ground.

"Had to check if she was dead," he mumbled.

"Seriously?" Packer asked, "Look at her."

He breathed out hard.

Given the rain, forensics probably wouldn't have gotten anything anyway, but it was still sloppy policing.

Stepping cautiously across the ground and careful not to get any closer than a metre from the body, he squatted down, holding the torch beam in front.

This close, the dark marks across her back were easier to identify.

They were tyre marks.

"Jesus," Packer said.

"I know," Perry said from behind him, "Poor girl. They continue over this way."

Packer shone the torch across the bloody path along the ground.

"She was dragged along," Perry said, "There's a trail of blood running from the point where the car impacted with her."

Packer followed them with the torch.

Something struck him.

"Look at the direction the marks in the blood are running," he said, holding the torch on them, "Same direction as the footpath."

Packer shone the torch beam on the back of the dead woman again.

"Now look at the direction of the tyre marks across her back," he said.

There was a moment of silence.

"So?" One of the uniforms asked, eventually.

"They're going the wrong way," the other uniform said, working it out.

Packer nodded. "Yeah. The driver hit her and left her, then ran over her again to finish her off."

There was a low grunt of disgust from Perry and the first uniformed officer swore.

"I think we can rule out accident," Packer said.

He moved the torch beam over the body once more.

Something on the left arm caught his eye. There was a mark there, but he couldn't quite make out what it was.

He stood up and moved around the body, then knelt down on the other side, with the building at his back.

Holding the torch beam down at a lower angle, he leaned forward.

The woman had a tattoo on her arm. A flower outlined in dark blue ink, with the petals filled in with yellow and red highlights. It was quite tasteful, as far as these things went.

"Fairly distinctive tattoo on her arm," Packer said, "Should help us ID her."

He stood back up and moved away from the body again.

Following the bloody smear along the ground, he walked over to the tyre marks. He couldn't see a clear print anywhere and the rain had washed over a lot of it. Forensics might still get something they could match, though.

Packer followed the tyre marks back to the road. All the way along the street were steel posts to prevent cars from parking on the footpath, spaced about twenty metres apart.

The tyre marks faced in from the road at a sharp angle.

"What is it?" Perry asked.

"It's up on the footpath inside the bollard. The driver would have had to turn straight in towards the wall to hit her."

"So, he was aiming at her?"

Packer nodded.

"Bastard," Perry hissed.

Packer straightened up and looked around.

On one side the road was the Supreme Court and the surrounding gardens, completely black apart from a couple of security lights across the front of the building.

On either side of the road where they were standing were office buildings. The lights were all out in the offices and the windows were black.

"Are there any nightclubs or anything at this end of town?" Packer asked.

Perry looked around as she thought about it, then shook her head.

"I think there used to be a couple of places up past the mall, but that was a few years ago. Nothing down here now."

"What was she doing down here, then?"

"Heading for the train station, maybe. Elizabeth Quay's closer, though. Don't know why she'd walk all the way down here instead."

Packer looked along the darkened street a moment longer.

"Have you spoken to the witness?" he asked.

Perry gave a wry smile. "I tried. He wanted to wait for you."

Packer frowned. "Why?"

"You'll find out when you meet him."

Packer followed Perry along the footpath under the slight shelter of the overhanging roof towards the patrol car with its flashing blue light on top.

There were a couple of metres between the footpath and the car, meaning they had to duck through the rain to get there. Packer was already soaked, but Perry was still relatively dry and muttered about getting wet.

As Packer got closer to the patrol car, he could see a darkened shape in the back leaning up close to the glass window looking out at him.

Packer put his hand on the back door handle and pulled it open.

The smell was so strong it made Packer recoil. Stale sweat tinged with alcohol and the unmistakeable stench of urine.

Packer pulled back slightly and grimaced, but the occupant inside the car didn't seem to notice. He leaned forward out of the car towards Packer.

His head was bald on top but lank, greasy hair hung down to his shoulders at the sides. Loose skin hung down on either side of a toothless mouth and there seemed to be dried food around his chin. He was wearing four or five shirts over the top of each other, the collars all equally sweat-stained, and bright red rubber boots.

"Are you the Chief Inspector?" demanded the man in the back, his high-pitched shrill voice carrying some kind of European accent.

"What?" Packer said, recoiling slightly at the smell of the man's breath.

"Are you the Chief Inspector? I'm not talking to any more frigging monkeys. I want the organ grinder. Don't give me any more bloody monkeys."

"I'm Detective Senior Sergeant Packer. What's your name?"

"Sergeant? Another bloody monkey! Get me the Chief Inspector."

The man in the car reached for the door handle and tried to pull the door shut, but Packer put his hand on the edge of the window frame and held it open.

The man glared at him and tried to pull the door shut again.

"Okay, look," Packer said, "I'm sure you've seen this stuff on TV, but we don't have Chief Inspectors in Australia. I'm a Senior Sergeant. I'll be running this investigation if we decide it's a murder."

"If you decide it's a murder?" the man shouted, "Of course it's a bloody murder! I saw that evil devil run that poor girl down. Deliberate it was! What else do you call that if it's not a bloody murder? Hmm. Tell me that!"

Spittle was flying out of the man's mouth as he shouted, and Packer leaned back to avoid any of it landing on him.

"It would probably help us decide if you told us what you saw," Packer said, trying to remain patient, "but I'll need some details first. Let's start with your name."

"Why do you need my bloody name?"

"It's standard procedure," Packer said, "Like on TV."

The man stared at him for a moment with wild eyes, considering this.

"Right, well," he said, eventually, "I suppose there's no harm in it. Dominic Brakovich is my name."

Perry had her notebook out and was holding it against her lower chest, as she leaned over to protect it from the rain. Dominic Brakovich leaned forward out of the car towards her.

"That's spelled D-O-M-I-N-I-C B-R-A-K-O-V-I-C-H," he yelled.

"Right, Mr Brakovich," Packer said, "Let's start with the basics. What were you doing down here?"

"Me? I thought you were asking about that poor, little girl that got murdered."

"I am asking about her," Packer said, "but I'm just trying to get some background. Were you sleeping near here somewhere? Over in the gardens maybe?"

Brakovich's eyes widened.

"How do you know that?" he demanded.

"Lucky guess," Packer said, "It's a popular spot. Not great weather for it at the moment, though."

"No," Brakovich agreed, "and that's why I decided to move along. Can't sleep near the train station, because they've got the jack-booted stormtroopers who like to shove you about after they close. Some of the buildings down the road are okay, though."

"There's a couple of shelters along Hay Street," Perry said, "and the ones near Wellington Square. Why don't you go to one of those?"

"Oh, you'd like that, wouldn't you?" Brakovich shouted, his temper re-emerging, "You'd like that!"

"Alright, well, never mind about that," Packer said, trying to calm him down again, "So you said you were walking along the road here, looking for someone to sleep. What side of the road were you on?"

Brakovich sat there glaring daggers at Perry, and Packer didn't think he was going to answer the question.

Eventually, though, Brakovich lifted one hand and jerked a thumb behind him at the opposite side of the road to the body.

"I was over there."

"Okay," Packer said, "Walking along. Then what happened?"

"I heard the almighty racket of the engine. Gunning it as hard as he could, he was, sinking the boot all the way to the floor. I looked up and saw him go rocketing off the road up on to the footpath. That poor, little girl didn't have a chance. Never even saw what was coming. He went barrelling straight into the back of her."

Brakovich shook his head in disgust.

"Oh, it was horrible, it was. Never seen a thing so horrible in all my life. Dragged her right along the ground, he did. Most horrible thing I've ever seen. But that wasn't the worst of it. Oh, no. After he ran her down, he stopped, then reversed and ran over her again."

"What did the car look like?"

"A huge white one, it was."

"Did you see what the make was?"

"I don't know what the make was. Just a big white sedan."

"Did you see the number plate?"

"Too hard to see in the rain. I couldn't see it at all. What about the reward?"

There was no change in his tone of voice and the question came so unexpectedly that Packer wasn't sure what it meant at first.

"What?" he asked.

"There'll be a reward, won't there?" Brakovich asked, "For helping capture that maniac?"

"That's not how we do things, Mr Brakovich."

"What?" Brakovich's voice was rising again, "I've seen rewards advertised in the papers for giving information to the police. Are you saying it's all a bloody scam to trick people? I bloody knew it! You filthy lying bastards. I knew I should have waited for the chief inspector! No use talking to the bloody monkeys."

The rant showed no sign of ending and Packer was confident they'd got as much useful information as they were going to.

He began pushing the door shut.

Brakovich pushed back against it.

"Don't you bloody close the door! I haven't finished talking. You promise me a reward for helping, then you tell me it's all lies. Trying to trick me, you bloody monkey-"

Brakovich was pushing hard against the door, but Packer was stronger. He flicked on the child-proof lock and pushed the door closed. Brakovich immediately began tugging at the door handle inside, but couldn't get it open. He thumped his fist against the glass and continued shouting, as Packer and Perry walked away.

"Quality witness there," Packer said, "Well done."

"Sorry, boss. I did try to warn you."

Packer stood under the overhanging lip and looked over at the woman's body again. The two uniformed officers stood beside her, looking back to him.

"What he says matches the tyre marks," Packer said, "Deliberately speeds up to run her down, then backs over her to finish her off. Not sure a big, white sedan's all that much help, though."

"Better than nothing."

He looked along the street.

"I wonder if there's CCTV in the area."

"Bound to be cameras closer to the mall."

Packer nodded.

"Alright. I'll stay and wait for Scenes of Crime to turn up," he said, "You go home and get some sleep. You're going to need it."

Chapter 3

Packer watched Claire Perry walk down the road to the plastic tape barrier that the uniformed officers had erected to block the road. She stopped briefly and spoke to one of the uniformed officers at the barricade, before ducking underneath and walking to her car, which was parked just beyond.

After the heavy downpour that had met Packer as he neared the scene earlier in the night, the rain had dropped back to a lighter, but persistent drizzle.

He put up the umbrella and stepped out from under the overhanging lip of the building.

As soon as he stepped away from the building, the wind began pulling at the umbrella.

Annoyed, he closed it up and left it on the ground near the wall. The rain was much lighter now and he was already soaked through anyway.

Squinting slightly, he walked further along the footpath, giving the body and the tyre marks a wide berth.

The barricade where he had entered was blocking off the entrance to The Esplanade from Barrack Street. He stood on the footpath near its edge and looked around.

To his left, the road continued up towards the casino, then crossed the bottom of the Hay Street Mall and continued on towards the train station.

In the opposite direction, the road continued down towards the tall, blue spire of the Bell Tower and the dark expanse of the Swan River that lay beyond.

Where was the woman going to?

The Elizabeth Quay Busport and train station lay behind him. Was she heading there to catch public transport? There was nothing else in that direction at this time of night.

And where had she come from?

Perth Underground Station lay on the other side of the mall and would have been much closer to Northbridge or any of the clubs in the city. Assuming she had been looking for a bus or train, there would have been no reason to walk all the way down here, rather than going to the Underground.

Packer turned to look down towards the river.

If she had come from there, she had to have walked along the footpath to get to here.

Packer walked off the edge of the footpath and into the gutter.

Looking back towards the footpath, he walked slowly along the gutter, watching for anything that had been left on the footpath as he went.

It was a five-minute walk to the Bell Tower, but Packer spent twenty minutes slowly pacing the distance in search of any traces on the footpath.

He found nothing.

If there had been anything there, it was gone now, washed away by the rain and the wind.

Packer walked past the buildings and down towards the river.

On his left loomed the circular spire of the Bell Tower and the shallow moat that surrounded the building. There were a handful of parking spaces on either side of the road, all empty now.

A couple of restaurants, souvenir shops and the ticket office for the Rottnest Ferry lined the edge of the wharf, bathed in shadow.

Packer stood there for a moment looking around.

There was no sign of life anywhere at this time and nothing to be found here.

He turned and walked back along the street towards the barrier.

The uniformed officer standing guard at the plastic tape fence watched him approach, but said nothing.

Packer returned to the narrow overhang and leant against the wall to wait for the forensics officers to arrive.

It took another hour.

Finally, the sound of a car moving along the road could be heard. The white shape of a police van crawled to a halt outside the barrier and the uniformed officer lifted the plastic tape to allow it in.

The van drove just inside the tape and stopped.

Packer walked over to meet it.

"Have ye been swimming, lad?" asked the gaunt, bald-headed figure getting out of the passenger side of the van, in a thick Scottish brogue.

Packer hadn't seen Alistair Goodge in over a month. He kept his face blank, but was shocked at how badly the man had deteriorated in that time.

Despite the chemotherapy that Goodge was on, the cancer was clearly winning the battle.

"Stepped in a puddle," Packer replied.

"A puddle? Must have been a great big sod of a puddle."

Packer watched the driver get out of the van. He was a much younger forensics officer. Packer couldn't remember his name, but he seemed to have become Goodge's minder, and they always travelled together now. He nodded to Packer, then headed for the back of the van.

"Took your time getting here," Packer said, looking at his watch, "Have you been on your tea-break?"

"Sorry," Goodge said, "Got tied up with a smash and grab over at Burswood. Lifted a ton of jewellery from one of the places along the highway."

Goodge walked along to the back of the van, with Packer behind him.

The younger officer handed Goodge a disposable paper suit and began to put one on himself.

"What have ye got here?" Goodge asked Packer.

"Hit and run. A woman. Two hours ago, or close to. Witness says the car deliberately accelerated to run her down, then backed over her."

"Christ a'mighty," Goodge said, "Not a wee accident, then?"

Packer shook his head. "There're tyre marks running in both directions. Matches what the witness says."

"Are there, eh? Let's see what else we can find, then."

"Uniform walked all over the scene before we got here."

Goodge grimaced. "Useless great lumps. Ah, well. Cannae be helped now, eh? Let's have a wee look."

The three of them pulled on shoe covers and walked away from the van. The younger officer carried a tool case in one hand and a large plastic sack in the other.

As they walked along the bitumen, Packer noticed that Goodge was now walking with a noticeable stoop and was growing short of breath. He had a sudden flash of Goodge before he became ill, a huge bearded man with arms as thick as logs. He bit down on the memory.

When they got closer to the woman's body, Goodge reached down to his belt and unclipped a torch. He switched it on and held it up. The torch was surprisingly powerful and the scene was lit up in its intense glare.

"Oh, dear," Goodge said, "That's a nasty smear of raspberry jam there. Looks like she travelled a fair way along the ground."

He used the torch to direct the younger officer, who took a series of photographs of the area using a camera with a ring of lights mounted around the lens.

After photographing the body and surrounding area, Goodge and the other officer followed the tyre marks back along the footpath, just as Packer had done earlier. The younger officer photographed them as they went.

"Here's where your man came up off the road," Goodge said, holding the torch over the edge of the road between the bollards, "You see the angle they're at?"

"I saw them," Packer said.

"Aye. I think you can safely say it was deliberate."

Goodge crouched down on the ground beside the marks on the road.

"Your car's wearing Bridgestones."

Packer grinned. "You can tell that from the tyre marks?"

"Very distinctive tyre pattern," Goodge said, "You see the shape of the ridges, there? And there? They're fairly new, too, which makes life easier. It's a medium-sized car, too. Not one of your wee hatchbacks."

"Witness says a big white sedan."

"Aye, well, I can't help ye with the colour, but a sedan sounds about right."

Goodge half-stood, so that he was in a crouch over the road. He shuffled sideways along the wet bitumen with the torch held out in front of him.

Packer and the other forensics officer followed along behind.

After a few minutes, Goodge stopped and squatted down again. He was close to the centre of the road, just behind the white line.

"There's your Bridgestones again," he said, shining the torch down at the road surface.

Packer could see a slight black mark on the road.

Goodge swivelled around and moved the torch beam until he found another mark on the other side of the centre line.

"And there's the other wheel."

He pointed towards the barrier.

"Your big sedan was coming in this direction. Right about here, he accelerated, leaving these marks on the road. You see how they're on either side of the dividing line? He was turning away, lining himself up to drive between the bollards over there."

Goodge pointed back towards the woman's body. There was almost a clear line of sight from where they were standing to the bollards.

"I'd say your car was driving along here, watching your lass," Goodge said, pointing along the road, "Made his decision right about here. Put his foot down and swerved up there." He pointed at the footpath between the bollards.

"Then - bang! That's the end for your lass on the ground, poor thing."

Goodge took out a tape measure and measured the distance between the tyre marks, making a note in his notebook.

He spent another half hour searching along the road but found nothing. If anything had been there, the rain had taken it away.

"Well, good print of the tyres, anyway," Goodge said, "not that it'll do you much good now, mind. But if you find your vehicle, I'll be able to tell you whether the tyres match. Should be some help with building a case against your driver once you pinch him."

Following the direction of the tyre marks, Goodge moved along the road. When he reached the bollards, he went around the marks leading up off the road, and followed them across the footpath to the woman's body.

"There's a footprint here," he said.

Packed moved closer to look at the area where Goodge was shining the torch. There was a tiny indent, little more than a rounded crescent.

"Is it?" Packer asked, unable to make anything out.

"Aye. You see at the end there, there are two parallel lines curving around? That's where the sole meets the outside of the shoe. And the rows of lines there? That's the tread under the instep. They're trainers of some kind. Your poor lass here is wearing heels, so they're not her footprints."

"They're definitely not from the first responders?"

"Not unless they're wearing trainers with their polis uniforms. Those aren't the soles of polis-issue boots, lad."

"There's a drunk bloke who saw it happen. He was wearing rubber boots, like rain boots."

"Not him either, then."

"Could have been here before she was hit."

"No," Goodge said, "Look at the edge here. It crosses over the top of the tyre mark. The shoe's come down in some mud and then left it behind afterwards. Your lass has been hit and knocked down, then somebody has stood here next to her while she was on the ground."

Packer thought through the implications of that. Somebody had been to look at the woman after she had been hit. Was she dying at the time? Was it the driver who had stood there?

"Can you match the shoe if I find another one to compare it with?"

"Mebbe. There's not much of a print left, though, and nothing distinctive about it. Find me a shoe when you find yourself a suspect and I'll see what I can do."

Goodge got a small L-shaped ruler from his pocket and placed it beside the imprint of the shoe so the other forensics officer took photographs from various angles.

After a moment, Goodge held a hand out to Packer. Packer helped him stand up, neither of them mentioning the fact that even this was becoming difficult for Goodge now.

"Right. Well, that's us, then," Goodge said, peeling off the blue rubber gloves.

"The car that hit her," Packer asked, "Would it have been damaged in the collision?"

Goodge pushed his lips together while he thought about it.

"Depends," he said eventually, "The front of a car's hard and a human body's not, so it's not like hitting another car or hitting a wall or summat.

"I had one a few years ago where the body bounced up over the bonnet, across the windscreen and onto the roof before sliding off onto the ground. Not a mark on the car. Few wee marks on the body, mind.

"Your lass over there has been dragged under the car and along the ground, so she must have folded up when the car hit her. Otherwise, she'd have been bounced up onto the bonnet. They don't put bumper bars on these cars any more like they did in our day. It's all fibreglass panels and they flex, instead of denting, or split if the impact's hard enough. I'd say there's probably some damage to the front from the impact on the car that did for your lass, but I wouldn't be completely surprised if there wasn't either."

"Is that a 'yes' or a 'no'?" Packer asked.

"It's an 'I can't tell you, you sarky bastard,'" Goodge said, "but I'll guarantee there's some blood and skin left on it. Find a car for me to look at, and I'll see if I can get something from it."

Packer nodded. "Thanks."

"Aye. Nae bother. Stay lucky."

Goodge turned back towards the van.

"And change your clothes, lad. You'll catch your death out here."

Chapter 4

Dawn was rising and it was just before 7:00am by the time Claire Perry arrived at the East Perth Police Station, after snatching a few hours' sleep at home.

The rain had stopped, although grey clouds still filled the sky, threatening to begin the downpour once again.

She parked in the underground carpark and made her way up to the team's incident room.

Her wavy, blonde hair hung down to her shoulders and she had changed into a grey skirt suit that was neatly pressed, although much tighter than it had been a year or two earlier.

Packer was in his office already, wearing a dry shirt and trousers. He didn't have a dry pair of shoes in his locker, so was barefoot.

"Morning, boss," she said, standing in the doorway, "Did you get home last night?"

Packer shook his head. "Forensics didn't arrive for an hour. Took another half hour after they finished for the mortuary to turn up."

"Forensics have anything useful to say?"

"Not really. The rain had washed away anything on the road, and uniform had walked all around the body. Goodge says it's a car, which matches what Mr Brakovich says, and he reckons it was following the victim, before lining her up."

"God. That's nasty."

"If we find the car, Goodge should be able to match the tyres."

"Righto," Perry said, "I'm making coffee. Do you want one?"

"Yeah, thanks."

Detective Constable Seoyoon Kim arrived shortly after Perry, her glossy hair pulled back into a neat ponytail and her black suit freshly pressed.

Detective Senior Constable George Thompson arrived a few minutes later. His heavy bulk was squeezed into a dark suit, his tie flapping over buttons that strained to hold his large stomach in place.

He gave Packer a nod as he headed for the coffee machine in the corner. "Boss. Ladies."

His words steadfastly retained his Belfast accent, despite having left the city over twenty years earlier.

Detective Constable Mickey Simmons was next to arrive, his blonde hair fashionably disarrayed and designer stubble covering his chin.

"Morning, all," he said, sitting at his desk and switching on his computer, "You're not wearing any shoes, boss."

"Really?" Packer said, hands around the coffee cup, "Someone should make you a detective."

"I've got a spare pair in my locker, boss," Thompson said, "Took them to get the heel repaired and forgot about them. Might be a bit small, though."

"They'll do. Thanks, George."

"Have we got a job on?" Simmons asked.

Packer nodded.

The incident room had a row of three whiteboards across the back wall near the entrance to Packer's office. One in the middle was blank. Packer picked up a whiteboard marker from the tray at its base and began making notes as he spoke.

"Alright," Packer said, "Here's what we've got. There was a hit-and-run last night on The Esplanade near the Supreme Court Gardens. A witness at the scene said it was deliberate, so uniform called us. Claire was on call, and went down for a look, then called me."

"What happened?" Thompson asked.

"Looks like the driver followed the victim along the street, then steered up off the footpath to hit her, then dragged her along the footpath for about five metres. He then backed over her to finish the job."

"Oooh," Simmons grimaced.

"That's horrible," Seoyoon added.

"It was deliberate, so assume we're looking for someone who knew the victim," Packer said.

"Have we got an ID on the victim?" Thompson asked.

"No," Packer said, "No handbag or belongings on the body. She's got a tattoo of a flower on her left arm just below the shoulder, though. I ran that through IMS this morning and nothing shows up, so it doesn't look like we've dealt with her as a POI on anything. Seoyoon, I want you to ring around and see if anyone's got any missing persons reported. This only happened a couple of hours ago, so there probably won't be anything reported yet, but put an alert on the system."

"Okay, boss," Seoyoon said.

"Anything on the driver?" Simmons asked.

"Big white sedan," Perry said, "No make. No number plate."

"Oh, good," Simmons said, "Can't be too many of those in Perth."

"There are no CCTV cameras on the street where the incident happened," Packer said, "There's likely to be something up near the casino and the mall, though. Mickey, see if any of the local businesses have got anything."

"What about the witness?" Seoyoon asked, "Has someone taken a statement?"

"He was drunk as a skunk last night," Perry said, "He's probably sobered up enough to get a statement from now, though.

"I can do it," Simmons said.

"You'll regret it," Perry said, "Dominic Brakovich. Homeless alco who was sleeping in the Supreme Court gardens, but headed off to find somewhere drier when the rain got too heavy."

"Probably better if you do it, George," Packer said, "He wanted to talk to 'the chief inspector' last night. You look more like someone senior than Mickey does."

"Looks old, you mean," Simmons said, grinning.

"He means I look like I know how to do my job," Thompson corrected.

"You might actually get something useful out of him," Packer said, "He was ranting a bit last night, but what he says seems to match up with the tyre marks at the scene."

"Tell him you're the commissioner and there's a reward in it for him," Perry said, straight-faced, "He'll probably be more helpful."

"Alistair Goodge found a muddy footprint which was over the top of the tyre marks," Packer said, "That would mean someone stood there after the woman was knocked down. See if Brakovich saw anyone after the collision."

"The driver?" Thompson asked.

Packer shrugged. "Maybe. Nobody else seemed to be around except Brakovich, but someone else might have walked by."

"Okay, boss. I'll see what he says."

"What was she doing there at that time of night?" Seoyoon asked, "especially when the weather was so bad."

"Yeah, I wondered that, too," Packer said.

"Meeting someone?" Thompson suggested.

"Maybe," Packer said.

"She must have wanted to see them pretty badly to meet there at three in the morning in the pouring rain," Perry said.

"Are we assuming the person she was meeting was the killer?" Seoyoon asked, "Lured her there, then ran her over?"

"We're keeping an open mind," Packer said.

"Her handbag was missing," Simmons said, "Robbery?"

"Running someone down and backing over them so you can pinch their handbag seems a bit extreme, don't you think?" Thompson asked, with an eyebrow raised.

"Yeah, fair enough," Simmons muttered.

"Besides, we don't actually know she had a handbag," Thompson added.

"It would be unusual if she didn't, though," Seoyoon said, "You've got to carry your purse, phone and other things somewhere."

"I agree," Perry said.

"Maybe she lived nearby," Thompson suggested, "If she was out on foot, she wouldn't have needed all that."

"She still would have needed front door keys," Perry said, "and she didn't have any."

"Aye. That's true."

"The footprint tells us someone stood there after she was run over," Seoyoon said, "so if it was the killer, he might have taken the handbag."

"So, it could have been a robbery then?" Simmons said.

"Not necessarily," Seoyoon said, "The handbag would have had ID in it. Maybe that's why it was taken."

"Makes it harder to ID her?" Simmons said.

Seoyoon nodded.

The team fell into a silence as they ran short of further ideas.

Packer waited a moment to see if anything emerged. When it didn't, he stood up.

"Alright," he said, "Let's get started."

The incident room had a single office at the end which was Packer's. He got up from the chair and walked across the room to the office, then sat behind the desk.

A small, hard shape dug into Packer's thigh through the inside of his trouser pocket as he sat down. McCain's USB drive.

A little over two months ago, Packer had replaced Detective Senior Sergeant Frank McCain as head of the team. McCain had left without warning, apparently as a result of some kind of health scare, although nobody had been able to confirm that and nobody seemed to know exactly what kind of health scare it had been.

Even more odd, McCain seemed to have disappeared off the face of the Earth. He had left no forwarding address and had been uncontactable.

McCain's office, now Packer's office, had been completely gutted after he left. Everything in it, from the files he was working on through to the stationary, had been removed. Through blind luck, Packer had found a USB drive hidden up underneath the cabinet behind his desk.

The USB was password protected and the files on it were named using some form of code. From what Packer could make out, McCain seemed to be running an investigation of his own that he was keeping quiet about.

Packer was still trying to get a handle on exactly what McCain was investigating, but it appeared to involve Jim Carlton, the member of parliament for Rockingham. The implications of that were deeply disturbing.

At this stage, Packer had nothing concrete to suggest McCain's covert investigation had anything to do with his apparent disappearance, but he was keeping it under wraps until he knew better.

Since finding the USB drive, Packer had been reluctant to leave it anywhere it could be discovered by someone else, and had kept it on him at all times.

He had planned to do some further digging, but that would now have to wait.

Packer's attention was diverted by a single knock at his office door. He recognised it before he looked up.

Inspector Harold Base walked into the office.

As always, Base looked immaculate, his tie perfectly square and his trousers freshly pressed. He was carrying the cap of his dress uniform, which he placed on Packer's desk, top down.

Pinching the front of his trousers, he tugged them upwards to preserve the crease before sitting down.

"A hit-and-run, I hear," he said, "and you think it's suspicious?"

Packer nodded.

"Are you certain about that? It was raining cats and dogs out there last night. It would have been easy enough for a driver to lose control in the wet. If it was an accident, then traffic branch should be dealing with it."

"She had two sets of tyre tracks across her back, going in different directions. She'd been run over twice."

"How is that possible?" Base asked, frowning.

"The driver hit her, then backed over her to finish her off."

Base tutted. "How horrible. What else have you got?"

"Not much. There was a witness at the scene who says he saw a white sedan."

"Well, that's something."

Packer shrugged. "Maybe. He's a homeless alcoholic, so I'm not putting much stock in it. He's all we've got for now, though."

"Are there forensics at the scene?"

"Tyre tracks that support it being deliberate. Nothing else."

Base let out a sigh. "Do you want uniform for a door knock?"

Packer shook his head. "I can't see the point. Nobody was out and about in the storm last night."

"Alright. Well, keep me posted."

Packer nodded.

Base collected his hat and left Packer's office. The incident room fell silent as he walked back through it to the door.

"Was that the pep talk?" Thompson asked, leaning back in his chair to look into Packer's office.

"At least he didn't tell us he wanted a quick result."

"Learned his lesson after last time, maybe?" Thompson asked with a grin.

Packer shrugged.

At the desk behind Thompson, Seoyoon was on the phone while writing with her free hand. She said thanks, then hung up the phone.

She said something to Simmons at the desk beside her, but it was too quick for Packer to catch.

Seoyoon stood up and hurried over to Packer.

"Belmont had a mis-per reported this morning, boss," she said, "Kacey Stewart. Twenty-six years old. Went out to her cleaning job yesterday after dinner, leaving her mum to babysit her daughter. She was supposed to be home around 4:30 this morning, but didn't return."

Packer could see there was something else on the way.

"Part of the description from her parents was a flower tattoo on her left arm."

Chapter 5

Kasey Stewart's house was much like all the others in that part of Belmont. A rundown single-storey house in a long row of rundown, single-storey houses.

While the southern end of the suburb was undergoing redevelopment, that had yet to catch up with the northern area. There was a high level of unemployment and a large amount of government housing. Yards were overgrown and neglected, fences had collapsed and been left unrepaired.

"Number 43," Perry said, pointing, "It'll be here on the left somewhere."

Packer slowed as they drew closer. He watched the street numbers and finally found a faded set of numbers on a letterbox.

The grass in the front yard needed mowing and the concrete driveway had tufts of weeds sticking up from the sides. A children's tricycle lay in the centre of the yard, with a Sesame Street ball a metre away.

Incongruously, a late-model Mercedes Benz sedan was parked in the driveway, its metallic blue paintwork clean and its tyres shining. A silver BMW was parked behind it in the carport.

Packer parked in the gutter outside the house. He and Perry got out and walked through the front yard towards the house.

Thompson's spare shoes were at least two sizes too small for Packer. They pinched as he walked, and he swore to buy a spare pair of shoes to keep in his locker when he found the time.

There were two steps leading up to the front porch, which was a wide concrete slab without railings. A couple of pot plants sat on either side of the door, but these were neglected and far past reviving.

Perry pressed the doorbell.

The wooden door was opened from the inside and a woman of about sixty stood on the other side of the security grill looking out.

"Yes?" she asked, anxiously.

Packer and Perry both held up their identification.

"Mrs Stewart? We're Detective Perry and Detective Packer from Perth Detectives," Perry said.

The woman undid the lock on the security door, and pushed it open.

"Please come in," she said, standing back for them.

Perry stepped inside, with Packer behind her.

The door opened onto a lounge room with two cheap settees and an armchair arranged to face a television. Children's toys lay around the edges of the room, although they were tidied into orderly piles and the rug in the centre was clear.

A girl of about three or four years old was lying on her stomach and elbows, propping up her chin with her hands. Her eyes were glued to the television which was playing a cartoon.

An overweight man in his late fifties was sitting on the settee behind the girl.

He got up as Packer and Perry walked in and took a step forward.

"Have you found her?" he asked, anxiously.

"Mr Stewart, is it?" Perry said, "Why don't you sit down?"

"Oh, no," the man said, his shoulders slumping, "She's been hurt, hasn't she?"

He rubbed at his eyes and gave a sigh that was almost a moan.

The woman inhaled sharply and sat in the armchair.

"Please, sit down," Perry said again, pointing at the settee.

The man sat in the settee beside the armchair, breathing hard.

Packer and Perry sat in the other settee, so that they were facing towards the other two at an angle.

"Can I ask for your names first?" Perry said.

"Bill Stewart," the man answered, "Felicity's my wife."

Perry began taking notes in her notebook as they spoke.

"Have you found her?" Bill Stewart asked again, "Have you found Kasey?"

"I need to tell you that we have located a woman's body in the early hours this morning," Perry said, keeping her tone neutral.

Stewart gave a low grunt of distress.

"Oh."

"At this stage, we have not identified the woman," Perry said.

"So, it might not be Kasey?" Stewart said, his voice rising, "It could be someone else."

"We can't be certain," Perry said, "As I said, we have not yet identified her. She wasn't carrying any identification on her when she was found."

"So, what makes you think it's Kasey?" Stewart asked.

"When you contacted police, you said that Kasey had a tattoo?"

Stewart breathed out through his nose and nodded. "That bloody thug made her get it."

"Can you describe the tattoo for us?"

He lifted his arm and pointed at the upper part with the finger of the other hand. "It's a flower. A yellow and red one."

"The woman we located this morning has a tattoo which matches that description."

Stewart stared at her. "A lot of women have tattoos now. It's fashionable, isn't it?"

"Yes," Perry said, neutrally, "That's true. A lot of women do have them. Even so, your daughter has a tattoo, and the woman we've located has a matching one in the same place."

"Well, that can't be enough to say it's her."

"No. It's not. We'll need some more details."

"We just want Kasey found."

Perry nodded. "Of course."

She looked around the lounge room. "This is Kasey's home, is it?"

Stewart nodded.

"You live here with her?"

"No. We're in Como," Felicity said, "I come to look after Jessie while Kasey's out at work."

Her eyes strayed towards the girl on the floor. Perry followed her gaze. The girl was still glued to the television screen, oblivious to what was going on behind her.

"Where does Kasey work?" Perry asked.

"A cleaning company," Stewart said.

"And she cleans at night?"

"It has to be then," Felicity confirmed, "After all the businesses are closed and the offices are empty. They can't clean during the day, because it would interrupt business."

Perry nodded. "So, this is a regular job?"

"Three nights a week," Felicity said.

"She's much too smart to be doing cleaning work," Bill said, "She went to uni, studying accounting. But then she met that useless idiot who ruined things."

"Who's that?" Perry asked.

"Deon DeSouza," Bill said, almost spitting the name out.

Stewart's dislike was so clear that it was almost physical.

"Kasey's boyfriend?" Perry asked.

"Her husband," Bill said, "Or I should say ex-husband, thankfully. Although even now, he's still trying to destroy her life."

"How's that?"

"He's taking her through the Family Court. Trying to take Jessie away."

"Did you try calling him this morning?"

"Him? Why on Earth would we?"

"Well, he might know something about Kasey."

"No," Bill said, "The don't speak to each other. There's an order preventing them from having any contact."

"Right. How long have they been separated?"

"Six months probably. Something like that."

Perry nodded.

"So, Kasey was at work last night?" she asked, looking at Felicity.

Felicity nodded. "I got here at about half past eight. Kasey put Jessie to bed and went out soon after that. I went to bed myself about ten. Kasey should have been home at about half past four this morning, but when I woke up, she wasn't home. I tried phoning her, but she didn't answer, so I called Bill."

"We've been calling all morning," Stewart said, "but she's not answering. We should have called you earlier."

He looked over at Felicity with a glare. She looked away, frowning.

Clearly this had been the subject of an argument before they arrived.

"Has she ever stayed out before and not come home in the morning?" Perry asked.

"Never," Felicity said, "She knows I have to get home."

"What was she wearing when she left?"

"Tracksuit pants. White, I think. And a blue T-shirt. There's no uniform, because it's night work."

"Do you have a recent photo of Kasey?" Perry asked.

Stewart stood up and retrieved his mobile phone from his pocket. He tapped in his pin number, then thumbed through it for a moment.

He leaned forward to show Perry and Packer a photograph.

"We took this one to show the court," Stewart said, "The solicitor said it would help to show that Kasey has family support."

He held out a photo that showed Kasey standing up on the porch outside the house they were in. Bill Stewart was standing beside her, wearing a suit and tie that was stretched over his heavy bulk. He had one arm holding Kasey's. She was standing stiffly beside him, wearing makeup and a formal-looking dress.

Perry nodded.

"Have you got another?"

Stewart turned the phone back to face himself and thumbed through it again.

After a moment, he held out the phone again.

The image showed Kasey and Jessie sitting on a wooden sun chair. The background was a paved area with potted palm trees and an in-ground swimming pool behind them. Jessie was sitting on Kasey's knees, laughing as Kasey played some kind of game with her tiny hands.

"That's from last weekend," Stewart said, "At our home."

Kasey's hair was down. It matched the body on the road that they had seen hours before. Kasey's arm was raised, as she played with Jessie's hand. Although her arm was partially hidden by the angle of the photo, Perry could see the side of the tattoo.

A flower with yellow petals and red highlights.

It was clearly the same one she had seen last night.

Perry looked at Stewart, careful to keep her expression completely neutral.

"I saw the tattoo on the woman we found," she said, "and I'm sorry to tell you that it looks the same as Kasey's to me."

"There must be dozens of women with flower tattoos," Stewart insisted, "Hundreds."

"Yes, but it does look identical," Perry said, "and so does Kasey's hair and her build."

She paused a moment to let Stewart consider that.

"I'm very sorry," Perry continued, "but I think you need to prepare yourself for the worst."

Stewart looked hard at her, and swallowed.

"It can't be Kasey," he said, his voice shaky, "She was only going to work."

"We will need one of you to view the woman we found to see if it's her."

"You mean look at her?"

Perry nodded. "Or you can view photographs if you'd prefer, but we will need a visual identification."

Felicity drew in a breath. "Do we both have to look, or..?"

"One of you will be enough," Perry said,

There was a silence while this sank in.

"Okay," Stewart said after a moment, "When do we have to do it?"

"We'll need to make some arrangements," Perry said, "but we would like it do it this morning."

Looking down at his feet, Stewart nodded, resigned to the fact. Felicity stared ahead, her eyes glazed.

Perry looked over at Jessie.

Her gaze was still fixed on the television, oblivious to what was going on.

Chapter 6

Despite it being a Sunday, the traffic in Perth's CBD was surprisingly heavy. Riverside drive and part of the city centre were blocked off for a charity marathon, and a car accident along St Georges Terrace had caused a two separate traffic jams that merged somewhere in the middle. Uniformed officers were doing their best to clear the roads, but there was little noticeable progress.

Simmons and Thompson had managed to get caught in the line of backed-up vehicles, and their movement was painfully slow as the line crawled along. It took them long minutes to get through each traffic light they crossed along the way.

"We should have just walked," Thompson grumbled, "It would have been quicker."

"Yeah," Simmons agreed, "Probably should have."

They stuttered along the road a little further, the traffic moving slowly.

"What do you reckon about the boss?" Simmons asked.

"What about him?"

"I don't know. He's a bit, well, grumpy, isn't he?"

"Maybe you just get up his nose, lad," Thompson suggested, and then added in a lower voice, "You certainly get up mine."

"And he's a bit closed off," Simmons continued, ignoring the remark, "I mean, you never really know what he's thinking."

"How d'you mean?"

"When we were looking for Abby Hanford, he knew a lot more than he was letting on."

"Aye," Thompson said, quietly, "He did."

"I mean if he had a theory about that, why keep it to himself? We're supposed to be working as a team. And then organising the DNA test so that Phil Hanford found out he wasn't the girl's real father was a pretty shitty thing to do."

"It was that," Thompson agreed, "although Hanford did know who took the girl and wouldn't tell us."

"Yeah, but his wife got burned, too. And Sean and Janey Griffith."

"It led us to the girl. And set us straight about Mosley."

"That's what I'm saying, though," Simmons said, "The boss had figured out a lot of this, but kept it to himself."

"He did."

"I mean, it turned out the boss was right and Hanford did know what had happened to the girl, but what if he was wrong about that? Someone could have got seriously hurt."

"Aye."

"And going to tackle Leon Abbas with just us was risky. TRG should have gone in, not us."

"TRG are a mob of cowboys," Thompson said, "If they'd gone in with guns blazing, the girl might have got hurt."

"You got hurt instead."

"I got a whack in the nose. Hardly out of the ordinary in this job."

"Abbas had a gun."

"It wasn't loaded. I doubt he even had bullets, stupid sod. He was just trying to be a bloody gangster."

"Even so, we shouldn't have been in there. The boss put us at all at risk. And Abby Hanford too."

"Why are you telling me this?" Thompson asked, turning in the seat to face him, "Are you just whining for the sake of it or you got something you want to say?"

Simmons fell silent.

The traffic crawled along very slowly, and he nudged the car forward before being forced to stop again.

"I don't want this to go any further, George," Simmons said, quietly.

"Alright."

"It's just between you and me, right?"

"Aye."

Simmons was silent a moment longer.

"Abbas took off from the house and the boss chased him. I lost them, but I caught up with them a couple of streets away. When I got there, Abbas was on the ground and the boss was hitting him. Like, really laying into him. Abbas was basically knocked out and the boss was still hitting him."

Simmons swallowed. "If I didn't stop him, I reckon he might have killed the bloke."

He turned to glance at Thompson, expecting Thompson to be looking at him with a look of scorn.

Instead, Thompson was staring straight ahead through the windscreen. His eyes were on the car in front, not on Simmons.

"I mean Abbas deserved what he got," Simmons said, almost defensively, "but, shit, that was going a bit far."

"You didn't report what happened?" Thompson said.

"Nuh," Simmons said, "Base asked how Abbas got the injuries. I told him he was kicking off and the boss had to subdue him."

"So now you're part of it, too, then?"

Simmons nodded. "Yeah, I suppose I am."

"So why not tell Base the truth?"

"I dunno. It felt wrong ratting out a senior officer."

"Mmm" Thompson gave a non-committal grunt.

There was a silence as they continued on, crawling slowly along. The cars in front nudged forward slightly before stopping again.

"I went with the boss to arrest the cleaner who killed the African lass," Thompson said, quietly.

"Emily Mtuba?"

"Aye."

There was a pause.

"The boss got a bit carried away then, too," Thompson said.

"Yeah?"

"Yeah. To be fair, he gave the boss and me a fair old whack with a steel post first, so he was resisting. But I had to call the boss off."

"I didn't know that."

"No, well, I didn't go broadcasting it. I wasn't actually sure what happened, to be honest."

"Twice is a bit of a coincidence."

"Maybe."

"And he never leaves work. He sleeps in the office when there's a job on. Who does that? It's weird."

Thompson sighed. "He's a good copper, lad. Granted, he's a miserable prick, and his communication skills could use some work, but he knows his stuff. I wish I was half as good a detective as he was."

"Yeah, until he beats someone to death."

"Steady on," Thompson said, "He gave a couple of bastards a kicking, but he wouldn't be the first copper to do that, would he? It was almost standard procedure when I started in the job."

"You're saying it's okay, then?"

"No, I'm not saying that."

"So, what are you saying?"

"I don't know," Thompson said, sighing, "I don't know."

"It was completely different when Sergeant McCain was in charge."

Thompson looked at him with a wry grin. "Frank McCain pulled a few strokes in his time, lad. Believe you me about that. There were a lot of crooks didn't want to be in the same room as Frank and a phonebook."

Simmons looked at him blankly. "What's that mean?"

"Phonebooks spread the blow. Give you a nasty whack but don't leave a mark."

"What?"

"Oh, never mind," Thompson said, giving up, "Anyway, Frank's gone. Packer's the boss now. He might be a moody bastard and he might be a bit handy with his fists, but he's a good detective."

"Okay. Whatever."

"What about the rest of the team?" Thompson asked, "Anything else you want to get off your chest?"

"What do you mean?"

"I don't know. Anything else you want to tell me?"

"No."

"Right then."

They fell silent, and continued crawling slowly along.

It took them another fifteen minutes to make it closer to the city's centre. Simmons passed the area where the body had been found last night. It was now fenced off with police tape and a council truck was parked half across the kerb next to it, the hazard lights blinking. Two uniformed officers stood guard, while three council workers cleaned the area where the body had been located with a high-pressure water hose and mops.

"Glad I haven't got that job," Simmons said.

"Aye. Me, too," Thompson agreed.

Simmons was unable to find a parking space, but stopped in a loading zone fifty metres away. A council inspector would inevitably be along to place a ticket on the vehicle, but once he checked the system, it would show up as a police vehicle.

"Do you want me to get the recording from the casino?" Simmons asked.

Thompson nodded. "I'll do the town hall. We'll do the rounds after that."

Behind them, the steady flow from the high-pressure cleaners ran off the kerb into a nearby drain, the water carrying a brownish tinge with it.

Chapter 7

Bill Stewart sat in the back of the car while Packer and Perry drove to the hospital.

"What other steps are you taking to find Kasey?" Stewart asked, as they passed the shopping centre.

"I'm sorry?" Perry said, turning in her seat to face him.

"Are there foot patrols out looking for her or something? There must be some steps being taken to find her, surely."

"Perhaps we can discuss that after you've seen the woman we located."

"But we don't know that this woman is Kasey," Stewart insisted, "She could still be out there somewhere. Injured or anything."

"Let's just take it one step at a time, Mister Stewart."

Perry turned back to face the windscreen again. She expected Stewart to go on arguing, but he fell silent. She could hear him clicking his teeth and tutting as they drove.

The traffic was fairly mild at this of day and it took them about twenty minutes to reach the city. There was a snarl of traffic closer to the city centre, though, and it took another twenty minutes to drive the last few blocks to Royal Perth Hospital.

Packer parked in one of the spaces reserved for police vehicles, then he walked through into main entrance, with Perry bringing Stewart behind him.

Packer showed his identification at the front reception and they were let into the building. After a few minutes, a mortuary nurse in a dark blue uniform came to collect them. They followed him along the winding corridors down to the mortuary level at the bottom of the building.

There was a long corridor on the lowest level, with offices opening off on one side. Along the other were three viewing rooms, each with a waiting room beside them.

The nurse showed them into one of the waiting rooms. Its walls and ceiling were painted a dull grey, but a white vase with a fresh bouquet of brightly-coloured flowers sat on a coffee table in the centre of the room.

Against the far wall was a low table that contained a rack of pamphlets on grieving, and contact numbers for counselling services. Perry had always thought this seemed tacky.

Packer left Stewart with Perry in one of the waiting rooms, while he went with the nurse to sign the paperwork.

Then they returned to the waiting room.

"I'll take you through in a moment, Mister Stewart," the nurse said, his voice low, "but I must warn you that this may be a very distressing experience. It is very confronting to see someone who has passed on. It's even more confronting when it is someone we know and love. It can be extremely emotional. In this case, there has been some injury, and we have had to use partial covering of the face. This may make things even more difficult."

"This woman could be anyone," Stewart said, "We don't know if it's Kasey."

The nurse gave a small nod. "Of course. But it's important that you prepare yourself."

He paused for a moment.

"Is there anything you would like to ask?"

Stewart looked at him for a moment, then gave a single, abrupt shake of the head.

"Won't you come this way, please?" the nurse said, his voice low and steady.

Stewart stayed in the chair for a moment, his expression blank.

Then he took a breath and let it out, nodding.

He stood up, tugging at the front of his shirt to straighten out the wrinkles, then straightening the collar and lapels of his jacket.

He nodded again and took a step forward.

Calmly, the nurse led him out of the waiting room and back into the corridor.

Packer and Perry followed behind.

The nurse opened the door to the viewing room and stepped inside. He stood back against the wall and held the door open for Stewart.

The inside of the room was a darker shade of grey. The lighting was dim, filling the room in a muted twilight, apart from a light in the centre of the room which cast a bright cone below it.

The room was empty, other than a table in the centre, which was covered with a pale cloth that fell all the way to the floor, completely concealing the table.

Lying on the table was the woman's body, covered in a pale cloth which matched the one covering the table. The cloth was peeled back on one side to reveal the flower tattoo on her arm.

One side of the face was covered over with a smaller pale cloth. The other side was exposed, the skin cold and pale, the eye closed.

Hesitantly, Stewart took a step inside.

Packer and Perry waited by the door.

Stewart walked forward, his steps unsteady.

He stood looking at the body on the table for a long moment.

Stewart's breathing grew harder. He sucked in a breath through his nose, then let it out fast.

"That's not Kasey," he said, his voice rising, "It's not her. You've got the wrong bloody woman. Whoever this is, it's not my daughter."

He whipped his head around and turned to face them, his teeth clenched. His cheeks were beginning to colour, and a heavy frown knotted his brow.

He shook his head furiously.

"That's not Kasey," he shouted, spittle flying from the edge of his mouth, "It's not my daughter."

Packer said nothing, but looked at him impassively.

The nurse reached to put a hand on Stewart's forearm, but Stewart shrugged him off.

"Get your hands off me," he shouted, turning towards the nurse and pulling his arm away.

Stewart looked back at Packer, fury written across his face.

"How dare you do this?" he shouted, "Making me think it was Kasey here! Making me look at this... this... It's not my daughter. You bloody bastard! Dragging me in here and making me think my daughter was dead. How dare you.. how-"

His voice broke and he stopped. He rubbed frantically at his eyes, as he let out a loud wail. Tears began to flow beneath his large hands as he moaned loudly in distress.

He took a stumbling step forward, away from the table and stopped.

His head hung down, his hands clutching at his face.

For long moments, Stewart stood there moaning helplessly, as the tears ran down his face.

"Can you confirm this is your daughter, Kasey Stewart?" Packer asked.

Stewart moaned again, a loud mewling cry of helplessness.

He nodded.

Packer turned to look at Perry, then nodded his head towards Stewart.

She gave him a frown of anger, but he was already stepping out of the room.

Perry stepped forward and placed her hands gently on Stewart's arm. He allowed her to lead him out of the room and back along the corridor to the waiting room.

Packer stood outside the viewing room, watching them pass.

The nurse left the viewing room and closed the door gently behind him.

"Never easy, is it?" he said, keeping his voice low.

"Has she been examined?" Packer asked.

"Yes. Doctor Chandra did a preliminary examination this morning when the body was brought in. We'll need authority for a full PM, though."

Packer nodded.

"Would you like to speak to Doctor Chandra?" the nurse asked.

"Yeah."

"Follow me."

"It's alright," Packer said, "I know the way."

Leaving the nurse, Packer walked along the corridor. He had to pass the waiting room and stood outside for a moment.

Stewart was sitting in one of the chairs, with Perry beside him. He was slumped forward, his large bulk on the edges of the chair, with his arms wrapped around his stomach. His face was red and puffy, tears rolling down his cheeks.

"She can't be dead," he was mumbling, the words muffled by his distress, "She can't be dead. We're going on holidays to Exmouth. Giving her and Jessie a break. She can't—"

He broke off, another thought occurring to him.

"What will we tell Jessie?" he asked, looking across at Perry, "What will we tell her?"

"There's no hurry for that," Perry said, gently, "It can wait a few days."

"A few days?" he said, anger in his voice now, "What happens in a few days? Will Kasey come back to life?"

Perry said nothing but held his arm.

Stewart leaned back in the seat again, making loud groaning noises.

Perry looked around and realised Packer was standing in the doorway.

She looked up at him, her eyes hardening.

He left and walked down the corridor.

Offices lined one side of the corridor. The office at the far end had a small plaque reading, 'Dr Nishdha Chandra'.

Packer tapped at the door.

"Come in," called a voice from inside.

Packer opened the door and stepped inside the office.

Nish Chandra was sitting behind her desk, her hands paused over her computer keyboard. She was wearing a plain white blouse, and her long, brown hair hung down over her shoulders, dark against the pale cloth. She wore very little makeup and no jewellery. A pair of oval-shaped glasses rested on her nose.

Seeing Packer, the corners of her lips curled into a slight smile.

"Good morning," she said.

"Hello, Doctor," Packer said.

The smile faded, and she gave a slight sigh.

"Business then," she said, "The car accident victim?"

"I'm working on the basis that it wasn't an accident."

"No," Chandra said, "It doesn't appear that it was."

Packer sat down in one of the seats in front of the desk.

"You've done a prelim?" he asked.

"This morning. I was just making some notes, actually. Have you identified her?"

"Kasey Stewart."

"Good. I hate calling them by a number."

She tapped at the computer keyboard.

Packer waited silently.

"Both legs were broken," Chandra said, "The femurs were protruding through the muscle tissue and skin on one side, which suggests that was the point of impact. The knee on that leg, together with the lower part of the spine and the organs were crushed, which suggests one of the wheels ran over that part of the body. The shoulder on her left is also crushed, which couldn't have happened at the same time because of the positioning."

"Run over twice," Packer said.

Chandra nodded. "It appears so. The abrasions on the skin from the tyres support that. The facial tissue on the right side has been almost completely flayed off and so has the tissue along the right arm and shoulder. She must have been dragged a considerable distance by the car."

Packer waited. None of this was news.

"She'd had sexual intercourse very recently," Chandra continued, "There's lubricant inside the vaginal tract, but even with the lubricant, there's moderate inflammation to the inner labia and the entrance of the vagina."

"Which means what?"

"Which means she was not aroused when intercourse took place."

"Intimate samples?"

"No. There must have been a condom used."

"There was a lot of damage from the impact with the car," Packer said, "Was there any other violence?"

"Not that I could see, but there was a lot of damage from the impact. It may have masked other trauma if it was there. Why?"

Packer shrugged. "I don't know. She was hit on a footpath and the car had to swerve up to hit her, then ran over her twice. Could have been an argument or something if she was being chased."

"I can't tell you anything that would help there."

"Alright."

"I'll finish up the preliminary report and send it to you, but I'm not sure there's anything else I can add at this stage. There'll need to be a full autopsy, of course."

Packer nodded. "Probably not something to discuss with the father right now."

"No. Of course not."

"Okay. Thanks."

Packer stood up to leave.

"I'm assuming you'll be busy with this for the next few days."

Packer nodded.

"Will you let me know when it's finished?" she asked.

Packer gave a vague shrug. "Alright."

"It's been weeks."

"I've been busy."

Chandra let out a breath.

"Mina is with her father until the weekend," she said, "I want to see you."

Involuntarily, Packer's eyes flickered to the photograph of Chandra and her daughter on the shelf behind the desk.

"Yeah, maybe," he said.

"Which is it?" she asked, her voice hardening, "Yes? Or maybe?"

Packer looked at her for a long moment.

"I'm not really happy families material, Nish," he said.

"And I'm not a tap you get to turn on and off when it suits you," she said, her voice firm, "I'm trying with you, Tony, but you make it so bloody hard."

For a moment, they looked at each other across the desk, Packer's face blank, Chandra's marred by a frown.

Then Packer leaned forward across the desk. Putting one hand on the back of her head, he pulled her forward and kissed her.

She pushed back against him, her mouth opening for his.

As he leaned back again, she followed him. She held his upper arms in her hands, preventing him from straightening up.

Their faces inches apart, she stared into his eyes.

"Tell me yes," she said.

Packer let out a breath.

"Yes."

Chandra pecked his lips, then let him go.

As he straightened up, she watched him with a slight smile on her face.

"I'm worth it, Tony," she said, "Don't forget that."

Feeling the smile appearing on his face, he nodded.

He left her office and walked back along the corridor.

Chapter 8

When Packer returned to the waiting room, Stewart was sitting calmly, leaning back against the wall behind the chair. Perry was sitting beside him.

She looked up at Packer with a neutral expression, but her eyes showed her feelings.

"We're finished here, Mr Stewart," Packer said, "We'll take you home now."

Stewart didn't move, but his eyes focussed on Packer. He looked at him for a moment, before nodding.

"When can we...bring Kasey from the hospital?" Stewart asked.

"Soon," Packer said, "but not just yet. Some further examination will be needed."

"Further examination?" Stewart asked, "What for? Kasey's... she doesn't need examining."

"The doctor has only done a preliminary examination at this stage, Mr Stewart. Because of the circumstances, it will be necessary to do a full post-mortem."

Stewart frowned, confused. "What circumstances?"

"We don't believe Kasey's death was accidental," Packer said.

Stewart stared at him. "You mean someone did this deliberately?"

"There's some evidence that suggests that."

"What evidence?"

"A witness saw what happened. I've spoken to the doctor, and the nature of the injuries also suggests it was deliberate."

"That's ridiculous," Stewart said, his anger beginning to rise again, "Who could want to hurt Kasey? It's nonsense."

"We need to make some further enquiries, Mr Stewart," Packer said, "and I'm sorry, but Kasey will need to stay here for the moment."

Stewart looked at him, clearly ready to argue further.

But he stopped. He breathed hard for a moment.

"What about her things? Can I at least take those?"

"Her clothes were damaged, Mr Stewart, and we'll need to examine those, too."

"Her jewellery and handbag. Can I take them?"

"She didn't have a handbag with her, and she wasn't wearing any jewellery."

"You're sure?" Stewart asked, frowning.

Packer nodded. "Did she normally carry a handbag with her?"

Stewart rubbed at his face. "Yes, I think so."

"Was it always the same one?"

"Probably. I mean I don't really know. You don't take much notice of these things, do you?"

He squeezed his eyes shut, his mouth turning into a grimace.

"Oh, God," he moaned, voice breaking.

"Let's get you home, Mr Stewart," Perry said, putting her hand on his arm.

He stood up with her and she led him from the waiting room.

Packer followed behind.

Despite his earlier outburst at the hospital, Stewart was calm on the drive from the hospital back to Kasey's house. He sat in the back of the car, unmoving, staring out the window with unfocused eyes.

Packer parked on the curb outside the house and walked to the side to open the door for Stewart.

Numbly, Stewart walked up the driveway to the front porch, with Perry beside him.

Before they reached the door, Felicity Stewart came out to meet them.

The sight of her husband told her what had happened.

"Oh, my god," she hissed, her voice little more than a whisper, "It can't be."

She raised a hand to her mouth, her breath coming out in short bursts.

Despite her obvious distress, Perry did not think the news had come as a surprise to her. Clearly, she had accepted what Perry had told her in the morning about the tattoo, even if her husband had not.

Bill Stewart walked past her into the house without speaking and she watched him go.

"I'm sorry, Mrs Stewart," Perry said, "but I'm afraid Mr Stewart has confirmed that Kasey is the woman we located."

Felicity nodded, her face pale.

"What do we... I mean, what happens now?"

"We need to speak to both you and Mr Stewart again," Perry told her, "And the sooner the better. You obviously both need to process what has happened, but it's important that we get some details from you as soon as we can."

Felicity looked at her for a moment. "I don't know if... Can it wait?"

"It is important that we gather information as soon as we can."

"Bill's upset and we need to look after Jessie, too."

Perry nodded. "Take some time, Mrs Stewart. What if we speak to you again in a few hours? We can come back in the afternoon."

Felicity stared at her for a moment, then nodded. "Yes, very well."

She began to close the door, then turned back again.

"Thank you, Miss... er."

"Perry, Mrs Stewart. Please call me Claire."

"Thank you, Claire."

Felicity closed the door, and they walked back to the car.

Packer pulled out from the street and headed towards the city.

Perry sat in silence, as Packer drove.

Her anger was clear, though.

"Go on, then," Packer said after a few minutes.

"That wasn't fair, boss."

"He was upset. It needed your touch."

"Because I'm a woman?"

"Yes."

"Oh, don't be so bloody sexist."

"I'm being a realist," Packer said, "He needed a shoulder to cry on. He didn't want another man holding his hand."

Perry fell silent. She was still angry at being left to deal with Stewart, but she knew Packer was right.

There drove in silence for a time.

"What do you make of them?" Packer asked.

"Bill and Felicity?"

"Yeah."

"They're not a happy couple. They've just lost their daughter, but neither of them tried to comfort the other at all."

"No."

"He was shocked when you told him it was deliberate."

"He was pretty keen to take the body."

"He wants to bury her," Perry said, sharply, "which is understandable. And grief was certainly strong," Perry said, then added in a lower voice, "Believe you me."

Packer ignored it.

"He clearly doesn't like the ex-husband much," Perry said, "although, that's probably not surprising, I suppose."

"Probably not."

"Are we talking to him next? There's a lot of emotion following a split."

"They split up six months ago. That's a long wait if he was angry about the split."

"I suppose it is."

"I'm more curious about the clothing."

"What about it?" Perry asked.

"Felicity Stewart said Kasey was went out to her cleaning job wearing tracksuit pants and a T-shirt. She was found wearing a dress and high heels."

***

When they returned to the incident room, Simmons and Seoyoon were both watching grainy CCTV on their screens.

"Where's this from?" Packer asked, standing behind Simmons.

"St Georges Terrace, near the casino," Simmons said.

"Does it get any better?"

"It hasn't so far."

The heavy rain was running down over the protective casing that covered the camera, obscuring the vision. The footage showed little more than a grey fog with dull patches of light visible in places.

"Have you found other footage?" Packer asked.

Simmons nodded. "There was a camera on the corner near the Supreme Court Gardens. It looked the same as this. There's another one from further along St Georges Terrace that I haven't looked at yet."

Packer turned to look at Seoyoon.

"There's a camera near the train station that's undercover, so it's clearer," she said, "but I haven't found the white car yet."

Packer nodded. "Alright."

He moved over to the whiteboard and wrote, 'Kasey Stewart,' at the top.

"We've got a definite ID on the body. Her father confirmed it at the morgue this morning. Claire and I will speak to the parents again this afternoon, see what else we can find out.

"In the meantime, Mickey you keep going with the CCTV."

Simmons rolled his eyes, but said nothing.

"Seoyoon, I want you to pull her phone records, see who she was speaking to yesterday and in the last few days. While you're at it, check with the service provider to see if they can track the phone. I'm guessing the answer will be that it's switched off, so no go, but let's make sure."

Seoyoon nodded. "Okay, boss."

"She's married, but there's a divorce in progress. Family Court, too."

"Do we know anything about the husband?" Simmons asked.

"Not yet, but we'll find out."

"My money's on him," Simmons added, "Ugly divorce."

"I'm glad you're not jumping to any conclusions before we get any evidence," Packer said, his tone flat.

"Well, I'm just saying," Simmons said defensively, "Divorces are ugly, aren't they? I mean... you know."

He trailed off under Packer's glare and turned back to the computer screen.

The door of the incident room opened and Thompson walked in. The knot of his tie was loosened, the top button of his shirt undone. He looked tired.

"Rough day?" Perry asked.

Thompson gave her a warning shake of the head.

"I've been wasting my bloody time!" he said, imitating an eastern-European accent.

"Ah," Perry said, grinning, "How is Mr Brakovich?"

"Letting the useless prick sober up was a mistake," Thompson said, "I'm sure he makes more sense when he's pissed as a parrot."

"That bad?" she asked.

"Even worse. I spent the first half-hour trying to convince him that we didn't pay anyone a reward for information, no matter what he'd seen on TV. We had to stop twice so he could take a bathroom break and then have his second breakfast for the day.

"After an hour, I finally got him to start talking about last night."

He shook his head.

"It just got worse from there."

"Did he at least give you a description of the car?" Perry asked.

"Oh, yes," Thompson said, "He remembered the car very clearly. A shiny red car, it was, like a racing car."

"What?" Perry asked, frowning, "He said it was a white sedan."

"Aye. I reminded him about that, but he wasn't having it. Definitely a red car with lots of chrome pipes. Just the sort of car the devil drives."

"Shit," Perry said.

"He remembered the driver, too. Got a real good look at the driver. A big man with dark glasses. He stopped the red racing car, got out and stood by the body, ranting and raving while the girl tried to crawl away. Then he stomped on her a few times to make sure."

"No."

"Yes. Then he turned and looked straight at Brakovich. Pointed his finger and told him he was next if he let anyone know what he'd seen. Knew Mr Brakovich by name, too, it seems."

"But he was so sure last night," Perry said, "He told uniform it was a white sedan, then he told me, then he told the boss."

Thompson held out his notebook to her. "Well, I haven't signed him up yet. Why don't you have a go? I'm sure he'd love to see you again."

For a moment, Perry looked at him, considering whether it was worth trying to get a statement herself.

"Oh, don't be stupid," Packer said, impatiently, "Even if he went back to the original version, how the hell could we ever trust it?"

He turned to Thompson. "Get him out of the station. If he causes any grief, tell him we'll charge him with wasting police time if he doesn't piss off."

"Boss," Thompson said, nodding.

He turned back to the door out of the incident room.

"Shit," Perry hissed, "He was so sure."

"Well, look on the bright side," Packer said, "At least we won't have to pay him any reward money."

Chapter 9

In the afternoon, Perry rang Felicity Stewart to arrange to speak to them again. Felicity told her that they had returned home to their house at Como and taken Jessie.

Perry and Packer drove across the Causeway and along the road heading towards South Perth. It was still too early for school pick-ups, but the afternoon traffic was growing as they drove.

Como was a large suburb. The area closest to the city had older houses which were being steadily replaced by luxury townhouses and apartments. Closer to the river, the housing was much more upmarket. Large houses sat on large blocks, surrounded by high fencing. Footpaths were lined with trees that hung over the road and the cars in the driveways were all recent and high-end models.

Bill and Felicity Stewart's house was not on the riverfront, but the river could be seen at the end of the street. A high brick fence with ornate wrought iron grills separated the house from the footpath.

Packer stopped the car in the driveway outside the gate.

They got out and Perry pressed the buzzer on the intercom.

"Come in," came Bill Stewart's voice over the speaker after only a few moments.

There was a buzz and the gate beside them clicked as the lock was released.

Perry and Packer walked up the path towards the house. The front yard was paved over and well-manicured gardens lined the walkway leading up to the ornate pillars on either side of the front door.

Bill Stewart was waiting for them at the front door.

He was much calmer than he had been earlier in the day, but his face was gaunt and his eyes puffy.

He stood back from the door to let them in.

"We thought it best to bring Jessie back here," he said, wearily, "We didn't really want to stay in Kasey's house."

"No, of course not," Perry said gently.

The entrance room at the house was clearly designed to impress. The floor was covered with wide marble tiles and the walls held two large paintings. Perry recognised them both as having been painted by local artists. Sunken lights in the ceiling cast a soft glow over the room.

"Come through," Stewart said.

He led them out into a lounge room on the other side.

More artwork hung on the walls and a row of mahogany cabinets lined one wall. Pale leather lounge chairs circled a glass-topped coffee table. A sheet had been placed over one side of the couch to protect the surface and a pink child's backpack sat on the seat beside a large stuffed rabbit.

Jessie was sitting on the floor, eyes glued to a huge television that was playing children's programs. A colouring book and a pencil case sat untouched on the ground beside her.

Felicity Stewart sat on the couch behind Jessie. Like her husband, she too looked upset and clearly exhausted.

"Can we get you tea or coffee?" Felicity asked.

"Oh, I'm fine, thank you," Perry said.

Felicity looked at Packer, who shook his head.

"Please sit down," Stewart said.

He sat beside Felicity, who shifted aside slightly to make space for him. Perry and Packer sat on the lounge opposite.

Perry took out her notebook.

"We'd like to ask you a few questions about Kasey," Perry said.

"About Kasey?" Stewart said, frowning slightly, "Why? Shouldn't you be out there looking for the maniac who killed her?"

"There are other officers making other enquiries," Perry said, "but learning more about Kasey might help us to narrow down who might have done this."

Stewart looked at them for a moment, confused.

Then realisation dawned.

"You think she was killed by someone she knew?"

"It's possible."

"That's ridiculous," Stewart snapped, "She was such a lovely girl. Nobody who knew her would want to see her dead."

"Even so," Perry said, gently, "It's something we need to consider."

"You're wasting your time. You should be out there, looking for a drunk driver or idiots high on drugs. I don't know why you people don't do something about them, instead of this nonsense."

Perry did not reply. She looked at Stewart in silence until he had calmed down.

After a moment, he gave a resigned shake of the head.

"Alright," he said, "What do you want to know?"

"You told us this morning that Kasey was doing night cleaning," Perry said, "Who does she work for?"

Stewart looked over at Felicity.

"Prestige Industrial," she said, "They clean offices and business premises."

"How long has she been working there?"

Felicity shrugged. "A few years now, I think."

"What does that matter?" Stewart asked.

"It doesn't appear that she was at work, Mr Stewart," Perry said, "Otherwise, she wouldn't have been down near the river."

"She must have been cleaning an office down there, then."

"What time were you expecting her home?" Perry asked, looking at Felicity.

"Half past four, or thereabouts. Her shift always finishes at about that time."

"When was..." Bill began, "What time did-"

"Kasey was found at 3:45am," Perry said.

"Well, there you are, then," Bill said, "She must have been on her way home."

Perry nodded. She looked at Felicity again.

"Did Kasey usually change her clothes before returning home?"

"Her clothes? No. Well, I don't think so anyway. I was always in bed asleep when she came home, but I can't think of any reason she would."

"Do you know if there were any difficulties at work? Did Kasey mention any problems there?"

"No," Stewart said, "but if she was on her way home, then it can't have had anything to do with her job, can it? Stands to reason. Asking around at her workplace is pointless."

Perry nodded, letting it go.

"You babysit Jessie while she's at work, Mrs Stewart?"

"Yes."

"Is it always you? Not Mr Stewart?"

"It's always me."

"So, what are the arrangements there? What normally happens when you're babysitting?"

"I drive over to Kasey's house at about half past eight. Usually, Jessie's in bed by then, or Kasey's just putting her down. Kasey leaves to go to work and I stay over. I have a bed in the spare room. I don't usually hear Kasey come in, but she's there in the morning, so I leave."

"Is that always the routine?"

Felicity thought about it for a moment. "Yes, usually. There have been a couple of times when Jessie's been ill or something. I've had to get up to her in the night or she's been upset and wanted Kasey. Luckily, it doesn't happen very often."

"And was there anything different on Saturday night?"

"No, I don't think so."

"What time did you get to Kasey's house?"

"The usual time, I think. I left here at about eight, just as usual. I didn't look at the clock when I got to Kasey's house, but it must have been about half past. Jessie put Kasey to bed. We said our goodbyes and off she went."

"How did she seem?"

Felicity gave a slight shrug. "Happy enough. Nothing out of the ordinary."

"Did she say anything to you?"

"Not really. Just goodbye."

"What happened after that?"

"I tidied up the lounge room. The place always looks like a bomb's hit." Felicity gave a slight grimace of annoyance. "Then I read a book until about ten o'clock and went to bed. You know the rest."

"What time did you wake up?"

"Seven o'clock. Something like that."

"And Kasey wasn't there?"

"No. I walked past her bedroom on the way to the bathroom and the bedroom door was open. It's usually closed, so I thought she must have been in the kitchen. She wasn't, though, so I tried Jessie's room but she wasn't there either. I looked outside and the car was gone, so I realised she hadn't come home. I tried phoning her a few times and got no answer. Jessie was out of bed by then, so I had to organise breakfast for her. There was still no sign of Kasey, so I called Bill."

"What time was that?"

Felicity thought about it. "I don't know. Probably about eight o'clock."

"So, an hour after you got up?"

"That's right."

"Why wait so long?"

"Well, I thought she might come home. She's not normally late, but I didn't really think there was any reason to worry."

"And I called the police when I got to the house," Stewart said, "I was worried. Even if I was the only one who was."

Felicity glared at him, but said nothing.

Perry nodded.

"You mentioned Deon DeSouza. That's Jessie's father, is it?"

Stewart nodded. "Yes. And if he his way, she'll never see her mother again."

"You mentioned the Family Court this morning," Perry said.

"That's right. He's trying to get sole custody over Jessie so he can take her away with him. Trying to steal her away from Kasey."

"There are actually custody proceedings on foot, are there?" Perry asked.

"Yes, there are. They send some woman out to talk to Jessie and do reports. It's going back to court again soon, I think."

He looked at Felicity for details.

"It's not for another couple of months," she said, "End of November some time."

"Do you have contact details for Mr DeSouza?

"There'll be court documents at Kasey's house that have it on them," Stewart said.

Perry nodded. "That's okay. We'll find it."

Stewart looked hard at her.

"Do you think he did this?"

Perry shook her head. "We're just getting some background, Mr Stewart."

Stewart looked away, frowning. "The man's complete garbage, but I wouldn't have thought he'd go this far."

"We're not suggesting he's involved, Mr Stewart," Perry said again, "We're just gathering background information."

"It would make things easier for him to get hold of Jessie, though, wouldn't it? I mean if he knows he's going to lose the court proceedings, this would be an easy way to get hold of her."

"Mr Stewart," Perry said, more firmly, "Let me be clear. We are not suggesting that Mr DeSouza is responsible. We haven't even spoken to him yet. We are simply getting some background information on Kasey."

Stewart looked at her again. "Well, you should be talking to him."

"And we will do. We'll be talking to everyone we think might be able to tell us something."

Stewart looked at her for a moment longer, before nodding. "Alright."

"Kasey is separated from Mr DeSouza. Does she have another boyfriend? Anyone like that?"

Stewart shook his head. "No, there's no boyfriend. I think she learned her lesson after that thug. All she needs is her family."

"Is there anyone else Kasey is in regular contact with?" Perry asked, "Close friends?"

Stewart shook his head. "I don't think so."

"There's Alicia," Felicity said.

Stewart gave a slight snort.

"Alicia?" Perry asked.

Felicity nodded. "They've known each other since high school."

"What's Alicia's last name?"

"Martin."

"Does Kasey see Alicia regularly?"

"Yes, she's like a spare shadow," Felicity said, "She's often at the house and Kasey mentions her a lot."

"She's a bad influence that girl," Stewart said, "Why Kasey insists on letting her hang around all the time is beyond me."

"Bad influence in what way?" Perry asked.

"I don't like her," Stewart said, "Never have."

"Does she live locally?" Perry asked.

"Yes, I believe so," Felicity said, "She and Kasey often do things together. Alicia has a child about the same age as Jessie. A boy, although I couldn't tell you his name."

Perry noted this down.

"Okay. Anyone else you can think of?"

"She was a popular girl," Stewart said, "Everyone who met her liked her. I'm sure there are a lot of people who knew her."

"Anyone specific apart from Deon DeSouza and Alicia Martin?"

Stewart shrugged.

Felicity shook her head.

"Okay. Well, if you think of anyone else, please let us know."

Perry made some more notes.

"We'll need to have a look at Kasey's home, too," she said, "Do you have her keys?"

"Why should you want to look there?" Stewart asked.

"There may be something there that helps us," Perry said.

"Like what?"

"I don't know, Mr Stewart, but there's nothing to be concerned about. It's all perfectly routine."

"I don't want you poking around in Kasey's things," Stewart said, "I mean, it's private. You've no business doing that."

"We're trying to get to the bottom of what happened, Mr Stewart."

"And how does digging your noses into Kasey's private business help you do that? Get out and look for the driver."

"Oh, stop it, Bill," Felicity said, impatiently.

"The cheek of it," Stewart said, glaring at her.

"They're the police, Bill. They know what they're doing. Let them look at Kasey's house if it helps them."

"I won't have it."

Felicity opened her mouth to argue, but Perry interrupted.

"I can understand that it's unpleasant, Mr Stewart," she said, firmly, "but it is necessary. Mrs Stewart can come with us to the house."

"Why her, not me?"

"It's clearly making you very emotional, Mr Stewart. We all want to find out what happened to Kasey. It's important that we do every single thing we can to do that."

"Phone me when you want to see the house," Felicity said, "I'll meet you there and let you in."

Stewart glared at her in silence. He looked unwilling to let it go, but said nothing.

After a moment, he snorted and shrugged dismissively.

"Do you have a recent photo of Kasey that we can take?" Perry asked.

"What do you want that for?" Stewart asked, "You know who she is."

"It might help if we need to show it to any witnesses, Mr Stewart. Again, it's completely routine."

She looked over at the mahogany cabinets behind them. There were a few framed photographs sitting on the top.

After a moment, Stewart got up. He walked over to the cabinet and picked up a small frame, then returned and handed it to Perry.

"I'd like this back when you're finished with it."

"Of course."

Perry looked at the photo. It was a portrait photo taken at a photographic studio. Kasey was sitting against a hanging backdrop of a garden, her hands resting on crossed knees. She was smiling at the camera, but there was something forced about it. The smile did not reach her eyes.

Perry closed her notebook.

"Is that it?" Stewart asked, seeming surprised.

"For the moment," Perry said, "I'm sure we'll need to speak to you again, but we'll follow up on these things."

She and Packer stood up. Stewart looked like he was about to say more, but didn't.

"What about Jessie?" Felicity asked.

"I'm sorry?" Perry said.

"What happens to Jessie?"

"Well, she'll stay here of course," said Stewart, looking at his wife.

Felicity looked at him for a moment, then back at Perry.

"I'm not sure what will happen long-term," Perry said, "It's not up to us. Family Services will decide what the best thing for Jessie is long-term, but there's no need to worry about that for now."

"The best thing is for to stay with us, of course," said Stewart, "What else?"

"As I said, there's no need to worry about it for now," Perry said.

She turned and took a step towards the entrance room. Packer followed her.

"Thank you for your help, Mr Stewart," Perry said, as the door.

"Just find the maniac who did this," Stewart said, his voice starting to crumble.

He closed the door behind them.

They returned to the car.

Packer backed out of the driveway and they began the drive back to the police station at East Perth.

"Definitely not a very happy couple," Perry said.

"No," Packer agreed.

"I didn't once see them reach out to the other. Not once."

"There's something off about him."

"What?"

"Too aggressive," Packer said.

"Well, he's just lost his daughter, boss. It's not that unusual to be angry about it."

"No," Packer agreed, "but he didn't like her ex-boyfriend or the school friend and he didn't want us looking at her things."

"Doesn't sound like he's got any reason to like the ex if there's a custody battle going on. Could be something similar with the school friend."

"Maybe."

"You don't think so?"

"He's a bit possessive."

"Some fathers are very close to their daughters, boss. It's not that unusual. The grief this morning at the hospital seemed genuine enough."

"I'm not sure that means much," Packer said.

"Meaning what?"

"Grief is often mixed with regret."

"You surely don't think it was him?" Perry asked.
"I'm just saying we'll keep an open mind at this stage."
"Okay. I'm not getting the 'close parent' vibes from the mother, though."
"Nor me."
There was a silence as they drove on.

Chapter 10

When they returned to the incident room, Perry updated the whiteboard in the incident room, noting down what they had learned from Bill and Felicity Stewart.

Packer removed the photo of Kasey from the frame and attached it to the top of the whiteboard with a magnet.

He stood looking at the photo for a moment, before turning back to the room.

"Seoyoon," Packer said, "I want you to find a contact number for the manager at Prestige Industrial. It's the cleaning company Kasey Stewart worked for. It's a Sunday, so you won't get an answer now, but try them tomorrow. Find out who her supervisor is at work and see when we can talk to them."

Seoyoon nodded. "Right, boss."

"Kasey was driving when she left home, but she was on foot when she was hit, so her car must be somewhere. See if you can find a make and registration number for her car. Get an alert out."

"Maybe she parked it somewhere nearby," Perry suggested.

"It's been nearly twenty-four hours if she did. Seoyoon, phone around all the parking places in the city. See if they've got a car that's been there since Saturday evening. Try the council, too. If the car was in street parking, they will have towed it away this morning."

"Okay."

"Could the killer have used her car?" Simmons said, with sudden excitement, "That would explain why it's missing and why she's on foot."

"How's that work?" Thompson asked.

"Maybe she was out with someone after work, and had some kind of argument with them," Simmons suggested, "She ended up out of the car. He chased her, ran her down and took off."

"And the evidence of that is..?" Thompson asked.

"Well, the car's missing," Simmons said, feebly, "That's it, I suppose."

"Bit slim, lad."

"Let's see if we can find the car," Packer said, "before we jump to any conclusions."

"What about the clothes?" Perry said. "Felicity Stewart said Kasey was wearing tracksuit pants, maybe white, and a blue T-shirt when she left home. That's not what she was wearing when she was found, so she must have changed them somewhere."

"Going clubbing after work?" Simmons suggested, "Changed her clothes at work before she left?"

"She finished work at four in the morning. Not many places open then, are there? Or down that way."

"No," Simmons agreed, "There's not."

"What was she wearing, exactly?" Thompson asked.

"A strapless dress," Perry said, "mid-thigh. And stiletto heels."

Thompson snorted. "Sounds like a street-walker."

Packer and Perry both looked at him.

"What?" Thompson said, defensively, "I'm just saying."

Then he realised why they were looking at him.

"Jesus," he said, "Do you think she *was* working as a hooker?"

"It would explain the dress and the heels," Perry pointed out, "and why she was out at that time of night."

"It's a bit far from Northbridge, though," Seoyoon said, "I've never heard of any girls working the streets down near the Bell Tower."

"Could have been a house call," Perry said, "although there aren't many apartments near where she was hit. It's all offices and commercial along that street."

"It would only be a ten-minute walk to the nearest ones, though," Thompson, "There are a couple of tower blocks up near the mall and more down past Langley Park."

"There's the big one near the Bell Tower," Thompson said, "The Towers? Is that what it's called?"

He looked at Packer. "What do you think, boss?"

"It fits what we know," Packer said, "It's too late to start looking now, but check with the restaurants and shops near the Bell Tower tomorrow. See if you anyone's got CCTV."

"Nooo!" Simmons said, holding up his fingers towards Packer in the sign of the cross, "Not more CCTV."

Packer ignored him. He looked at his watch.

"Alright. Let's call it a day. Back again in the morning."

The team began to say goodnight and file out.

Packer remained in front of the whiteboard, reading over the notes and thinking through the two discussions with Bill and Felicity Stewart.

None of the others thought it odd that Packer was remaining in the office at the end of the day. After several months of working with him, they knew he would not leave when they did.

After they left, Packer moved over to the coffee machine and switched it on.

He waited for the cup to fill, then took it back to his office.

He nudged the mouse to activate his computer screen. There were a handful of e-mail messages waiting for him. Most of them were management messages and he deleted them without opening them.

There was a message from Alistair Goodge with the subject line, 'photos,' and Packer clicked on that one.

The message was blank, other than Goodge's automated signature block at the bottom. Attached to the message were thirty or forty image files.

Packer clicked on the first and found it was a photograph of Kasey Stewart's body taken by the younger forensics officer while Goodge and Packer stood nearby. The next was a closer-up image of the body.

Packer clicked through each of them, peering at each image closely and searching for some tiny detail he might have missed earlier, or any further clue to what had happened the night before.

The streets in all of the photos were soaked. Rain water had pooled up in the gutters, where the drains had not been able to cope with the heavy downpour. Wide pools of water were backed up against the walls of the building where the huge amount of water had not run away.

The storm had been intense, emerging suddenly and dropping a massive amount of rain across the dark streets.

Kasey Stewart's dress was stuck to her body, the material completely saturated and running down over her pale skin to leave pools of water beneath her cold flesh.

He clicked through the images until he found one that gave a better view of her clothing.

The dress was tiny, barely covering her body at all. The hem only came down to halfway between her knees, exposing a good proportion of her thigh, while the top was low, leaving her cleavage on display.

Could George be right about her being a street-walker?

It certainly fitted with changing her clothes after she left her mother at home. But the area where she was killed was a long way from anywhere prostitutes plied their trade.

Packer clicked to the next image. It was a close-up image of Kasey's hand. The back of her hand lay against the concrete, the fingers curled up towards the sky. The fingernails had been painted, but were short and irregularly-shaped. They were fingernails that were not well cared for.

Packer drained the last of the coffee as he worked his way through the images. The caffeine did nothing to reduce the tiredness he felt.

Using the mouse, he zoomed in on one of the images. The photo had been taken at a low angle and showed a close-up of one of Kasey's feet. She was wearing black high heels with a high back on them that ran up past her ankle. There were two straps that wrapped around her lower leg and fastened with small buckles. It was hard to tell from the angle, but the stiletto heel would have been eight or ten centimetres high.

Packer zoomed out slightly, trying to get a better view of the shoe. With such high heels, the shoes must have been very difficult to walk in. Clearly, they had not been chosen for comfort, and were designed solely for the effect they would have on men who saw Kasey in them.

Why had Kasey worn them? If she had been standing on a street corner trying to attract potential customers cruising the gutters, the shoes would have become torturous very quickly. If it was a home call, the customer had already been lined up, so there was no point wearing the shoes to attract him.

Was it simply part of the service?

Something about that didn't sit right. They were not the sort of shoes a prostitute wore to a pre-arranged meeting with a customer.

They were the sort of shoes a woman wore for a night out with someone special.

Packer's eyes felt heavy and he rubbed at them as he moved through the photos trying to get a better image of the shoes.

Part of him suspected he was reading too much into this; they were simply shoes.

But another part of him knew to follow his gut instinct. It was right more often that it was wrong.

Who had Kasey worn the shoes for? And why?

Packer felt his eyes growing heavy.

Feeling the tiredness washing over him, he closed his eyes, giving in to the inevitable.

The rain was pouring down now, like a sheet or water hammering through the night. The sound was intense, a roar in her ears.

The wind slammed against her from behind, pushing her forward along the street as she ran. Her hair was whipped around her face in wet tendrils that slapped at her cheeks and stung her eyes.

Pools of water lined the footpath, the gutters backed up where the drains could not cope.

The shoes made it difficult to run in the rain, the high heels threatening to turn beneath her and send her flying to the concrete as she tore along the footpath.

The night was dark, the streetlights little more than dull glows in the haze. They did nothing to pierce the darkness.

And it was cold. The night air was freezing, the wind forcing the icy-cold rain against her naked skin. She shivered in the night, feeling the chill run through her whole core.

Through the murky haze of the storm, she could see lights up ahead. She ran on, heading towards them.

She was close now.

Not much further.

Not much.

Something slammed against the backs of her legs, and they folded beneath her. There was a split second of numbness.

Then the agony ripped through her, pain more intense than anything she could ever have imagined.

The ground rose up to meet her, slamming against her face.

She felt the wheels run across her back.

Packer jumped in the chair, the image fading as his eyes snapped open.

For a moment, he felt the same disorientation he always did, as reality forced its way back into his consciousness. He breathed hard, peering around the office.

The clock on the wall gave a dull, regular click, as the hand moved. There was the faint sound of a car on the road outside.

Packer lifted his hands and rubbed at his eyes.

He had seen lights in the distance. Just before she had been hit, there had been lights in front of Kasey. Did it mean something?

He sat there a moment longer.

Sniffing, he reached for the empty coffee cup and wrapped his hand around it. The cheap ceramic felt cold beneath his fingers, as he stood up and walked back out to the coffee machine.

Monday

Chapter 11

Packer spent the night in his office.

He was tired, but knew he would not be able to sleep.

He spent a few hours skimming over the forensic photos, searching for some tiny detail that might give some meaning to what he had seen, or provide some explanation for why Kasey had been there at that time of night.

Despite going through each of the photos several times, he found nothing.

Packer opened Google Maps on his computer and spent another few hours searching the area near where Kasey had been found. Where was she going?

The train station lay two blocks from where she had been killed, and the bus station just beyond that. Public transport began to close down at midnight, and nothing was running at 3:45am on Sunday morning. Kasey could not have used either, but could she have been confused about that? Was she heading there in the belief that she could catch a bus or train home? Or planning to wait there until the first service began?

Kasey left home in her car, but was on foot in the rain.

Was she trying to get back to it? Where was it now?

When she left for work in the evening, Kasey was wearing tracksuit pants and a T-shirt, not the tiny dress and heels. She must have changed somewhere.

Too much needed explaining.

Just before the dawn rose, Packer walked to the bathroom at the end of the floor and showered, then changed into fresh clothes from his locker.

He shaved in the tiny sink. As he watched his reflection in the mirror, it occurred to him that he could not recall the last time he had shaved at home. It was always here.

He returned to his office and sifted through the photos yet again as he replayed the conversations he had had with Bill and Felicity Stewart the day before. For parents who seemed so heavily involved in their daughter's life, there was something odd about both of them. Felicity seemed distant and Bill seemed too close. It was a strange dynamic.

The team began to arrive at the station as the morning began.

Seoyoon began phoning around parking garages in the city, and Simmons began calling local businesses in search of CCTV.

Packer wondered if anything would turn up.

He ran his eyes over the whiteboard, at the scant information they had.

He turned away.

"George, I want you to search Kasey's house," he said, "Phone Felicity Stewart to meet you there with the keys. Bill Stewart didn't like the idea, so make sure she's not bringing him along to make things difficult."

Thompson nodded. "Okay, boss."

"Take Mickey with you. Leave the CCTV for the moment."

Simmons practically jumped out of his seat at the excuse to avoid sifting through CCTV.

"We'll go and talk to the spare shadow," Packer said to Perry.

***

Thompson phoned Felicity Stewart and arranged for her to meet them at Kasey's house. She had clearly been expecting the phone call and agreed to meet them at Kasey's house.

Thompson and Simmons left the station and drove north along the freeway. It took them about twenty minutes to get to Belmont. They parked outside to wait.

It took Felicity another fifteen minutes to arrive.

"Morning, Mrs Stewart," Thompson said, "Detectives Thompson and Simmons."

They held up their identification and Felicity gave them a cursory examination.

"Thank you for helping us," Thompson said.

"Do you need me to come in?" she asked.

"No," Thompson said, "In fact, it's best you don't. You can go somewhere for a coffee if you like. Or we can drop the keys back to you when we're done."

"I'll go home," she said, "You can return the keys later."

"Okay. No problem."

Felicity walked to the front door. She unlocked the security screen with one key, then the wooden door with another and pushed it open, leaving the key in the lock.

"Thank you," Thompson said again, "We'll drop these back when we're finished."

Felicity nodded without saying anything and walked back to her car.

Thompson watched her go.

"What is it?" Simmons asked.

"I don't know," Thompson said, "Just seemed a bit flat or something. Disinterested."

"Well, she's still in shock. Her daughter's just been killed."

"Aye. I would have expected her to be more upset about it, though."

Felicity started the engine and left.

"Alright," Thompson said, "Let's get started, shall we?"

He and Simmons both took out blue rubber gloves and pulled them on.

The house was messy, but some attempt had been made to tidy the lounge room, with toys pushed back against the walls or arranged into heaps out of walkways. There was a small plastic tub of books next to one of the armchairs that was full of children's books.

Thompson looked at the cover of the book at the front for a moment, then knelt down and began to sift through the others.

"How old's the daughter?" he asked.

"Three or four, I think. Why?"

Thompson shook his head. "Don't know. These books just seem a bit simple, is all. Bit easy for a three- or four-year-old."

"Maybe she's not much of a reader."

There was a bureau against one wall with a row of cabinets at the bottom and drawers above them. Shelves on the top held a couple of photographs. Most of them were photos of Jessie and Kasey. One was a photo of Bill and Felicity Stewart standing with Kasey and Jessie.

Simmons opened the cabinets and found they were almost empty, apart from a couple of vases and some chinaware.

He opened the first of the drawers and found it was full of bills, a licence renewal and a couple of letters from the council.

The next drawer had a large pile of letters and legal documents. A few of the letters had the logo of a solicitors' firm at the top and the court documents bore the seal of the Family Court.

"The Family Court stuff's in here," Simmons said, "Are we bringing it?"

"Yeah," Thompson told him.

The kitchen was tidy but not particularly clean. The benches felt greasy and there were a couple of patches on the floor where food had been dropped but not cleaned up.

The pantry had a few tins and a lot of snack food.

The fridge, too, was almost empty. Soft drink cans and juice boxes were on the shelf in the door, while the shelves contained a few packets of ready-to-cook meals. The freezer had a couple of stacks of frozen meals.

"She wasn't much of a cook," Thompson said.

Simmons shrugged. "Single mum. Working nights."

"Even so. Not a trace of fruit or veg in here, or fresh meat."

"Maybe she was planning to do the shopping this week."

The bathroom was similarly in need of a clean. The glass doors of the shower screen were opaque with soap scum and the grout at the bottom contained thick black patches of mould. The sink had orange stains around it and there were drops of dried toothpaste on the top near the toothbrush rack.

The towels hanging on the rack were in need of a clean, as was the crumpled mat next to the shower.

One of the bedrooms clearly belonged to Jessie. Toys lay on the floor and on top of a low shelf under the window. A couple of Disney posters were sticky-taped to the walls, next to some drawings made with felt pens or coloured pencils. Again, Thompson thought they looked like the work of a much younger child.

A set of drawers contained children's clothing, but it was an odd mix. There were dozens of pairs of socks still in the packets, but very few shirts. Nothing was arranged in any sort of order, just pushed into the drawers.

A second bedroom contained a single bed and a cupboard that was empty apart from a spare pillow and some linen.

The main bedroom lay at the back of the house.

The bedclothes had been pulled roughly over the bed, but left untidy. There was a faint smell to the sheets and the doona. They clearly had not been washed in some time.

Thompson opened the cupboard and found a few dresses hanging beside coats and jackets. Several pairs of shoes were on the bottom of the cupboard in disorganised piles.

He opened a chest of drawers beside the cupboard. Underwear was in the top drawer, much of it lace, and some of it lingerie.

The second drawer contained T-shirts and shorts, mixed with leggings and socks. Like the child's bedroom, things were piled in without any sort of order.

"George," Simmons said, from behind him.

Thompson turned.

Simmons was kneeling on the floor beside the bed. He had been working his way through the bedside cabinet.

Thompson got up and walked over to him.

"What is it?"

Simmons pointed. The middle drawer of the bedside cabinet was open. There were a couple of paperback books at the front and a pair of socks. Behind them was a black, plastic box with a hinged lid.

Simmons held the lid open for Thompson to see inside.

A small glass pipe with a round bulb lay next to a clip-seal packet of white powder.

Thompson took a pen out of his shirt pocket.

Carefully, he inserted it into the end of the pipe and lifted it up. Leaning forward, he held the pipe in front of his nose and inhaled.

"Meth?" Simmons asked.

"Aye," Thompson said, "and that's not a small bag either. Looks like the lass had a fair old habit, doesn't it?"

Chapter 12

Alicia Martin lived in an apartment building on the edge of Maylands. It was part of a basic, but pleasant block of twenty a couple of streets back from the main road.

The front of the building had a secure door and an intercom system.

Perry found the button for Alicia's apartment and pressed it.

It took a few moments before there was an answer.

"Hello," came a voice over the speaker, sounding tired and washed out.

"Police," Perry said, "Detectives Perry and Packer. We're looking for Alicia Martin."

"That's me."

"We need to speak to you. Can we come in?"

It took a moment before there was a reply.

"Okay. I'm on the third floor."

There was a buzz and the front door was unlocked.

Perry pushed it open and they walked into the foyer of the building. It was a narrow space with an elevator and a door at the end marked, 'No entry'. A couple of bicycles and a folded pram rested against the far end beside a large pot plant.

They took the elevator up to the third floor.

It opened onto a long corridor with a bare concrete floor. Windows faced out over one side and a row of apartment doors were on the other.

They walked along to 34 and Perry knocked on the door.

Alicia Martin opened it.

She was in her mid-twenties and overweight, with long, blonde hair that was messy and gathered into a loose pony-tail at the back. She was wearing a Taylor Swift T-shirt and tight leggings.

"Come in," she said, holding the door open for them.

The lounge room inside was a mess. Cheap toys covered the floor and a large cardboard box at the back had been converted into a cubby house with windows cut in the side and a garish rainbow of paint covering its surface.

Sitting on the floor pushing a plastic truck along the ground was a boy of about four. He was sucking on a dummy and wearing a shirt, but no trousers over his underpants.

"I'm sorry about the mess," Alicia said, picking up clothes and toys from one of the lounge chairs to make space for them, "Jakey goes to daycare a couple of days a week and I tidy up, but it's not one of his days."

"Don't worry about it," Perry said, smiling, "Every house with a toddler in it looks the same."

She smiled and waved at Jakey, who was now sitting up and looking at them with curiosity.

Alicia stood there with the clothes and toys in her hand, unsure what to do next.

"Um, so what's this about?" she asked.

"We need to ask you a few questions," Perry said, "Maybe Jakey can watch some TV for a little while."

Alicia looked at her for a moment, then gave a nod. "Yeah, sure. Sorry. Sit down. Do you want a drink or...?"

"No, that's fine," Perry said.

Packer shook his head.

Perry and Packer sat down on the couch, careful not to stand on any of the toys around the floor in front of it. Alicia moved over to the TV set against the far wall and switched it on. Jakey moved across eagerly to position himself in front of the TV while Alicia fiddled with the hand control until a children's cartoon appeared on the screen.

There was another lounge chair beside the one Perry and Packer were sitting on, and she pushed aside a couple of stuffed animals and plastic cars to make space to sit down.

Alicia looked at them blankly.

"You're friends with Kasey Stewart?" Perry asked.

Alicia nodded. "Kasey? Yeah."

"I'm sorry to tell you we have some bad news."

Alicia's eyes widened. "Oh, no. Has something happened to her?"

"I'm afraid so," Perry said, "There's no easy way to tell you this. Kasey was hit by a car on Saturday night."

"Oh, God," Alicia said, shocked, "No. Is she hurt?"

"I'm sorry to tell you she was killed."

"What?" Alicia said, her voice rising.

Jakey looked around from the TV. He stared at her for a moment, then returned to watching TV.

Alicia was shaking, her breath coming out in short, hard bursts. "I don't understand. How could this... She was here on Friday. We went to the play centre. Oh, God."

Alicia began crying, arms wrapped around her body as she rocked on her chair.

"I'll get you a drink," Packer said, and disappeared into the kitchen.

Perry felt her annoyance rising again, but pushed it away.

She did her best to comfort Alicia. It took some time to calm her down enough to speak.

Packer returned with a glass of water and handed it to Alicia, before sitting down again.

"Do you know..." Alicia asked, "who did it?"

She swallowed hard, her face crumpling again.

"Not yet," Perry said, "but we're following up a few things. How long have you known Kasey?"

"Since we were kids," Alicia said, "We met in, like, grade four or five at school and became friends. We stayed like that all through high school."

"Right," Perry said, "A long time, then. You must have been very close."

Alicia nodded. "Like sisters."

"What was she like as a child?"

"Always happy. She was always smiling. I mean, we had arguments sometimes. Like kids do, but it never lasted long."

"You were at the same high school as well?"

Alicia nodded. "Different classes, so we didn't see each other as much, but we always spent lunchtimes together and hung out after school. We kind of lost touch near the end, though."

"Oh. What happened?"

Alicia frowned. "When we were... fifteen or sixteen probably, Kasey went through this kind of, I don't know, strange patch. She got sort of withdrawn and secretive. It was harder to talk to her. We started arguing a lot, and she just wanted to spend more time alone."

"What was that about?" Perry asked.

"Just teenage girls, I suppose," Alicia said, shrugging, "I kind of thought something must be wrong and I tried talking to her about it, but she kept saying there was nothing wrong. She used to get angry, so I stopped asking. After a while, we just kind of drifted apart. I made other friends and we lost touch.

"I ran into her again a couple of years ago at the Transport Department. I was down there to renew my driver's licence, and she was sitting down in the waiting area. Just about fell over when I saw her again after nearly ten years. She didn't see me, and I kind of ummed and ahhed about going over to talk to her, which seems really stupid now. But as soon as I went over, she got up and hugged me. It was like we were kids again. Straight back to being best friends. It's been like that ever since."

Alicia was smiling now.

Then she suddenly remembered why the police were here.

Her mouth crumpled into a grimace and tears began to run down her cheek again.

"Oh, my god."

Packer and Perry waited while she cried silently for a few moments, wiping her face on her T-shirt.

"Alicia was still married when you resumed your friendship?" Perry asked, when Alicia had recovered enough to continue.

Alicia gave a slight snort and a weary smile.

"Yeah," she said, "Yeah, she was still married to Deon when we got back in touch again. I was still with Jordan then, so we used to go to each others' places a bit or out for a drink. We both had kids, so we used to go to the park and stuff with both families."

"Did you get along with Deon?"

Alicia looked at her for a moment, then shook her head.

"He used to be an okay guy," Alicia said, "and I think he really did care about Kasey at first. Like, they were really happy together. But he was pretty nasty to Kasey sometimes. Shouting at her for stuff. She had bruises a couple of times and used to have these reasons that sounded made up."

"You think Deon was hitting her?" Perry asked.

Alicia shrugged. "She never told me that, but I thought so sometimes. I don't know. It got worse once Kasey's parents came back on the scene. Kasey and Deon were arguing more than before. There was always friction between him and Kasey's parents, which made things really hard. And he turned into a complete arsehole after they split up, too, trying to take Jessie off her."

"What kind of friction between Deon and Kasey's parents?" Perry asked.

"Bill's always been a bit, I don't know, possessive or something. When we were kids, it was always him driving Kasey to parties and things. If we went shopping, he always took us there and waited in the car. That was cool when we were ten or twelve, like having our own taxi service. But it was kind of weird later. Even when we were fourteen or fifteen, he was still hanging around.

"Felicity's always been weird. She always used to put Kasey down, like whatever Kasey did wasn't good enough, you know. There were a few things she did when we were kids that were really nasty. I remember in grade seven, Kasey got an award at school for maths, like the best in the school. The school principal gave it to her at an assembly and the whole school clapped. She was really excited about it. When we got home after school, she showed Felicity and Felicity just kind of laughed about it. Said it was just a participation award, and they had to give one to everyone. Kasey just shrugged it off, but I could tell she was upset about it.

"When Kasey and me met up again a few years ago, I asked about her parents. She'd stopped contact with them, hadn't seen them in years. I wasn't surprised. I was glad about it, actually.

"But then she got in touch with them earlier this year. They found out about Jessie and wanted to see her, so they started hanging around all the time. Kasey thought it was great at first, but it soon got to be a problem. Felicity was back to putting her down all the time and Bill was kind of taking over everything like when we were kids."

Alicia fell silent. She stared over at the TV.

"You said this caused problems with Deon?" Perry prompted.

"Huh? Oh, yeah. Sorry. Um, yeah. They didn't like Deon. Didn't think he was good enough for Kasey - although nobody would have been. I was at Bill and Felicity's place a few times with Kasey when Deon wasn't there, and as soon as his name came up, they'd start having a go at him. Kasey just said nothing, but it was obvious she didn't like it.

"Deon didn't like them either. He used to avoid them. He went to dinner at their place a couple of times, but then, I think he had this big argument with Bill about something and that was the end of it. Kasey used to go on her own after that. If they were coming to Kasey's place, Deon would go out."

"That must have made things hard for Kasey."

Alicia nodded. "Yeah. At first, she was kind of defensive about it, sticking up for Deon and that. But after a while, she started agreeing with what her parents were saying. Although, by then, she was..."

Alicia broke off suddenly, glancing up at Perry and Packer, then looking away.

"Anyway, she started arguing with Deon. They split up not long after that. And then he turned into a complete bastard, trying to get custody of Jessie. I mean Kasey had some problems, but instead of trying to help, he was just making things worse."

"What kind of problems?" Perry asked.

Alicia shrugged, not looking at her. "A few issues she was sorting out."

Her face hardened. "And then the arsehole started trying to take Jessie away. As if Kasey didn't have enough problems without him doing that to her."

"When did they split? Kasey and Deon?"

"Um. What is it now? December. So, they must have broken up in about June, July maybe. Something like that."

"And there was a custody issue?"

"Yeah. I think Kasey kind of assumed that neither of them would see Deon again. He left and that was it. That was what Kasey thought anyway. Then the next thing, she gets these Family Court papers served on her and he's trying to get sole custody. Saying she's not a fit mother. Family Services got involved and started doing home visits and stuff. It just caused this huge blow-up. All Deon had to do was say he wanted to share custody and it would have been fine, but he was trying to take Jessie away instead. Pig."

"How did Kasey take that?"

"How do you think she took it?" Alicia asked, widening her eyes, "She was so pissed off with him.

"It was a really difficult situation, though, 'cause Kasey got her parents involved. She had to tell Family Services that her parents were helping her, so that they would let her keep Jessie until the Family Court stuff was sorted out, but I don't think she really wanted them around. It was this huge stress trying to keep Family Services happy and her parents, too."

"And this was all in the last few months?"

Alicia nodded. "Yeah. I suppose Deon'll be happy now."

"Why?"

"'Cause he'll get Jessie, won't he? That was what he wanted."

"I'm not sure it'll work that way," Perry said, "It'll be up to the Family Court to work out what's best for Jessie."

Alicia frowned. "She'll just go to Deon, won't she? He's her father."

"Not necessarily," Perry said, "They look at the child's welfare. There's a lot of things to take into account. Jessie will be looked after though."

Alicia was clearly surprised about this, but said nothing further.

She frowned at Perry, a thought occurring to her.

"Why are you asking all this stuff about Kasey? Why do you want to know this?"

"We're treating Kasey's death as suspicious."

"What do you mean suspicious?"

"We think someone hit Kasey deliberately."

Alicia's frown deepened with surprise. She stared at Perry.

"Like, someone meant to kill her?"

Perry nodded.

"Oh, my god," Alicia said, her voice little more than a whisper.

"Can you think of anyone who might have wanted to hurt Kasey?" Perry asked.

Alicia shook her head.

"No," she said, "No one. Why would anyone want to do that to Kasey?"

Chapter 13

When Packer and Perry returned to the incident room, Simmons and Thompson were back from Kasey Stewart's house. They filled in Perry and Packer on what they had discovered.

"Drugs?" Perry asked, "A bit of weed of something?"

Simmons shook his head. "Meth."

"Really?"

"It was quite a bit, too," Simmons said, "Half a gram maybe."

He looked at Thompson who nodded. "Thereabouts."

Perry gave a slight snort of surprise. "I wouldn't have expected that."

"Half the people in Perth have tried it one time or another," Thompson said, "You know that."

"Yeah," Perry agreed, "and she'd be the right age group, I suppose. It just doesn't seem to fit with what we've heard about her."

"I'm not sure about that," Thompson said, "If she was on the game, it makes sense. Most of the girls are using something."

"They are," Perry agreed, "but the girls working the streets in Northbridge are usually on their own or with a boyfriend who kicks the shit out of them before taking half their earnings for himself. Kasey had a daughter and her parents were helping her out."

"She's got to pay for the meth habit, though," Thompson said, "which can't be easy if you're only working three nights a week. She couldn't exactly ask her parents for a few dollars to buy drugs, could she?"

"Actually, it sounds like things were a bit difficult with her parents," Perry said, "according to Alicia Martin anyway."

She relayed the conversation that they had had with Alicia Martin.

"This is all Alicia's perception, of course," Perry said, "She doesn't like Bill and Felicity Stewart, so she didn't have much nice to say about them. But Felicity was babysitting three nights a week and Bill was pretty distraught at the hospital. I'm not sure I believe what Alicia says about their relationship with Kasey being strained."

"Not sure I agree with that," Packer said, "Felicity didn't seem as upset about losing her daughter as she could have."

"I thought that, too," Thompson said, "when she came to the house to let us in."

"Yeah?"

"Aye. Like it was more of an annoyance having to help us out."

"Well, to be fair," Simmons said, "She's just lost her daughter, like I said at the house."

"Different people grieve in different ways," Seoyoon said, backing him up, "Not everyone breaks down crying when they lose someone."

"I suppose not," Thompson said.

"Where's she getting the drugs from?" Packer said.

"Nothing at the house to tell us," Thompson said, "but meth dealers aren't exactly a rarity in Perth, are they? Especially somewhere like Belmont. I mean, they get arrested at the shopping centre sometimes."

Packer nodded.

He turned to Seoyoon.

"Have we got the records for Kasey's phone?"

Seoyoon nodded, "They arrived this morning. I just started going through them now."

"Anything?"

"I haven't really looked much yet. I was just going through the Saturday she was killed. There's an exchange of text messages with Alicia Martin in the morning and one from her father in the afternoon. There are a few other calls, but they're not numbers we know. I haven't IDed them yet, but I will."

Packer nodded. "Okay."

"I wonder if Alicia Martin knew about the drugs," Perry said, "She said they were best friends. It's the sort of thing a best friend might notice."

"Why not tell you if she did?" Simmons asked, "I mean Kasey's dead, now. She doesn't need to protect her if she did know."

"I'm not sure she'd see it that way," Perry said, "She only just found out Kasey was dead. She'd still feel protective."

"Probably wouldn't have told you if Kasey was on the game to pay for her drug habit, either," Thompson said.

"No," Perry said, "She probably wouldn't."

The incident room door opened.

Inspector Base entered, holding his cap under his arm.

"Progress?" he asked.

"Some," Packer said.

"Right," Base said, "We'll discuss it in your office, shall we?"

Without waiting for an answer, he headed across the incident room to Packer's office.

Packer followed behind him.

"Did he sound more polite than usual?" Simmons whispered to Seoyoon.

"He didn't get the promotion," she whispered back, "Maybe he's working on his communication skills."

"Still got some way to go, if you ask me."

"Haven't you two got work to do?" Thompson asked.

Still grinning, Simmons and Seoyoon turned back to their computer screens.

Base sat down on the chair in front of Packer's desk.

Packer walked around to sit at the back.

"So, where are things at?" Base asked.

"We've IDed the victim as Kasey Stewart," Packer said, "26, single mother. Told her mother she was going out to her job as a night cleaner at nine o'clock, leaving the mother to babysit the daughter. George and Mickey searched her house this morning. She had meth in her bedroom."

"Family Services seem to be involved."

"Do we know why?" Base asked.

"Not yet. There seems to be a custody battle going on with the ex-husband. He's got a history for assaulting her and a couple of others."

"He seems like a good bet."

"Maybe," Packer said, "Doesn't explain what she was doing down at the Bell Tower at three in the morning, though. There's something odd about the parents, too."

Base raised an eyebrow. "Another of your 'feelings', Tony?"

Packer shrugged.

Base pressed his lips together. "Alright. Well, I suppose they've panned out in the past."

Packer remained silent.

"I thought you said there was some progress?" Base said, "This sounds like more questions than answers. Well, keep on it. Let me know when you're got a suspect."

"Sir."

Base collected his hat and left Packer's office.

"Good work, everybody," he said, as he headed back through the incident room.

They watched him in silence.

He closed the door behind him.

"Who was that?" Thompson asked, "It looked a lot like the inspector, but didn't act much like him."

"There were some difficult discussions with the commissioner over Harold Mosley's arrest," Perry said, "That's what I heard anyway."

A month earlier, Base had insisted that they arrest a known sex offender for a girl's abduction and had called a press conference to announce it. The man had later been cleared, much to Base's embarrassment.

"That can't have done his prospects of promotion much good," Thompson said.

"No," Perry agreed, "I don't think he's completely out of the running for Superintendent Canning's job when he retires, but it hasn't improved his chances."

"He'll never get that," Simmons said, from the other side of the room, "Not after the balls-up with Mosley."

Thompson looked around with mock surprise. "Did you say something? I was having a private discussion with Claire."

"I'm just saying I agree," Simmons said, slightly chastened.

"Have you finished on that CCTV?" Thompson asked, "Do you need something else to work on?"

"No," Simmons muttered, returning to his computer screen.

Thompson looked across at Seoyoon, who was watching him.

He winked at her, and she shook her head, before returning to her own computer screen.

***

It took Seoyoon an hour to sift through Kasey's phone records. She called Packer and the others over to her computer to summarise what she had found.

"Kasey made a few calls on the day she was killed," Seoyoon said, "Most of them look irrelevant. There is this one, though."

She tapped the screen.

"Just before ten in the morning, she rang Miriam Todd, and spoke to her for nearly thirty minutes."

"Who's Miriam Todd?" Thompson asked.

Seoyoon moved the mouse on her computer and pulled up another window which was open at a website.

"She runs this place," Seoyoon said, "Sunrise. It's a women's drop-in centre. Counselling and support groups. That kind of thing. The address is not far from Kasey's house."

Seoyoon moved back to the phone records. "Kasey seems to have been a regular caller. She phoned or texted Miriam Todd several times a week."

"When did she start doing that?" Packer asked.

"The first call's about six months earlier."

"Around the time of the split with the ex."

"Makes sense," Perry said, "She's going through a rough patch and needs some help. I'm sure there were things she'd prefer not to discuss with her parents."

Packer nodded.

"Anything else of interest?" he asked.

"Not yet," Seoyoon said, "but I'm still working my way back through the records. I just focused on the Saturday she was killed to start off with."

"Okay," Packer said, "Keep at it."

"I've got something, too," Perry said, "I did some background on the ex-husband."

"And?"

"I hate to stick up for Mickey," Perry said.

"Geez, thanks," Simmons muttered.

"But look at Deon DeSouza's record."

Packer moved over to stand behind her desk.

"Five previous convictions for assault," Perry continued, "and about a dozen complaints. Look at who the complainant is."

Packer didn't need to.

"Kasey Stewart for all the recent ones," Perry continued, "The three before that are for a different complainant and one more before that is for a different complainant again. I'm guessing previous girlfriends."

"There you are then," Simmons said, triumphantly, "It's the ex. I told you."

"It's certainly ringing one bell anyway," Perry said.

"Alright," Packer said, "Get a current address for him."

"I bet he drives a white sedan," Simmons asked.

"I think you'll find it was a red sports car," Thompson said, then added in an Eastern-European accent, "with lots of chrome. The vehicle of the devil, it was! The devil!"

"George, you and Mickey go and talk to Miriam Todd," Packer said, "Find out what she and Kasey spoke about on Saturday morning."

"Right, boss."

"Claire, you and I'll go and talk to the ex-husband."

Chapter 14

Packer slowed down as they drove along the side street. Rows of workshops and industrial units lined either side of the street.

"There it is," Packer said, seeing the sign atop the building.

There was no parking outside, so he drove forward another thirty or forty metres and pulled in beside the footpath. He and Perry got out and walked back along the street.

The building was a large workshop. Three roller doors were rolled up and a car was parked below each of them inside the shed.

In the area outside, there were another four cars parked. Each of them had been modified in some way, lowered suspension, wider tyres or hood scoops on the bonnets.

There was a blue car in the left-hand side of the shop that was up on a raised platform and the bonnet had been removed. One man in work pants and a T-shirt was leaning over the bonnet with a socket wrench, while another was on his back under the engine with a power tool.

A radio blared incessantly in the background, the tinny sound of rock music playing through the workshop.

Packer and Perry walked into the workshop.

The man under the bonnet saw them approaching and stood up.

They were in plain clothes, but his expression clearly showed that he recognised them as police officers.

"Can I help youse?" he asked, warily.

"Is there a Deon DeSouza working here?" Perry asked.

"In the office," the man said, nodding towards a door at the side of the workshop.

"Thanks," Perry said.

She and Packer walked across to the office.

The man standing beside the car stood and watched them in silence.

The door to the office was open.

Inside was a narrow room with a desk across the centre. A row of three filing cabinets lay across the back wall next to a door marked, 'Toilet,' and a line of plastic documents trays holding a jumble of paperwork sat on top of them. Cardboard boxes were stacked in places, and shiny engine parts wrapped in plastic lay amongst them.

Posters of heavily-modified street racers were pinned to the wall with the logos for automotive parts manufacturers printed across their tops.

Sitting behind the desk was a man in an AC/DC T-shirt. Both forearms were heavily tattooed. His head was shaved down to the skin, leaving a blue rash of growth across the surface, and he was wearing large gold earrings in each ear.

He was on the phone, but looked up as they entered. He continued talking on the phone, but eyed them as he did so. Clearly, he recognised them as police officers, too.

The man continued the conversation on the phone, obviously in no hurry to end it. He was discussing engine work, making a few notes on a sheet of paper on the desk, asking for specifics and giving estimates of prices. After a few minutes of this, he started asking about the caller's plans for the weekend, turning the conversation away from work. This continued on for another few minutes, as he ignored the waiting police officers.

"Rightio, buddy," he said cheerfully into the phone, "Good luck with that. Let me know how she goes, and bring her back into the shop if anything gets fucked up. I'll sort her out for you. No worries. Catch ya."

He hung up the phone and wrote some more notes on the paper in front of him.

"Deon DeSouza?" Perry asked.

"The boys in blue, eh?" DeSouza said, turning his attention to the computer screen on the desk. He began tapping at the keyboard with his index fingers. "What do youse want?"

"Just a few questions," Perry said.

"Go on then."

DeSouza peered down at the keyboard, searching around for the keys and tapping at them with one finger.

"We want to speak with you about Kasey Stewart."

DeSouza looked sideways at Perry, smirking knowingly, then back to the screen. "It's all bullshit."

"What's all bullshit?" Perry asked.

"Whatever she says I done. I haven't been anywhere near her."

"She was run over by a car on Saturday night," Perry said bluntly.

The grin disappeared as DeSouza turned in his chair to look at her. A frown of concern appeared on his face.

"Yeah?" he asked, "Is she alright?"

"I'm afraid she's dead, Mr DeSouza," Perry said.

"F-u-c-k," DeSouza said, drawing out the sound of the word, "Really?"

Perry nodded.

He sat there for a moment, staring out the window to the carpark outside. He gave a slight shake of his head.

"What happened?" he asked, turning back to Perry.

"We're still making enquiries," she said, "but it appears to be deliberate."

"Deliberate?" he said, frowning.

A look of sudden realisation appeared on his face. He held up his hands.

"Well, I didn't fuckin' do it," he said, "I'm not even with her any more. We split up months ago."

"You still have contact with her, though?"

"No. None at all. The solicitors are sortin' out all that shit with Jessie."

"This is the custody issue with your daughter?"

DeSouza nodded. "Yeah, we're in the Family Court sortin' it out."

"When was the last time you spoke to Kasey?"

DeSouza thought about it. "I don't know. Two months ago, probably. We went to a mediation. Waste of fuckin' time, though. Either I get Jessie or Kasey does. Not much there to fuckin' mediate, if you know what I mean. But you gotta do what the court's tellin' you to do."

"Is there some hostility between you and Kasey?"

DeSouza grinned humourlessly and gave a slight roll of his eyes. "Yeah, you could say that. It's her being hostile, though, not me. I just want to look after me own daughter, you know? Get her away from that crack-head."

"Kasey's a crack-head?"

DeSouza nodded. "That's part of why we split up. She's smoking so much of that shit that she doesn't know what time of day it is most of the time."

"When did this drug use start?"

"Months ago. Came out of nowhere, too. I don't know why she started doing that shit. Well, I do. I mean, I can guess."

"And why is that?"

"Her fuckin' parents."

"What does that mean?"

"Talk to them and you'll see what I mean."

"Why don't you tell us what you mean?"

DeSouza rolled his eyes and shook his head. "Forget it."

"That's not very helpful, Mr DeSouza."

"Yeah? Well, pardon me."

A thought seemed to occur to him. "If Kasey's been... I mean, where's Jessie?"

"Bill and Felicity Stewart are looking after her."

"Oh, get fucked. She should be with me. Not that pair."

"As I understand things, Kasey has custody until the Family Court proceedings are resolved."

"Yeah, and that's bullshit, too," DeSouza said, "I wanted to take Jessie with me, but Kasey wouldn't let me. So I called Family Services. I wasn't trying to cause trouble for her, but I mean, what the fuck's happening to Jessie when I'm not there, you know? She's not safe with a fuckin' junkie looking after her.

"But that didn't solve the problem, either. They let her keep Jessie and made her do fuckin' rehab or some shit. So now we have to go through the Family Court bullshit to sort it out."

"What did you think would happen with Family Services?" Perry asked.

"I thought they'd give Jessie to me. I mean, how can you say she's better off with a mum who's shooting up drugs than she is with her own father?"

"Did they give you a reason why they wouldn't place Jessie with you?"

DeSouza shook his head, but he looked away. There was clearly something evasive about him, now.

"Have you ever been in any difficulty with the police?" Perry asked.

DeSouza glared at her, clearly angry about this.

He shrugged. "Alright. Well, you obviously already know, don't you? Yeah, I've got a couple of convictions for hitting Kasey. It didn't happen like she said, though. I wasn't beating her up."

"So what did happen?"

"We had an argument. She started pushing me, and I pushed back. She fell over and hit her face. I didn't punch her, which is what she fuckin' said."

"And this happened more than once?"

"Yeah. When I saw youse here this morning, I thought that was what you were here for. Thought she'd made up another bullshit story to help her with the Family Court stuff."

"This is all in her imagination, is it?"

DeSouza threw his hands up, and shook his head.

"Yeah, see, this is what I fuckin' mean. You cunts just take her side, like fuckin' Family Services. She was using drugs, right? I mean, I didn't know that at the time, but I do now. We argued and she got aggro with me. Always her. Every time. And then she hurt herself and said it was me. It was bullshit."

"What reason would she have for doing that?"

"She was a druggie. I don't know. Look, she just completely changed in the last few months. She wasn't the girl I was with for five years. She started acting crazy. She was depressed and then she was angry. You never knew what was going to happen with her. That's why I had to leave in the end. It wasn't a good place for Jessie either."

"So the last time you had any contact with Kasey was at the Family Court mediation two months ago?"

"Yeah. Pretty sure it was."

"Did you speak to her apart from that?"

"No. There's a court order saying we have to speak through the solicitors."

"What sort of car do you drive?" Packer asked.

DeSouza looked at him.

He stood up and pointed out the window to the carpark.

"The maroon one."

Packer and Perry turned to look out the window. A maroon-coloured Subaru WRX with dark-tinted windows and a hood scoop was parked closest to the street.

"Anybody else have access to it?" Packer asked.

DeSouza shrugged. "I let the guys use it sometimes. Sometimes we have to give a customer a lift or get some rags from Bunnings or something."

"Where were you on Saturday night?"

"What time?"

"After midnight. The early hours of the morning."

"After midnight? Home in bed asleep."

"Alone?"

"Yeah."

DeSouza rolled his eyes. "Why? You think I fuckin' run her over?"

Packer and Perry looked at him with blank faces.

"Get fucked," he said, realisation dawning, "You really do think I did it."

"Well, it sounds like you had a reason to," Packer pointed out.

"Look, I didn't want her to get killed. I spent five years with her. We've got a kid together."

"And now you don't have to worry about the Family Court proceedings."

"Alright. Well, no. I suppose I don't. But I didn't fuckin' kill Kasey."

"Drug users are unstable, Mr DeSouza," Packer said, "You know that from your own experience. When you argued, Kasey would stumble over and injure herself. If you went to talk to her on Saturday night, she might not have been acting rationally. Accidents happen."

DeSouza shook his head. "Nuh. Didn't fuckin' happen, mate. I wasn't anywhere near there."

"Near where?"

"Wherever she got run over. I don't fuckin' know. I was at home in bed."

"But nobody can confirm that?"

"It's the truth."

Packer looked at him for a moment.

DeSouza stared back.

After a long moment, DeSouza raised his eyebrows and held out his hands.

"Is that it?" he asked.

"For now," Packer said.

He turned and left, with Perry behind him.

As they walked across the carpark, Packer crossed over to DeSouza's car, and moved to the side. Then he walked to the front and squatted down. He leaned towards the front, looking over the grille and the front moulding.

"What are you looking at?" Perry asked.

"Wanted to see if there was any damage."

"Why?

Packer looked up. "Because this looks like a red sports car with chrome on it. And it's got Bridgestone tyres."

Chapter 15

Simmons and Thompson drove north along the freeway and out towards Belmont once again. They continued past the shopping centre and into the industrial area that ran through the blocks beyond.

They drove past tyre fitters and automotive parts, whitegoods retailers and a line of charity shops.

The address for Sunrise was a unit along a side street.

"Bit of an odd place for a drop-in centre," Simmons said.

"Close to the bus stop and the shops," Thompson pointed out.

Simmons pulled into the parking lot and slowed down.

A row of businesses lined the road with a row of narrow parking spaces between them and the road. He managed to find a park near the middle and pulled in.

He and Thompson got out and walked along to the end of the row.

Most of the units were painted in tasteful colours with professional-looking signs across the tops of the units.

By contrast, Sunrise was painted in a bright purple colour, with a sign reading, 'Sunrise,' comprised of different-coloured and different-sized letters arranged in an arc. Below this, in neater, but still rough, writing was a sign reading, 'A Place of Safety'.

Thompson and Simmons exchanged glances.

"After you, lad," Thompson said, "and don't worry. You're safe."

Simmons pushed open the door and walked in, with Thompson behind him.

The inside of the unit was a large, open space. Heavy grey industrial carpeting covered the floor, but the walls were painted in bright blues and yellows. Two doors at the back led to bathrooms. Beside them in the back corner was a cluttered desk and a row of mismatched cabinets that looked like they had come from charity shops and had been painted in bright, gaudy colours.

At the front of the room was a large Turkish rug surrounded by big cushions, beanbags and chairs of different styles. Large baskets containing children's toys sat beside a TV set.

At one end of the rug was a fit-looking woman in Lycra gym gear, who was cross-legged with her arms raised overhead in some form of yoga pose. A group of women sat facing her, imitating her pose with various degrees of success. A few small children crawled around them or pushed toys along the floor, and there were two strollers with sleeping babies at the end.

A small bell on the back of the door gave a tinkling sound as Simmons and Thompson walked in.

A woman at the back of the rug looked up at the sound.

She was probably in her late thirties and heavily overweight with pink-framed glasses and her long, curly hair spilling down over her shoulders. She was wearing leggings pulled tight over her huge thighs and a baggy top.

Seeing the two detectives in the doorway, she lowered her arms and pushed herself to her feet with some effort.

She walked across to them, smiling.

"Hi there," she said, "Can I help?"

Simmon and Thompson produced their identification and her smile disappeared.

"Detectives Simmons and Thompson," Simmons said, "Are you Miriam Todd?"

"Yes," the woman nodded, looking back anxiously at the rug.

Nobody else seemed to have noticed them, and continued with the exercises.

"Is there somewhere we can talk?" Simmons asked.

Miriam took his arm in her hand and steered him towards the back of the room. Thompson followed.

Still clutching Simmons's arm, she took them to the desk at the back of the room.

"Take a seat," she said.

Rather than sit down behind the desk, she pulled out a chair at the front, so that the three of them were sitting together in a group.

"How can I help?" she asked.

"Sorry to interrupt your class," Simmons said, "Yoga, is it?"

"Pilates," Miriam said, "We run a class here each week. Sonia comes in each Monday."

"Right. I thought this place was like a women's refuge or something."

"Sunrise is a support centre," Miriam said, sounding like a sales pamphlet, "We offer support to any woman who needs it for any reason. Exercise and meditation classes help to boost self-esteem and a sense of belonging.

"We also offer counselling or legal advice. A lot of the time, we're just here to be someone to talk to."

"Right," Simmons said, "And it's, what? Government-funded or something?"

"We get a tiny grant," Miriam said, "but we rely mostly on donations and volunteers. The local churches help out."

"It's you running the place, is it?"

"I'm Sunrise's manager, but we have volunteer staff. People like Sonia, who have a professional skill, donate their time when they can."

Simmons nodded. "Right. We wanted to ask some questions about Kasey Stewart. Does she come in here?"

Miriam's face remained friendly, but neutral. "Did she tell you she does?"

"Not exactly," Simmons said, "but your number came up in her phone records fairly regularly."

"I don't mean to be rude at all. But I'm not comfortable discussing anything about Kasey unless she's given me permission to. Anything we've spoken about together was in confidence."

Simmons nodded awkwardly.

"I'm really sorry to tell you this," he said, "but we've got some bad news about Kasey."

Concern showed on Miriam's face.

"Is Kasey in some sort of trouble?" she asked.

"It's a bit worse than that, actually," Simmons said, nervously.

Miriam looked at him expectantly.

Simmons opened his mouth, but had trouble finding the words.

"Kasey was involved in a hit-and-run incident," Thompson said, taking over, "I'm afraid she's been killed."

"Oh," Miriam gasped, her hand going to her mouth, "Oh, no."

She looked between the two of them, with wide eyes, as tears appeared.

She closed her eyes and rubbed at them, sniffing hard and giving a low sob.

Thompson and Simmons gave her a few minutes to take in the news.

"How? I mean what happened?" she asked, after a while.

"We're still trying to get to the bottom of that," Thompson said, "but at this stage, we believe it was deliberate."

Miriam looked at him with shock. "Deliberate? You mean she was killed on purpose?"

"It looks that way, yes."

"Who did it?" Miriam asked, "Was it Deon?"

"We're trying to find out who did it, Ms Todd," Thompson said, "Why do you suggest Deon?"

"He was making things so hard for her. Trying to take Jessie away from her."

"Kasey discussed that with you, did she?"

Miriam stopped talking. She looked at him, swallowing and breathing hard.

"Um, I'm sorry," she said, shaking her head, "but I don't know if I should talk about that."

"I can understand your concern about breaking confidences," Thompson said, "but Kasey's gone now. We need to find out what happened, so that we can get justice for her. Anything you can tell us would be a great help."

Miriam looked at him for a moment longer.

"Can I just have a moment to think about that?"

"Aye, of course."

Miriam looked across the room. She watched the exercise class for a while, but did not appear to be focused on what was actually happening.

Eventually, she turned back towards them.

"I'm not sure how much I can tell you," she said, "but I'll answer what I can."

"Thank you," Thompson said, "That's very good of you."

"Was it... I mean, was Kasey in pain for long?"

"We believe it was very quick," Thompson said, "She died at the scene and we've no reason to think she suffered at all."

"Thank God," Miriam said, "How awful."

"The incident happened on Sunday morning around 3:45 am," Thompson said, "Down near the Bell Tower. Have you any idea why Kasey might have been down there at that time of morning?"

"She does night cleaning," Miriam said, "There must have been some offices or something down there that she cleaning."

"We don't believe she was doing cleaning work," Thompson said, "She wasn't dressed for it. She was wearing a brief dress and heels. Can you think of any other reason she might have been there?"

Miriam shook her head, frowning. "At three in the morning? I suppose she might have been out for a night on the town or something, but it would be very unlike Kasey."

"She's not a clubber, then?"

"Her focus is Jessie. That's all she cares about."

"Did you speak to her last Saturday?" Thompson asked.

"Um," Miriam said, thinking about this, "Yeah. Yeah, I did. She phoned me in the morning."

"What did you speak about?"

"Nothing in particular. Kasey often called without any specific reason. She just liked to talk if she was feeling anxious or depressed."

"Is that how she was on Saturday? Anxious or depressed?"

Miriam thought about this. "I suppose so. Something was bothering her, but there often was with Kasey. There was a lot going on in her life."

"What sort of things?"

"Oh, the custody fight mainly. She was very worried about losing Jessie, and her ex was being very hostile about it. There were problems with her parents, too."

"Did she talk to you about the custody issues?"

"A lot. The only thing that really mattered in Kasey's life was Jessie. If she had lost Jessie to Deon, she couldn't have handled it. Trying to take her away was such a horrible, vindictive thing to do to Kasey. He used to assault her during the marriage. Trying to take Jessie was just an extension of the same violence, another way to hurt Kasey."

"What about her parents? You said some problems there, too?"

Miriam nodded.

"That was very difficult. Kasey cut off contact with them when she was in her late teens, and moved interstate. She came back to Perth with Deon when Jessie was small. I'm not sure how they found her, but her parents resumed contact. Kasey had very mixed feelings about that."

"Mixed how?"

Miriam let out a small breath. "It was something that Kasey and I had begun to work through together, but it was a very difficult issue for her. She wouldn't have got back in contact with her parents if it was up to her, but now that it had happened, she was trying to make something positive of it. She thought Jessie should have grandparents."

"Why did she cut off contact with her parents?"

"I don't know," Miriam said, "There was something there that she was had just begun to share with me. It was something we were going to explore together in the future."

Her face creased slightly and she began to cry again. "Oh, it's so awful that she's gone. Poor Kasey."

A thought suddenly occurred to her. "What about Jessie? Has she been told about what happened to Kasey?"

"I'm not really sure," Thompson said, "Jessie's with Kasey's parents. I don't know what they've said to her."

Miriam frowned. "Bill and Felicity have Jessie?"

Thompson nodded. "Aye, that's right."

Miriam said nothing.

"Is that a problem?" Thompson asked.

"I'm not sure how Kasey would have felt about it."

"How do you mean?"

"I don't know if Kasey would have been happy with them taking Jessie."

"Why not?"

"Oh, I don't know. As I said, there were some difficulties between Kasey and her parents. She was still unsure about having them in her life again. She was very protective of Jessie and I don't know if she would have trusted her with her parents. Or anyone else, really."

She gave a small shrug. "But I suppose there's no alternative. There's nobody else, is there?"

"It's not really our department," Thompson said, "I gather Family Services are involved. The Family Court will have to sort out the custody issues at some stage."

Miriam shook her head. "Deon won't want to take Jessie. Trying to get custody was just his way of hurting her. He'll stop all that now that Kasey's gone."

"Did you ever meet Deon?" Thompson asked.

Miriam gave a wry smile. "No. But I feel like I know him, after my time with Kasey. What a terrible man."

"You said you were doing some counselling with Kasey?"

"Freeform exploration," Miriam said, "We talked about whatever she wanted to talk about. Sometimes I guided the conversation towards more difficult areas to encourage her to share with me."

"Right. You see a lot of troubled young ladies in here," Thompson said, "and I'm sure you see all sorts of problems with alcohol and drugs. Did Kasey have any difficulties like that?"

"Kasey had some issues," Miriam said evasively, "She and I were working through them together. I'm afraid I can't say more than that."

Thompson looked at her, wondering whether to push her. Clearly, this was not something Miriam was willing to discuss.

"Can we go back to this phone call with Kasey on Saturday morning?" Thompson said, instead, "You said she sounded anxious or depressed."

"Yeah, she did."

"Did she give you any idea why?"

"I don't think so. Nothing out of the ordinary."

"Just take a minute to think about exactly what Kasey said."

He waited while Miriam thought about it.

"Do you know," Miriam said, looking up, "She did say something odd. Just before she hung up. She said, 'There's no escape.'"

"No escape from what?"

"I don't know," Miriam said, "but that was what she said. 'There's no escape.'"

Chapter 16

Packer and Perry stood in the driveway at the workshop while they waited for the forensics unit.

DeSouza came out of the office and stood in the doorway looking at them. After a few minutes, he went back inside.

"Do you think they'll find anything, boss?" Perry asked.

Packer shrugged.

"There's no damage on the car," Perry pointed out.

"Nothing visible to us. But DeSouza's got a repair shop."

"Brakovich has no idea what he saw. First it was a big white car, then it was a red sports car and the driver got out to threaten him. It's all garbage."

"Probably," Packer said, staring at the window of the office, "but I was impressed by DeSouza's sunny disposition."

It took another half hour for the forensics van to arrive.

"You're keeping me busy, lad," Goodge said, as he got out of the passenger seat. He looked tired and was walking with a noticeable stoop. The same officer from Sunday morning was driving.

"Although maybe it was worth the trip after all," he said, seeing Perry, "Have you done something different with your hair, lass? It looks lovely."

Perry gave a tutt of frustration and turned away.

"What have you got, then?" Goodge asked.

"WRX over there," Packer said, pointing, "Have a look at it for me."

"Dark red one? I thought you were looking for a white sedan."

"There's some doubt about that."

"Is there? Aye, well. Let's a quick squizz, then."

Goodge pulled on disposable blue gloves while the younger officer retrieved a tool kit.

They walked over to the car with Packer.

Goodge knelt down in front of DeSouza's car and peered at the grill. He took a torch out from the tool kit and shone it over the grille, moving it up and down to change the angle.

After a few moments, he reached into the tool box and retrieved a mirror, which he held underneath the car, shining the torch up underneath with the other hand.

It didn't take DeSouza long to emerge from the office.

"What the fuck are you doing?" he snapped, walking over to them.

"Just admiring your car, Mr DeSouza," Packer said, "I assume that's alright with you."

"No, it fuckin' isn't. Leave it alone."

"Why?" Packer asked, "Is there something you don't want us to see?"

"No."

"Then what's the problem?"

DeSouza glared at him, but fell silent.

"How long's this gonna take?" he asked eventually.

"Not long," Packer said, "We'll let you know when we're finished."

He nodded meaningfully back to the office, but DeSouza made no move to leave. He stood there, fuming.

Packer turned back to Goodge, ignoring DeSouza.

Goodge lay on his back and tried to move under the bottom of the car.

"Give us a hand, will you, lad?" he asked.

The younger officer knelt down beside him and pushed him forward under the front of the car. He waited while Goodge looked around, then pulled him back out again.

"Nothing," Goodge said to Packer, "but there's moisture under there. I'd say it's been pressure-cleaned in the last day or so."

Packer turned to DeSouza.

"Any reason you've had your car cleaned recently, Mr DeSouza?" he asked.

"I clean it most days," DeSouza said, "It's good advertising for the business, so I keep it looking smick."

Packer turned back to Goodge.

"What about the tyres?"

"Right make."

"Can you match them?"

"Not here," he said, "but we'll compare them back at the lab."

He watched while the younger officer took multiple photos of the treads and the side walls of the tyres.

"Right," Goodge said, "I'll be in touch. Be lucky."

"Thanks," Packer said.

As Goodge and the other officer returned, Packer turned to DeSouza.

"I won't keep you any further, Mr DeSouza. Thanks for your help."

DeSouza said nothing as Packer walked out of the carpark and back to the street.

Perry got in the passenger seat and Packer started the engine.

"Do you think it's him?" Perry asked.

"Right attitude for it," Packer said.

"He sure has."

"I don't understand the timing, though. They split six months ago. If it was him, then something must have triggered it. We need to find out what."

"There could have been some development with the custody issue."

"Could have been. Did you speak to someone at Family Services?"

"I'm waiting for a call back."

"If it's DeSouza, that doesn't explain the drugs or the clothing, either."

"Coincidences?"

"No such thing."

***

The traffic grew increasingly heavy along the freeway as they neared the entrances to the city.

"There must have been a car accident up ahead somewhere," Perry said.

"Yeah," Packer agreed.

"I'm glad I'm not out in this heat, trying to clear it. I don't miss those days."

"You can't have been in uniform for long."

"No," Perry agreed, "I applied for the detective's course as soon as I could. Got into Joondalup at the next intake."

The police academy was located in Joondalup, a smaller city an hour north of Perth.

"Was Frank McCain teaching at the academy when you were there?" Packer asked.

"Frank?" Perry said, "I don't think he ever taught at the academy."

"Didn't he? I thought someone told me that."

"I don't think so. Frank didn't really have the temperament for being a teacher."

"No?" Packer asked, "Had a bit of a temper?"

"He sure did," Perry said, "It never lasted long, though."

"You worked with him for a while, then?"

"Yeah. Three or four years. He was in charge when I joined the team. George, too."

"Have you heard from Frank since he left?"

"No," Perry said, a slight scoff in her voice, "Frank wasn't the sort to keep in touch."

"You worked together for a long time, though. Bit strange that he hasn't at least said hello."

"Yes and no," Perry said, "He'd had enough of the job. After Genevieve died, he started to get a bit jaded with it all. Couldn't see the point any longer. I'm not that surprised that he wanted a clean break from it when he retired."

"So, what do you reckon with his time now?" Packer asked.

"I don't know," Perry said, "He wasn't the type to play golf."

"He can't have that many years left in the job. Never said anything about what he was going to do after he retired?"

"I can't remember him ever talking about it," Perry said.

She thought for a moment. "He had a property out bush somewhere. He went out for a holiday once."

"Yeah? Whereabouts?"

"Oh, I don't know. I don't think he ever told us. He had an aunt, I think, who was an Aboriginal bloke. They weren't married, but when he died, he gave the land to Frank. He didn't have any other family and got along pretty well with Frank."

"Was it a farm or something?"

"No, nothing like that. It was just scrap out in the middle of nowhere. There must have been a river running through it, because was talking about fishing. George was giving him a hard time about not having the patience for it. Told Frank he'd be in there threatening the fish if they didn't jump on the hook straightaway."

"Right."

"Why are you asking about Frank?" Perry said, turning towards him.

"I wasn't, really," Packer lied, feigning disinterest, "I was thinking about Bill Stewart. He's retired, too, and it sounds like his retirement plans involve running Kasey's life."

"Alica Martin said he was always like that, though," Perry said, "even when they were children."

"Yeah. Sounded like Kasey started to grow out of it, though."

"Alicia said Kasey started getting withdrawn and secretive. Do you think that's what she meant? Rebelling from Bill being too close?"

"Maybe."

They fell silent, as they continued driving on towards the city, through the densely-packed traffic.

Perry did not seem to have noticed Packer digging for information about Frank McCain, and seemed to have accepted his excuse for asking him. Pushing for more was risky, so he left it.

But he filed away the information about the remote property.

It was something to look into when he had a chance.

***

When Packer and Perry returned to the incident room, Simmons was sitting at his desk beside Seoyoon's. Thompson was perched on the edge.

"What did the prodigal husband have to say for himself?" Thompson asked.

"The course of true love never did run smooth," Perry said.

"What?" Simmons asked.

"Don't they teach you anything in school these days, lad?" Thompson asked, "It's Shakespeare. From *Romeo and Juliet*."

"*A Midsummer Night's Dream*," Seoyoon corrected.

"Is it?" Thompson asked. "Okay. How was Mr DeSouza's true love running?"

"Poor Mr DeSouza's the injured party," Perry explained, "Kasey treated him terribly."

She outlined what DeSouza had told them.

"What about Miriam Todd?" she asked.

"Bit evasive," Thompson said, "Knows more than she was letting on."

He, in turn, recapped on their discussion.

"She couldn't explain what Kasey was doing out there either," Thompson said, "Didn't think Kasey was the sort to go clubbing."

"She wasn't at work, either," Seoyoon said, "or at least, it doesn't look like it."

"Why?" Perry asked.

"I rang Prestige Industrial while you were out," Seoyoon said, "Kasey Stewart doesn't work there any more."

"What?" Perry asked, frowning.

"She used to. Worked there as a cleaner for over a year, doing three nights a week, but she left nearly four months ago. She didn't give any notice. Just didn't show up for a shift one night. And when the office phoned, she said she wasn't coming back."

"Did they say why?" Packer asked.

Seoyoon shook her head. "The manager said she was quite surprised, actually. Said Kasey had been a good worker and fairly reliable. It was completely out of the blue when she quit, and unlike her to quit without giving any kind of notice."

"So where was she going at night if she wasn't cleaning?" Perry said.

"Could she have changed jobs?" Seoyoon suggested, "I mean, there must be heaps of night cleaners. Maybe she just got a job working for a different one. Better pay or conditions."

"Her mother seemed pretty certain it was that one."

"Maybe Kasey didn't tell her that she'd changed companies," Simmons suggested, "or maybe the mother just got confused and told you the name of the old one by mistake."

"I suppose it's possible," Perry said, sounding unconvinced, "But Felicity seemed pretty certain. And if Kasey was just changing jobs, why not tell the old company or give notice?"

"Seoyoon, can you phone around other cleaning companies?" Packer asked, "See if anyone else has Kasey on their books."

"Okay, boss."

"You think she did just change jobs and Felicity got it wrong?" Perry asked.

Packer shrugged. "Not really. But let's make sure."

"Explains the clothes she was wearing when she was found," said Simmons, "She wasn't cleaning."

"She wanted Felicity to think she was, though," Perry said.

"Well, she wasn't cleaning floors, anyway," Thompson said, "Might still have been polishing some knobs, though..."

Perry grimaced at him and shook her head.

Packer walked over to the whiteboard.

Seoyoon had already updated the details in her tiny, neat handwriting. 'No longer working for cleaning company.'

He looked at the photograph of Kasey at the top of the board. She looked back to at him, her eyes guarded.

What was she hiding?

Chapter 17

The Department of Family Services had their offices in one of the tall office blocks between the Perth Arena and the train station that housed many government departments.

Packer and Perry made their way up in the elevator.

After speaking to the receptionist at the front counter, they were shown into a small waiting area. A row of lounge chairs sat on either side of the room with a water cooler and a door leading deeper into the building.

It took a few minutes for the door to open and a short, plump woman in a grey suit to emerge.

"Hello," she said, "I'm Abigail Moore."

Perry introduced them while they held out their identification.

Abigail Moore led them through the door into a corridor on the other side. Glass-fronted offices lined both sides of the corridor and she took them through to one near the end.

Her office was small, with a desk and computer and rows of filing racks. All of the racks were filled with hanging files and the desk was piled high with more files. Despite the volume of work, the office was tidy and appeared well-organised.

"Please sit down," Moore told them, pointing to two chairs in front of her desk. She picked up a pile of the files from the desk and put them on the floor to make space. The floor was already piled with more files and she placed these on top, making the pile wobble slightly.

"You look busy," Perry said.

Moore gave a small sigh. "There's no shortage of cases," she said, "and there's not as many of us here as we need."

She looked up at Perry. "I don't mean to be rude, but you said on the phone you wanted to speak about Kasey Stewart. You didn't say specifically what you want to discuss, though. Is she in trouble?"

Perry shook her head. "We're investigating her murder."

"Oh," Moore gasped.

Her plump face went pale, and eyes widened slightly. She looked at Packer, and then back to Perry again, seeking some sign that she had misheard.

"I'm sorry," she said, "Kasey's been murdered?"

Perry nodded.

"Could there be some mistake?" Moore asked.

"I'm afraid not," Perry said.

"Oh," Moore said again.

She stared across the room at nothing in particular.

"I'm so sorry," she said, "It's just such a shock. I just need a moment to process it."

"Of course," Perry said.

Moore shook her head slightly, and gave a small sigh. "Goodness. I mean you know these things happen, but you never think it might be someone you know. I was just speaking with her last week."

Perry and Packer waited for a few minutes, as Moore composed herself.

"Okay. Sorry. I'm fine now," she said.

Perry nodded.

"You're the case worker for Kasey Stewart and Deon DeSouza?" Perry asked.

"I'm the case worker for Jessica DeSouza," Moore corrected, "We prioritise the interests of the children where there is a possibility they're at risk."

"Right."

"Where is Jessica now, do you know?"

"With the grandparents," Perry said, "They've taken her back to their place."

Moore nodded, picking up a pen and making a note. "I see. We'll need to arrange a visit to make sure the house is suitable, but I suppose that's okay in the interim."

"How did you get involved with the family?"

"There was a report from Deon DeSouza about Kasey Stewart using drugs. He phoned Child Protection initially, and it was referred through to us. Kasey had the care of Jessica, so we investigated."

"And was she using drugs?"

Moore nodded. "Yes, she was."

"She admitted that?"

"Not at first. We did a home visit and there was enough to concern us. We asked for a voluntary blood test, but she refused. Once it was explained to her that we could get a court order requiring one and failing to cooperate with us would count against her if it came up positive, she admitted to amphetamine use. She said it was occasional, but the toxicology results suggested it was more frequent than she said."

"Jessie remained with her, though?"

Moore nodded. "We prefer to manage the situation, rather than separate the child from the mother. There were no risk factors apart from the drug use. The child was healthy and well-nourished. She was being well looked after and Kasey had family support from her parents. The house was in a bit of shambles, but there were no weapons or drug paraphernalia lying around.

"Kasey was required to attend rehab and provide weekly blood tests. She knew that if her compliance was poor, the consequence was likely to be that she would lose Jessica."

"And her compliance was good?"

Moore gave a twitch of the lip and shook her head. "Unfortunately not. It was patchy at first. She missed a few counselling sessions and returned a few positive tests. But that's very common. It's hard to get off drugs, to we give them a fair bit of leeway at first. We expect the compliance to improve over time, but it never really has with Kasey. The attendance at counselling sessions has remained sporadic and there are still a lot of positive drug tests."

"She kept custody of Jessica, though?"

Moore nodded. "Mmm. We were performing regular home visits and there were no signs that Jessica was at further risk. Kasey's parents are both retired and providing support which was a big factor. And Kasey has a friend, Alicia Martin, who is providing assistance with child-minding. The only other option was to take Jessica into care and place her with foster parents, which we're very reluctant to do unless there's a significant risk to the child. It's obviously very traumatic for the child, so it's a last resort."

"Was Mr DeSouza happy with the arrangement?"

Moore twitched her eyebrows and gave a slight smile. "No. He was expecting Jessica to be placed with him once Kasey's drug use was confirmed, so he was very unhappy when that didn't happen. There were a number of difficult discussions with him about that. But it was made clear to him that the department's decision was to leave Jessica with Kasey, and there would be consequences for him if he didn't accept it."

"Why wasn't Jessica placed with him?" Perry asked.

"His criminal history mainly," Moore said, "He has a number of convictions for assaults on Kasey and on previous partners. Nothing to suggest he was ever violent towards Jessica, but it still created an unacceptable risk to Jessica's safety."

Moore pursed her lips slightly. "It seems to me from my contact with him that he genuinely loves Jessica, but it's not a risk we can take. It'll count against him in the Family Court, too. He's asking for sole custody, but it will never be granted with his history."

"Is he aware of that?"

Moore nodded and rolled her eyes slightly. "It was explained to him repeatedly by his solicitor, and by us. But he just wouldn't accept it. He was adamant that he was going to get Jessica. Still is, I believe. But that's never going to happen. Never in a million years.

"In a way, it's a shame, because he was always compliant with our directions and with the Family Court's orders. He never put a foot wrong, unlike Kasey, and as I said, my feeling is that he genuinely loves Jessica."

"Kasey's Stewart's dead," Packer said, "What happens with Jessica now?"

She pursed her lips thoughtfully. "That's a good question. It will depend on the Family Court, of course, but we'll have to consider the options and make some recommendations."

"With Kasey gone, does that improve DeSouza's chances of getting custody?"

Moore shook her head. "No. As I said, the history of violence rules him out."

"He's the only parent left, though."

"Even so, the risk is too great."

"Would DeSouza understand that?" Packer asked.

Moore gave a wry smile. "I very much doubt it."

"Will Jessie go to Bill and Felicity Stewart, then?"

"In the short term, but only as a temporary arrangement. Their age means they're not suitable carers long-term."

"Would they understand that?"

Moore considered. "I don't think so. They've been heavily involved in Jessica's care up until now, so they will probably make the assumption that that will continue."

"So, what's the likely result?"

"We would have to find a foster family for Jessica. I can't really see another option. It's not ideal, but I think it's unavoidable now."

They thanked Moore for her time and left the office.

"What a terrible situation for that little girl," Perry said, in the elevator on the way down, "Losing her mother's terrible enough, but now she'll be placed in foster care."

Packer nodded. "Doesn't sound like anyone else really understands that, though."

"DeSouza?" Perry asked, "It sounds like he still believed he was going to get custody through the Family Court, though."

"Maybe he finally realised otherwise."

"He certainly seemed to think he'd get Jessie when we spoke to him."

Packer nodded. "Bill and Felicity Stewart seem to think they will, too."

Perry looked at him. "You're not saying you think one of them did it?"

Packer shrugged. "Something odd about them."

"Killing their own daughter to get custody of their granddaughter?" Perry said, dubiously.

"Or to prevent DeSouza getting her."

"But he wouldn't have."

"They might not have known that."

Perry considered this. "I don't know, boss. I can't see it. DeSouza seems more likely to me. He gets angry easily, too, which fits with the idea of running Kasey down, then backing over her."

"I don't know about that," Packer said, as the elevator doors opened, "Running someone over is a bit impersonal. DeSouza strikes me more as a man who'd prefer to get his hands dirty."

Chapter 18

"I think I've found something," Seoyoon said, when they returned to the incident room.

Packer and Perry stood behind her. Thompson and Simmons moved over, too.

"I've been back through Kasey's phone records," Seoyoon said, turning to the screen.

She had a table open on the screen. It had tiny print and was divided into columns, listing the phone number, date and time of the call and duration.

Seoyoon had colour-coded the rows, identifying each caller in a different colour. There were yellow rows, randomly interspersed with pale blue rows and pale green rows.

"There's a lot of calls and SMS message with Alicia Martin and a lot with both of her parents. There's a lot of calls to Miriam Todd at Sunrise. There's also fairly regular contact with Family Services and with a solicitor's firm."

Using the mouse, she scrolled upwards on the screen, moving the table backwards in chronological order.

She stopped scrolling and used her finger to tape the screen on a row that was marked in a pale grey colour.

"This number comes up a lot. It first appeared in late May this year. Only a few messages to start off with, then it increases within the first couple of weeks."

She began scrolling downwards. The grey lines began to increase in number as she went.

"Then there's a lot of messages over the next six months," said Seoyoon, still scrolling, "until here."

She stopped, tapping the screen again.

"About three weeks ago, the calls stop. There's a lot of messages from Kasey, but no reply from the number. She tried phoning it many times, but you can see the duration of the call was zero minutes and seconds, meaning there was no answer."

As they looked at the screen, they could see that Kasey had sent several messages to the number. On one day, there were over twenty messages from

Kasey but no replies, together with calls from Kasey that went unanswered. The following day had even more messages and calls. Over the next couple of days, they began to drop away, but Kasey was still trying to contact the number. After about a week, she seemed to have given up.

"Can you ID the phone number?" Perry asked.

Seoyoon's mouth curled up into a smile. "Sort of."

She moved the mouse across the screen and opened another window. It showed the identification details for the phone number Kasey had been trying to contact.

"I ran a subscriber check with Telstra," Seoyoon said, "The phone number is registered to 'William Schuester.'"

"Is there an address?" Thompson asked.

Seoyoon turned to look at him, still smiling. "It's fake, George. Will Schuester is the head of the Glee Club."

"The what?"

"The Glee Club. On the TV show?"

Thompson shrugged. "I'll take your word for it."

"She was pretty eager to get in touch with him, whoever he was," Perry said, "Even after he stopped talking to her."

"Boyfriend?" Simmons suggested, "Went cold on her and she couldn't accept it?"

"Are you speaking from personal experience?" Thompson asked him.

"No," Simmons said, "I'd never treat a girl like that."

"I think you've misunderstood me, son," Thompson said, straight-faced, "I assumed they stop answering your calls once they get to know you."

Seoyoon grinned, but said nothing.

"He's not a boyfriend," Packer said, "His phone's registered in a fake name."

"Who then?" Simmons asked.

"He's her dealer. That's why she was trying so hard to get in touch when he stopped answering her calls."

"That was three weeks ago," Perry said, "but she still had meth in her bedroom, so she must have found a new supplier."

Packer stared at the screen. "I think a better question is why the old one stopped talking to her."

"Ran up a debt she couldn't pay?" Simmons suggested.

"That's not how it works with dealers," Packer said.

"What do you mean?" Simmons asked.

"Drug dealers don't write off bad debts, son," Thompson said, "They write off the customer."

He looked at Packer. "Is that what you're thinking, boss? She got killed over a drug debt?"

Packer shook his head. "No. If it was that, the calls would be the other way around. The dealer would be chasing her and it would be Kasey not answering the phone. If someone was chasing her for money, she wouldn't be phoning them."

"What then?"

"I don't know."

"Maybe she found a new way to pay for her habit," Thompson said, "and I think we know what that is."

"So why did the dealer cut her off?"

"Maybe it wasn't a dealer," Perry suggested.

"Just someone else with a phone registered under a false name who Kasey-the-drug-addict rings regularly?" Thompson said, with an eyebrow raised.

"Yeah, okay," Perry conceded.

Packer stared at the screen.

He turned to Seoyoon.

"Get in touch with the Drug Squad. See if they recognise the name or the number."

"Okay, boss."

"We're missing something here," Packer said, "but this is three weeks before someone killed her. The timing can't be a coincidence."

***

"So, the only footage you have is the foyer?" Simmons asked, "Nothing at the front of the building?"

He was sitting in the office of the security officer at the Towers. It was a tiny, cramped space that smelled faintly of body odour and had a narrow desk with a computer, a TV set tuned to daytime television and a phone.

The security officer shook his head.

"No need for it," he said, "Each of the residents has an intercom system with a camera that faces the buzzer at the front. If someone wants to contact them, they push the buzzer and the resident can see who is out there."

"What if there's trouble? Like a robbery or something?"

The security guard shrugged. "Then they wouldn't go down, would they?"

"No," Simmons said, "That's not what I meant. If one of the residents is going out or coming home and someone's outside the building and decides to rob them or whatever, isn't there a security camera out there?"

The security guard shook his head. "My job's to look after security in the building, not the street. Keeping the streets outside safe is the job of the police."

The guard kept his face blank, but the stare he gave Simmons and the tone of his voice gave more than a hint of attitude.

Simmons was finding it difficult to remain patient. It had taken him ages to get the security guard's attention from the entrance outside the building, and then even longer to persuade the guard to let him in. Once inside, the guard had not proven any more helpful.

"Alright," Simmons said, producing a USB drive, "Can you copy the footage from the foyer for last Saturday evening and Sunday morning?"

"Why?"

"I've explained this already, mate," Simmons said, "We're trying to trace someone who might have been down this way."

"But you said you don't know where she went."

"No," Simmons said, "We're trying to find her."

"So how do you know she came in here?"

"We don't. I want to check to see if she did."

"This girl might not even have come in here."

"No," Simmons agreed, "but there's only one way to find out, and that's to check the footage."

It took another five minutes of circular discussion before the security guard reluctantly agreed to copy the footage for Simmons.

He slotted the USB drive into the front of the computer in his tiny office and they sat waiting for it to copy. His attitude filled the room.

Eventually, the guard handed the drive back to Simmons.

Simmons thanked him for his help.

The guard turned back to his desk in silence.

"Bloody wanker," Simmons muttered, as he left the building.

The glass doors slid shut behind him.

He stood looking out from the front of the building.

About twenty metres in front of him was the Bell Tower. It looked like a huge, space-age wine bottle with a wide bottom that narrowed to a tall spire high above. Rows of steel bands curled around it its frame. A shallow pond lay in front of the building and a wide, paved space in front of that. A narrow road circled around the building and the pedestrian space, with rows of short-term parking on either side.

Simmons turned left and headed away from the river towards the hotel next to it.

A row of square pillars lined one side of a strip of bitumen wide enough for three cars. On the other side was a wide row of steps leading up to sliding glass doors and the foyer of the hotel. Potted plants sat on either side.

The doors opened for Simmons and he walked into the foyer. A huge expanse of navy-blue carpet met him. Plush chairs were arranged tastefully around a small fountain on the far side and a dark wood counter lay against the back wall. A corridor between them led down to the elevators.

Simmons walked over to the counter and showed his identification to the concierge.

"Can I see the manager, mate?" he asked.

"One moment, please, sir," the concierge said, putting a slight emphasis on the word, 'sir.'

The concierge picked up the phone on the counter and mumbled into for a moment.

He looked up at Simmons. "Won't be a moment."

Simmons thanked him and stood by the counter.

After a few minutes, he heard the discrete chime of an elevator arriving and a woman walked from the corridor beside the counter.

She was wearing a dark suit and her hair was tied up into a neat arrangement behind her head.

As she walked towards Simmons, he reached into his pocket for his identification, but she raised a hand and shook her head slightly.

"Would you come this way, please?" she said, gesturing back the way she had come.

Simmons followed her around behind the counter and into the room behind. The woman closed the door behind them.

"I'm Maryanne Kinsley," the woman said, "The day manager."

"Detective Simmons," Simmons said, "We're making some enquiries into a suspicious death near here."

"How does that concern us?"

"We think the victim may have come down this way. Do you have CCTV cameras outside?"

"No."

"You don't?"

"We cater to an exclusive class of clients here, clients who value their privacy. We respect that and they respect the fact that we help maintain their privacy."

"What about if there any safety issues?"

"In the unlikely event that there is any difficulty within the premises, we have staff members who can deal with that," Kinsley told him, "If there were any difficulties outside the premises, we would contact police to deal with it."

It occurred to Simmons to ask whether she and the security guard in the building next door were comparing notes, but he bit his tongue.

Instead, he thanked her and left.

Simmons turned right and walked along the footpath towards the river thirty metres away.

A steel rail ran along the edge of the Swan River with gates leading out to the docks where the ships heading to Fremantle and Rottnest Island docked. Clustered on either side of the docks were rows of souvenir shops and restaurants.

Simmons walked along the rows of buildings looking for the telltale dome of CCTV cameras.

He spotted one outside the ticket window for one of the tourist places offering boat trips and waited until the cashier was free.

"Police," he said, producing his identification, "Can I have a word with your manager?"

He was shown into the narrow space and spoke to a middle-aged woman in glasses.

"Sorry," she said, after he explained what he wanted, "The camera records, but we only switch in on when we're open. It doesn't record at night when we're closed."

Simmons thanked her and left.

He tried the restaurant beside them and got essentially the same explanation.

A souvenir shop on the other side had a camera outside, but it was just for show. It had broken down months earlier and the shop owner had not had the money to get it fixed.

Two others had footage, though, and he downloaded those on to the USB drive.

The Chinese restaurant at the top of the pier had two cameras that faced out towards the street, and he copies the footage from both.

It took Simmons over an hour to canvas all of the shops and business along the water.

He stood by the water for a moment, before heading back to the car. The only thing waiting for him back at the office was several hours of staring at CCTV footage, so he was in no hurry to leave the docks.

It was a hot day, and he enjoyed the cool breeze coming off the Swan River, feeling it blow against his fashionably-tousled hair.

He watched as a bus turned the corner and began the slow circuit along the narrow road wrapping around the Bell Tower and its surrounds.

As the bus stopped at the nearby bus stop, Simmons looked past it towards the bottle shape of the Bell Tower.

There was a streetlight on the other side of the road, placed to illuminate the paved area beyond it after the sun went down.

On the top of the post, above the light, was the round dome of a CCTV camera.

Simmons briefly toyed with the idea of pretending he hadn't seen it and returning to the office to find something to do other than watching CCTV footage.

Then he sighed and began the walk up towards the city council building where the city's security cameras were monitored.

***

Packer's phone rang.

"Is this a pay week or is it next week?" Alistair Goodge asked.

"Next week, I think," Packer said.

"Have you got anything left over from last week?" Goodge asked.

"Is this your long-winded way of saying I owe you a bottle of Scotch?" Packer asked.

One of Goodge's running jokes was that he insisted on being paid in Scotch for the forensic discoveries that led to arrests. His course of chemotherapy prevented him from drinking alcohol, but he maintained the running joke and Packer, like everyone else, went along with it.

"Long-winded?" Goodge said, incensed, "Is that any way to speak to a man bearing glad tidings?"

"You got a match on the tyres?"

"I did," Goodge said, "There wasn't quite enough left on the ground where your lass was flattened to give you a perfect match, but I can give you one with ninety percent confidence."

Before Packer could respond, Goodge said, "I should caution you, though, lad. It's not an uncommon tyre. A lot of mid-size cars use them. We sometimes see something distinctive, like a rock stuck in the tread or heavy wear on the side or summat. There's nothing like that here. The tyre matches, but so would the tyres on a lot of other cars driving around Perth."

"Alright," Packer said, "Thanks."

He saw movement in the doorway and looked up. Seoyoon was standing there.

"It's up to you," Goodge said, "You can send over a Ballentine's or a Bell's now and save the Johnny Walker until later, or just wait and send me the red label once you make your arrest."

"Let me get back to you," Packer said.

"You tight bastard-" Goodge managed to get in, as Packer hung up.

He looked up at Seoyoon.

"I rang around all the parking garages this morning," she said, "and one of them's just called me back. They've found Kasey Stewart's car."

Chapter 19

Packer and Perry left the police station and drove west along St Georges Terrace. When they reached Barrack Street, Packer turned left towards the Bell Tower, then right onto The Esplanade.

The area where Kasey Stewart's body had been found was only a few metres ahead of them, and they both looked out the car window as they approached.

"You'd never know anything had happened here," Perry said.

"No."

A couple of pedestrians walked along the footpath under the overhanging lip of the building where Packer and Perry had sheltered only two days ago. A woman was walking a dog on a lead, and another was pushing a stroller with a small child asleep inside.

They walked over the spot where Kasey had been killed, completely unaware of what had happened here.

Only the dark brown stain on the concrete marked Kasey's death.

Packer sped up slightly after they passed the location. He was stopped at the traffic lights on the corner of the train station, and they waited for the line of cars moving south towards Riverside Drive to pass before being able to move off again.

They passed the bus port, one of the city's CAT buses waiting at the lights and another behind it.

Packer turned left at the next set of lights and drove onto the long stretch of bitumen that headed into the underground carpark for the Convention Centre.

The road separated into two lanes, each closed off with a boom gate. Packer stopped and reached out to the machine beside him to take a ticket. The gate swung upwards and he drove into the carpark.

He cruised slowly past the rows of parked cars. At the end of the rows, was a long, glass window with the word, 'Administration', written above it. Packer pulled into the loading zone beside it.

They had barely even managed to get out of the car before the door was opening and a man came out with a faint look of excitement on his face. He could not have been older than his early twenties and could even still have been in his late teens. The tail of his shirt hung out on one side and he had a rash of acne around his cheeks.

"Are you the police?" the man asked eagerly.

"Detectives Perry and Packer," Perry told him.

"Hi, I'm Nate," the man said, "I'm the Day Manager. Well, today anyway."

He held out a hand and shook both of theirs, looking between them eagerly.

"The car must have come in some time between 6:00pm on Friday night and 1:00pm Sunday," Nate went on.

"How do you know that?" Perry asked.

"Well, I was on duty on Friday until six and the car wasn't there then. When I got the call from Detective Kim this morning, I did a walk around and located it. I reviewed the CCTV for Sunday and for yesterday and it didn't come in during the day, so it must have been here before then."

"What about the footage for Saturday?" Perry asked.

Nate shook his head. "The system only keeps it for 48 hours, then records over it. There's only limited hard-drive space. We can transfer footage to another drive to stop it being lost, but we only do that if we're aware of an incident, like a break-in to a vehicle or a punch-up or something. As soon as Detective Kim rang me, I went back and reviewed what we had, and that was at 1:00pm, so I could only go back to 1:00pm on Sunday. If she'd rung me earlier, I could have gone back further, but the footage has been recorded over now."

"Didn't someone notice that the car was sitting there? I mean, it's been there for two days."

Nate gave a slight shrug. "To be honest, it could have been there for two months if Detective Kim hadn't rung. Drivers get a ticket at the gate when they come in and get charged by the amount of time they're parked here. They have to go back out through the same gate, and it only opens if they pay at the ticket machine first, so we've got no reason to check on the cars. We have a cheaper rate for all-day parking, so if someone wants to stay here for two days, that's up to them. They're paying, so they can stay as long as they want."

"What about if someone abandons a car here? Doesn't come back for it?"

Nate shrugged again. "It happens. But we don't usually notice it for a while. We only find out because we notice the tyres are flat, or one of the security guards realises it hasn't moved for a while."

"Where's the car?" Packer asked.

Nate turned to look at him. "Over this way."

He waved them forward and then turned towards the rows of cars. He set off through the car park at a fast past, clearly very eager to show them his discovery.

Perry exchanged a glance with Packer, grinning at him.

"Probably the most exciting thing that's ever happened to him," she said in a low voice.

"I doubt there's much competition working here."

They followed on behind Nate as he power-walked across the carpark and quickly drew ahead of the police officers.

Nate stopped up ahead of them and turned back towards them, waiting for them to catch up.

He was standing behind a pale blue hatchback. Three orange traffic cones had been arranged behind it.

"As soon as I located the vehicle, I cordoned off the scene," Nate said, "to preserve any forensic traces."

Packer said nothing as walked along the side of the car and peered in through the side windows.

"Will you get prints off it, do you think?" Nate asked, "or DNA?"

"Probably not after a few days," Perry said, "especially if there have been drivers on either side coming and going. And the crime happened elsewhere, so we're not looking for any forensics on the car."

"Oh," Nate said, obviously disappointed.

"Good job securing the car, though," Perry said.

She edged past Nate and stood beside Packer.

"Anything?" she asked.

"Clothes in the back," he said.

Perry looked through the window. She could see a pair of pale grey tracksuit pants crumpled into a heap on the back seat, beside a black T-shirt. A scuffed pair of pink sneakers sat on the floor with socks stuffed into them.

"Something on the front seat, too," Packer said, "What do you reckon that is?"

Perry could see a black, oblong case about twenty centimetres long and ten across.

"Box of some kind?" she suggested.

Packer took hold of the door handle and pulled it. It was locked.

He walked around to the passenger side and tried that, but it was locked, too.

"Let's get someone down here to open it," Packer said.

"I can do that," Nate said from behind the car.

Perry and Packer both looked at him.

Nate shrugged. "People lose their keys or lock them in the car all the time," he said.

Perry and Packer waited while he rushed back to the office. He returned minutes later with a long length of plastic cable that was folded into a loop.

They watched as he pushed the end of the loop between the glass and the rubber seal on the driver's window and began to wiggle it around.

With barely a few seconds of work, there was a click and Nate turned.

"*Voila*," he said, easing the plastic loop back out of the door and grinning triumphantly at them.

Packer stepped around him and pulled the door open.

He leaned down to look at the floor of the car, and then gave the rest of the car a once over, but could see nothing of interest.

He sat on the driver's seat and reached over to pick up the black case. It had a flocked surface and a hinge along one seam. He pulled open the case.

Inside was a black velvet lining shaped into an asymmetrical oval with a bulge in the middle.

"It's a jewellery case," Perry said, leaning in, "for a necklace."

Packer closed it and handed it to her. "Nothing in it now, though."

He opened the glove box of the car. There were a couple of CD cases, a small packet of tissues, a tube of lipstick and a half-empty packet of chewing gum.

The centre console had a charging cable for a mobile phone and more CDs.

No necklace.

He reached over and tried the passenger door. It was locked.

He pressed the central locking button on the door, then got out and walked around to the boot. Dark grey carpet covered the boot and was marked with dried mud in places. There were a couple of stray canvas shopping bags and some plastic beach toys, but nothing else.

Packer lifted up the edge of the carpet and found the spare tyre and the jack. There was no necklace hidden anywhere in there.

"Thanks for your help," Packer told Nate. He turned to leave.

"Is that it?" Nate asked, his voice clearly carrying his disappointment.

"Someone will be touch about towing the car away," Perry told him.

"Will I need to come to court?" Nate asked, "You know, as a witness?"

"We'll let you know if it's necessary," Perry said, keeping her face blank, "Thanks again."

She followed Packer back to the police car, leaving Nate's crestfallen figure behind them.

"Kasey wasn't wearing a necklace when she was found," Perry said, as Packer started the engine.

"No, she wasn't," Packer agreed.

"It's possible it was just an empty case, though. I mean we don't know if she put a necklace on when she changed her clothes and shoes."

"It was sitting on the passenger seat. And why carry an empty case around with her?"

"Maybe she had taken it to be repaired or something."

"And hung on to the case?"

"Alright. So, where's the necklace then?"

"Good question."

"Do you think the killer took it? After he ran her down?"

"Makes sense."

"I don't know, boss. Running her over so he could steal her necklace seems a bit unlikely."

Packer drove up to the boom gate and slipped the ticket into the machine's slot. It took a moment to read the ticket, then the screen flashed with the payment amount.

Packer held his credit card in front of the reader, wishing he had had the forethought to ask Nate to open the gate for them.

"A robbery doesn't seem likely to me, either," Packer said, as the gate opened, "but if she was wearing the necklace when she was killed, then whoever killed her must have wanted it."

"It would explain why Alistair Goodge found the footprint on top of the tyre tracks near the body."

"Yeah."

"So, what was so special about the necklace?"

"Good question."

Chapter 20

"A necklace?" Bill Stewart asked, "I can't think of one."

He was sitting on the couch in his lounge room, Felicity on the couch beside him.

Perry and Packer sat opposite, with the coffee table between them. The black case was on the top of the table.

"What kind of necklace?" Felicity asked.

"We don't know," Perry said, "We just found the case."

"Are you sure it's a necklace?" Bill asked, "If it was just a case, it could have had anything in it."

"It looks like a jewellery case to me," Perry said.

She leaned forward to the case on the coffee table in their loungeroom and opened it along the hinges, showing them the inside.

"You can see the shape of the inside," she said, pointing with her fingers, "The centre is raised to hold it in place."

Bill leaned forward in the chair to peer at the case.

"I don't know about that," Bill said, "It could hold anything. Earphones for a stereo, or computer cables or something."

"It's a case for a necklace, Bill," Felicity said.

He turned on the seat to look at her.

"Georgia has one like that for the piece Anthony gave her for their twenty-fifth wedding anniversary."

"Well, I've never seen anything like it," Bill said.

"No," Felicity agreed, "You've never bought a necklace for me. Or any jewellery."

There was a clear hostility in her voice, as she looked back at Bill.

"Have you ever seen this case before?" Perry asked, quickly, interrupting before Felicity's barb could turn into an argument.

Bill and Felicity both looked back at the case.

"No, never," Bill said.

"Mrs Stewart?" Perry asked.

Felicity was staring at the jewellery case. She shook her head.

"The necklace must have been quite expensive," Perry said, "It's a good quality case. Can either of you think of anywhere she might have gotten it?"

Bill shook his head. "Kasey didn't have much money. She was only working a few nights a week and that thug certainly wasn't giving her anything. Apart from misery, that is."

"It doesn't seem like something Kasey could have afforded to buy on her own," Perry said, "which is why we thought it might have been a gift."

"Well, not from me," Bill said, "If there even was a necklace in there in the first place, and not just earphones or something."

"It was a necklace, Bill," Felicity said, firmly.

Perry looked at her. "Can you think of anyone who might have given Kasey an expensive necklace, Mrs Stewart?"

Felicity looked at her for a moment.

Then she shook her head. "No," she said, "I can't."

"I suppose it might have been that man," Bill said, "He owns a mechanic's shop or something. Some men are prepared to spend a fortune on these souped-up cars they drive. He must be making a fortune out of that."

"It doesn't seem like he's doing very well at all," Perry said, "Barely making ends meet."

"Maybe that's what he told you," Bill scoffed, "but the man couldn't lie straight in bed. If you'd only heard the filthy lies he was telling about Kasey at some of those court hearings."

"In any event," Perry said, "We'll check with him, as I said."

She closed the case again.

"Will you test the case for fingerprints?" Felicity said, "or DNA matches or whatever it is?"

"Kasey left it in her car, Mrs Stewart," Perry said, "so we wouldn't find anything that helped us identify the driver."

"It might help you work out where she got it from," Felicity said, "Whoever gave it to her might have left their fingerprints on it."

"She said 'no,' Felicity," Bill said.

Felicity glared at him, but said nothing.

"Fingerprints and DNA don't last on surfaces for very long, Mrs Stewart," Perry said, "We would only find forensic traces if they had been left there very recently."

"We think Kasey was wearing the necklace when she was killed," Packer said, "Can you think of any reason why she would have put it on?"

"She was going to her cleaning job," Bill said, "Why would she have put on an expensive necklace for that? That makes no sense at all."

"We made some enquiries with the cleaning company," Packer said, "Kasey hasn't worked there for months."

"That's not right," Bill said, "She goes three times a week."

"She goes out somewhere," Packer said, "but not cleaning."

"Of course she does," Bill insisted, "Felicity sees her going out each time when she's minding Jessie."

He turned to look at Felicity. "Don't you?"

Felicity said nothing, but looked at Packer.

"And she certainly doesn't go out wearing expensive jewellery," Bill said, turning to Packer again.

"She wasn't wearing cleaning clothes when she was found," Packer said, "It appears that she changed out of her cleaning clothes in her car, and put on a dress, heels and the necklace."

"How could you possibly know that?" Bill asked.

"We found the clothes in her car. Along with the jewellery case."

Bill stared at him for a moment longer, a frown appearing on his face.

"If that's true, then where's this necklace?"

"We believe it was taken from Kasey," Packer said, "After she was struck by the car."

"By who?"

"By whoever struck her."

"You're saying someone ran her over just so that they could steal her necklace?"

"That's a possibility," Packer said, "or taking the necklace might have just been an afterthought."

"What do you mean?" Felicity said, "An afterthought?"

"There may have been another reason for killing her. Something other than stealing the necklace."

"What reason?" Felicity asked.

"We don't know yet," Packer said.

Both Bill and Felicity stared at him across the coffee table.

He looked back at them blankly.

"You said that man had money problems," Bill said suddenly, "Can't make ends meet or whatever. He must have taken the necklace. He used to beat her, you know. Filthy animal that he is."

Packer said nothing.

"Go and search his house," Bill insisted, his voice rising, "I bet you'll find the necklace there. He must have killed her and taken it."

"We will make some enquiries with Mr DeSouza," Perry said, "but what reason could he have for running Kasey over?"

"To steal her necklace," Bill said, "and to get hold of Jessie. Killing two birds with one stone. He..."

His voice trailed off, as he realised what he had just said. "Killing... Oh, god."

He swallowed hard, the colour draining from his face.

"Oh," he said, his voice breaking, "My girl. My little girl."

His voice broke down completely, as he began to weep. He leaned over the side of the chair, his back to Felicity and began to suck in deep breaths as he sobbed.

Felicity ignored him.

"Well, I'm sorry we couldn't help," she said, "Is there anything else?"

Perry looked at Bill weeping, then back at Felicity.

Felicity's eyes were cold.

"No," Perry said, "I think that's all for now. Thank you for your help."

She and Packer stood up to leave.

Felicity stood up, walking behind them as they headed for the door. She left Bill crying on the couch.

"Thank you," Felicity said, flatly, closing the door behind them.

Perry and Packer walked back to the car in silence.

"My god," Perry said, as she pulled her seatbelt on, "What a bitch. Leaving him to cry."

"Hmm," Packer grunted.

"I mean, I know people react to grief in different ways," Perry said, "but not even the faintest hint of sympathy. For her own husband. God, what kind of marriage must that be?"

Packer said nothing, as he started the car and pulled out on to the street.

***

They drove back to the police station and returned to the incident room.

The team sat in a circle, as Perry gave them a summary of what they had learned.

"So, she tells her mother she's going to work at nine," Thompson said, "Then she drives to the Convention Centre and parks there. Changes out of her tracksuit into the cocktail dress and high heels and puts on the necklace. That takes, say, half an hour, including the drive?"

Perry nodded.

"But she's not killed until 3:45am the next morning," Thompson went on, "That's about six hours in between."

"Now we know where she was going to when she was killed, anyway," Seoyoon said, "On her way back to the Convention Centre to her car. To change her clothes and return home again."

"Aye," Thompson said, "She definitely didn't want her parents to know what she was up to."

"Well, she wouldn't, if she was working as a prostitute, would she?" Simmons said.

"I'm not sure about prostitution any more," Perry said, "The necklace is the problem. Prostitutes don't wear jewellery, especially not expensive jewellery. It's just asking to get robbed."

"Maybe that's what happened," Simmons said, "She saw a client who liked the look of the necklace, so he followed her and ran her over, then stole the necklace."

"Why get in his car to do it?" Perry asked, "If he was going to rob her, why not just do it when he met her? Or on the street?"

"If it was a house call," Simmons said, "then she'd have known who he was. Maybe he ran her over in his car to hide his identity."

"Still seems a bit extreme to steal a necklace," Thompson said, "even an expensive one."

"It looks more likely, though," Simmons said, "I mean we thought it was just the handbag before. Now we know it was an expensive necklace, too."

Thompson gave a non-committal shrug.

"Are we sure she was wearing the necklace?" Seoyoon asked.

"Look at the case," Perry said, "Don't you recognise it?"

"Yeah, it's a necklace case," Seoyoon said, "That's not what I meant. Kasey doesn't have much money. She's only working three nights a week and she's got a meth habit to pay for. Could she have been selling the necklace to make some money? Fencing it?"

"Why change her clothes, though?" Perry said, "Or try and sell it at night?"

"No," Seoyoon said, "No, you're right. Doesn't make sense, does it?"

"I don't know," Thompson said, "Wearing expensive jewellery doesn't fit with the rest of her lifestyle."

He looked over at Packer, who was standing in front of the whiteboard, saying nothing.

Thompson suppressed a sigh of annoyance.

"Do you have a theory, boss?" he asked.

Packer was silent a moment.

Then he turned around.

"No," he said, shaking his head, "Seoyoon, can you check around all the jewellers in the city? See if you can find someone who sells jewellery in a case like that."

"It's a long shot," Perry said, "There must be dozens of jewellers who use them, and they must have sold hundreds of necklaces. Thousands, even."

Packer nodded. "Yeah, okay. You're right."

The phone on Seoyoon's desk rang and she went over to answer it.

"You said you don't think it was a house call," Thompson said to Perry, "and I can see why. So, if it's not that, what else could it be? Why was she out there?"

"Going to see someone," Perry said, "Someone she doesn't want her parents to know about."

"Say she meets someone at a nightclub," Simmons said, "Spends a few hours with them, then goes back to their place. And gets up in the morning to head home. That makes sense."

Perry nodded. "Yeah. It does."

"If she was-" Simmons began, but he was interrupted by Seoyoon.

"Boss," she called, hanging up the phone, "Sergeant Prior just rang. There's been a '000' call from Deon DeSouza's workshop. He's just been arrested for attacking someone."

Chapter 21

By the time Packer and Perry reached the industrial area at Balcatta, it was all over.

The late afternoon was growing darker, but blue flashing lights were evident as they turned the corner from the main street. Two patrol cars were parked across the street and a police van was stopped on the footpath.

Packer stopped the car twenty metres away and they walked towards the workshop.

A uniformed officer was standing on the footpath near one of the patrol cars to discourage passersby from stopping to watch. He recognised them as they approached.

"It's under control," he said, "We've arrested him and there's an ambulance on the way for the victim."

Packer looked past him towards the workshop. The two men they had seen working on the car earlier were both standing off to the side of the carpark furthest from the office, watching. A uniformed officer stood beside them.

Two more uniformed officers were standing outside the office. Seated on the ground between them was Deon DeSouza who was wearing handcuffs behind his back.

The office door was open and Packer could just make out the back of another uniformed officer inside.

A blue Mercedes Benz sedan was stopped across the middle of the driveway.

"What's the story?" Packer asked.

The officer turned back towards the workshop and pointed at the office.

"The driver of the blue Mercedes stopped the vehicle there. He got out, armed with a golf club and approached the two men working here, screaming that he wanted to see Deon. He's the business owner, Sarge. Deon DeSouza."

Packer nodded.

"The driver then smashed the front of the vehicle in the shed," the officer continued, "and went into the main office. He used the golf club to damage the inside of the office. There seems to have been some sort of struggle, and the business owner got the golf club off him. He then used it to attack the driver."

"Did you catch the driver's name?" Perry asked.

"I didn't, ma'am, but I've been on guard here."

"Bill Stewart," Packer muttered, heading towards the office.

As he got closer to the office, one of the uniformed officers nodded to him. "Sarge."

DeSouza looked up at him and glared.

He looked back down at the ground again.

"Is he injured?" Packer asked, pointing at DeSouza.

"No, he's not," the uniform said, "The bloke inside's in pretty bad shape, though."

Packer nodded.

He walked into the office.

The uniformed officer near the door moved aside to let him in.

The inside of the office was a mess. The door leading into the room had a glass panel in it that was now smashed, glass lying on the floor around it. The computer screen had been knocked from the desk and lay shattered on the floor. Chairs had been turned over and papers were everywhere.

At the far end of the office, Bill Stewart lay on the floor.

His eyes were closed and he was unmoving. Two uniformed officers wearing blue gloves knelt on the ground on either side of him, an open first-aid kit on the ground next to one. Stewart had a large white bandage taped to the side of his face, and a red stain was spreading across its surface.

A golf club lay on the ground beside him, its end bent at a strange angle. Droplets of blood stained the floor and were spattered across the wall behind Stewart.

"Is he alive?" Packer asked, nodding at Stewart.

"Unconscious," one of the officers said, "but he's still got a pulse. There's a head wound and a broken arm. I think chest injuries, too. Ambulance is on the way."

Packer nodded.

He looked up at the ceiling and followed it around the room. In the corner, he could see the tiny, black bulge of a CCTV camera.

He pointed up to it.

"Somebody get the recording for that," he said, "and check if there's a camera outside, too."

"Yes, Sarge."

He and Perry walked back outside.

A siren was now wailing in the distance.

They walked over to the two mechanics standing on the far edge of the car park.

Packer pointed at one of them.

"You. Over here."

Packer led the man into the workshop, so that he was out of the hearing of the other man. Perry remained with him.

"What happened?" Packer asked the man with him.

"I was working on the Hyundai and I heard tyres screeching. I looked up to see that Merc stopping there outside. This crazy cunt waving a golf club around comes running over shouting, "Where's Deon?". He starts smashing the front of the Hyundai with the golf club and shouting all this shit.

"Col told him Deon was in the workshop and he went running over there, yelling out.

"I seen Deon at the door of the office. When the crazy cunt got near him, Deon backed up to get out of the way. I could hear shouting and stuff getting smashed, so I rang '000'. Then me and Col went in to see what was going on.

"Deon had got the club off the bloke and managed to get him on the ground. That's it."

"Who stopped Deon attacking the bloke on the ground? You or your mate?"

The mechanic glanced away, then lowered his eyes, before looking at Packer again.

"He'd already stopped. Like, he was just defending himself. That bloke attacked him first. He was fucking crazy, mate. Fucking out of control. He could have killed someone."

Packer nodded. "Alright. Thanks. Go back and join your mate."

The mechanic went back to the officer and the other mechanic.

Perry walked over to join Packer, just as an ambulance arrived at the workshop and stopped behind the blue Mercedes. It had switched off its siren, but the red lights on the roof continued flashing.

"And?" Packer asked.

"Stewart turned up, yelling out for Deon. Smashed the car here, then went into the workshop and started smashing that up. Deon managed to get the club off him and Stewart then 'fell over and hit his head'. Deon definitely never hit him with the club, although I heard 'self-defence' mentioned four or five times. You?"

"About the same. We'll see what the CCTV shows."

"What do you reckon it's about?"

"At a guess, I'd say Bill Stewart's feeling a bit upset with DeSouza."

They watched as two paramedics hurried into the office, carrying a stretcher between them.

"Although, I think it'll be a while before he can tell us why," Packer added.

***

They waited while the paramedics carried Bill Stewart out to the ambulance on the stretcher. He was still unconscious, but now had an intravenous drip inserted in one arm and an oxygen mask over his face.

DeSouza looked at the ground as Stewart was carried past.

Perry arranged for Felicity to be told about what had happened.

Then she climbed into the back of the ambulance with Stewart.

After the ambulance left, the two officers walked DeSouza to the police van. He stood up and walked meekly between them, offering no resistance as he was placed in the back.

It took another half-hour for the officers to download the contents of the CCTV system's recorders onto a USB drive.

Packer waited for it before heading back to East Perth.

***

They stood behind Simmons's desk as he opened the CCTV footage on his computer screen and moved the mouse around. It took him fifteen or twenty minutes of playing around to find the right sections of CCTV.

"Here is he arriving," Simmons said.

The image on the screen showed a view of the concreted area in front of the workshop, with the street at the back of the screen.

Stewart's blue Mercedes could be seen driving past the entrance, then breaking hard, before reversing and turning into the front driveway. It moved quickly forward, then stopped abruptly.

The driver's door opened and Stewart got out. He was waving the golf club over his head and silently screaming abuse, his face a mask of fury.

He disappeared off the bottom of the screen out of the camera's view as he entered the workshop.

Simmons left the footage open in one window on the screen, then opened another.

This time the image showed the inside of the office from high up. DeSouza was sitting at the desk, one hand tapping at the computer keyboard, while he held the phone to his ear with the other and spoke animatedly.

After a moment, he turned his head towards the door. Still talking on the phone, he stood up at the desk and leaned forward, trying to peer outside.

He then hung up the phone and walked quickly around the desk.

Just as he got to the front of the desk, Stewart entered the room, holding the golf club in front of him. He jabbed the club at DeSouza, silently screaming at him.

He smashed the club against the door, shattering the glass panel.

DeSouza backed away as Stewart advanced.

Still yelling, Stewart swung the club at the computer screen, which exploded with a flash and a shower of shattered glass and was flung onto the floor.

Stewart jabbed the club at DeSouza again, then began smashing the furniture around him. A storm of paper flew across the room, followed by a fax machine and the phone from DeSouza's desk.

As Stewart swung the club towards the top of the filing cabinet, DeSouza rushed forward and shoved Stewart to the side.

Caught off balance, Stewart stumbled, but managed to stay upright by pushing against the filing cabinets with his free hand.

DeSouza began punching him in the head, still striking as Stewart fell to the ground. Stewart lost his grip on the golf club as he went over.

Bending down beside him, DeSouza snatched up the club.

Holding it over his head, he began pounding down on Stewart with it. Blood splattered across the floor.

"Oh, shit," Simmons grunted, wincing at the sight.

DeSouza continued raining blows down on Stewart, smashing the golf club into his head and upper body. Stewart tried to roll to one side to avoid the blows, but they continued. Blood splashed across the wall behind him. He rolled on to the other side, before lying still.

DeSouza continued to hammer Stewart's unconscious body with the club as he lay on the ground.

The two mechanics ran through the door and pushed against DeSouza, knocking him to the side. He struggled briefly as one of them held him down and the other picked up the golf club and moved it out of his reach.

After a few moments, DeSouza got up.

He stood beside Stewart's body, and ran one hand across the top of his shaved head.

Then the three men left the workshop and walked outside.

Stewart was left in a bloodied heap on the ground, unmoving.

"That's a man with one very bad temper," Thompson said.

"Maybe he was having a rough afternoon," Packer said.

Chapter 22

It was close to seven o'clock when Perry rang the incident room with an update.

"They've put him in the ICU," she told Seoyoon over the phone, "His heart stopped on the way here, but they revived him. He has a skull fracture, and a broken arm and rib."

"God," Seoyoon said.

"Yeah. It's pretty nasty. Heavy concussion, I'm told. He's unconscious and they're not sure whether he'll wake up. If he does, it won't be any time soon."

After she got off the phone, Seoyoon relayed all of that to the others.

"That's got to put DeSouza in the frame for Kasey's murder," Simmons said, "I mean, fucking hell. That was a brutal attack on Bill Stewart."

"Aye," Thompson agreed, "It was. But Stewart attacked him first."

"You're not saying it was self-defence?" Simmons asked, incredulously.

"No, of course I'm not," Thompson said, "Taking the golf club off him would have been understandable. Giving him a whack in return, even. Putting him in a coma's not. What I meant was, that it wouldn't have happened at all if Stewart hadn't gone around to try to give DeSouza a going over."

He looked at Packer.

Packer nodded. "Agreed."

"It's a bit different to following a lass in a car and running her down," Thompson said.

"Shows he's violent, though," Simmons said, "and he's got a history for beating her up."

"That's true," Thompson said, "but he didn't go around to Stewart's place. It was the other way around."

"Why did Stewart go around there?" Seoyoon asked, "I mean why now? Does he think DeSouza killed Kasey?"

"Seems likely," Thompson said, "I can't think of another reason. Doesn't sound like he liked the man much to start off with."

"But why do it now? If he was going to attack DeSouza, why not do it as soon as he found out about Kasey being killed?"

"Maybe he was bottling up," Thompson suggested.

Packer was still looking at the whiteboard.

"Was Felicity Stewart at the hospital when you spoke to Claire?" he asked.

"She didn't say," Seoyoon said, "but she asked me to make sure Felicity had been told, so she mustn't be there at the hospital."

Packer nodded, still looking at the whiteboard.

"Check with uniform. Make sure someone went around to the house to tell her."

Seoyoon picked up the phone.

Packer turned to Simmons. "Can you phone down to custody? Make sure DeSouza has been processed and offered a lawyer."

"Boss," Simmons said, picking up the phone.

Thompson walked over to the whiteboard to stand beside Packer.

"What do you think, boss?" he asked, "You don't think DeSouza killed Kasey?"

Packer shrugged. "I don't think we can rule it out. What you said about Stewart starting it is right, though."

He looked at the whiteboard. "I wonder what it tells us about Stewart."

"Boss?"

"He armed himself and went around to attack DeSouza," Packer said, "Must have taken him about forty minutes to drive to DeSouza's place, but he didn't calm down on the way. He still went through with attacking DeSouza. Or tried to."

"You think Bill Stewart's the driver? His own daughter?"

"There's something odd about him."

"He's just lost his daughter. He's not thinking too clearly. I can understand him wanting to lash out at someone."

Packer said nothing.

Seoyoon hung up to the phone.

"Two officers went to the house an hour ago and spoke to Felicity," she said, "They offered to take her to the hospital, but she said she had Jessie to look after, so would make her own way there."

Packer nodded. "Alright."

They waited for Simmons to finish on the phone.

He hung up.

"Sounds like DeSouza's being difficult," Simmons said, "Sergeant Prior arranged for a medical examination, but DeSouza refused to let the doctor see him. He's refusing a lawyer and he's refusing an interview."

"What a piece of shite," Thompson said.

"Not surprising, though," Packer said, "Alright, let him sit there overnight. See if that helps clarify his thinking."

"We've got enough to charge him on the CCTV alone," Thompson pointed out, "Attempted murder. Aggravated GBH at the least."

Packer nodded. "No hurry. We've got him for 48 hours."

He looked at his watch.

"Alright," he said, "Let's call it a day. Everyone get some sleep. We'll start again in the morning."

Packer returned to the whiteboard.

"See ya," Simmons said, as he left.

"Goodnight, Mickey," Seoyoon said.

"Night," Thompson said.

Thompson checked over some work on his computer.

Seoyoon straightened her desk and sent some e-mail. Then she shut down her computer and picked up her handbag.

"Goodnight," she said.

"Night, Seoyoon," Thompson said.

He watched her leave.

The door to the incident room closed and he waited a moment longer.

"There something going on with those two," he said to Packer.

"I noticed," Packer said.

"Are you going to say something? I mean it could cause problems down the road."

"They're both adults, George."

"I would have thought Seoyoon would have more sense."

"Maybe she doesn't find Mickey as annoying as you do."

"Clearly not. But that's not what I meant," Thompson said, "You don't shit in your own nest."

"They wouldn't be the first two officers who did."

"Aye. And they won't be the first two officers both trying to get transfers to other stations if something goes wrong."

"No," Packer said, "and I'm sure they've thought about that."

"Well," he added, "I'm sure Seoyoon has, anyway."

Thompson grinned. "I don't think the blood's going all the way to Mickey's head at the moment."

Packer nodded, with a faint grin on his face.

"Go home, George," he said, "I'll see you in the morning."

He turned back to the whiteboard.

"You staying here all night again?" Thompson asked.

Packer shrugged.

"Aye, well. Goodnight, boss."

"Goodnight, George."

Thompson collected his coat and left, closing the door behind him.

Packer looked over the whiteboard a few minutes longer before walking over to the coffee machine and switching it on.

He made coffee and drank it as he looked over the whiteboard again.

What had tipped Bill Stewart over the edge and made him go to DeSouza's workshop?

Stewart had leapt on the suggestion of DeSouza killing Kasey to steal the necklace when he and Perry had asked them about it, but that didn't seem like enough provocation - particularly when Stewart had initially had difficulty accepting that the necklace even existed.

And where had the necklace come from in the first place? As Seoyoon had pointed out earlier, Kasey was living on the edge of poverty. An expensive necklace would been out of her price range. Had someone given it to her? Had she stolen it?

He looked up at the photo of Kasey pinned to the top of the whiteboard.

She looked back at him with guarded eyes.

Packer spent another hour working over the evidence in his mind, trying to find a connection.

He was not particularly hungry, but knew he should eat.

He closed the incident room door behind him and walked along the corridor towards the elevators.

Packer was surprised to find that it was dark on the street outside, despite the season. Night had fallen.

He looked at his watch and discovered it was after nine o'clock.

There was an Asian noodle shop along Hay Street a couple of blocks up from the police station where Packer seemed to get most of his dinners.

He wasn't sure if he would find the place still open, but fortunately it was.

The shop was deserted, though. The woman who was usually behind the counter had gone home, and only the chef was still there. He was a large Chinese man, bald on top but with a moustache and couple of days of beard covering his chin. He was sitting behind the counter, watching the television on the wall which was turned to a reality TV show.

Packer picked something at random from the menu.

The chef gave a grunt in response and headed back out to the kitchen.

Packer sat down on the bench across the window beside the entrance to wait.

He leaned back and placed his head against the window.

The glass felt cool against his scalp.

Tiredness washed over him and he closed his eyes.

The wind tore at her dress as she ran, tugging at the hem. The thin material was completely saturated, sticking to her body, but the wind was so strong that it pulled the hem away from her and made it slap against her bare thighs.

It was cold, so bitterly cold.

The rain was freezing against her skin, making her shiver, and the wind whipped it against her, making it feel like knives digging at her skin.

She stumbled on the heels, one of her feet sliding beneath her.

For a heart-stopping second, she felt herself falling, as the long spike skidded along the wet concrete, then caught, turning below her foot.

The necklace slapped against the top of her breasts, the metal hard against her bare skin.

Stumbling, she stepped to the side, her handbag sliding down along the slick surface of her arm, but she managed to regain her balance.

She gave a low gasp of relief, the sound swallowed by the relentless onslaught of the storm.

She hurried forward again, running through the rain along the treacherous footpath, expecting her feet to slide out from under her at any second and throw her down to the hard concrete.

She turned the corner and there was the slightest respite from the wind driving behind her.

But it was an illusion.

Instead of hammering her from behind, the wind was now driving the rain against her front instead. It slapped against her face, trying to force her backwards and stinging at her eyes. It lifted the bottom of the necklace, making it slide along her neck and up to her shoulder.

Shivering hard, she forced herself to move forward into the torrent.

The cold was like a physical force, trying to drive her back.

She could see the lights up ahead. Not far now.

She managed to stagger forward another few metres.

Suddenly, the ground in front of her flared.

There were lights behind her, rushing closer.

In a flash, her shadow shot out in front of her, elongating rapidly as the lights drew closer.

She did not even have time to think.

Something hard slammed against the backs of her legs, knocking her feet away. She felt her ankles twist and turn underneath her, as her legs shattered.

Her face was slammed against the ground, agony howling through her body.

She tried to scream but her face was mashed against the ground as she was squashed flat.

Blackness took her.

For a time, she lay there, agony ripping through her broken body.

She could hear tapping in front of her.

It grew louder, footsteps coming closer, calm, measured.

There was silence.

She tried to turn her head, tried to open her eyes, but could not.

She felt fingers on her neck, cold, invasive.

But she was powerless to move.

The fingers slid over her skin.

They gripped the necklace and began to pull.

Packer felt something touch his shoulder, and he jumped.

The Chinese chef was standing in front of him, holding the cardboard box and a napkin in his hand.

He looked silently at Packer for a moment with dark eyes.

"Sorry," Packer mumbled, "I drifted off."

The chef grunted in response.

Packer took the box of noodles from him and left the shop.

Tuesday

Chapter 23

Packer stood by his office window until the dawn rose.

The Causeway and the murky stretch of the river gradually emerged through the gloom, as the sun forced its way into the sky over the city. It was still too early for traffic, but a solitary delivery truck rumbled along the road, crossing the bridge and heading west.

Packer drank more coffee before heading along the corridor to shower and shave in the tiny bathroom.

He had spent the night in the office, turning the pieces over in his mind, but making no progress. He had been over the CCTV footage from DeSouza's workshop several times now, watching the way the man's temper erupted.

Was he Kasey's killer?

Packer tried to picture DeSouza following Kasey along the street, the anger burning within him until the pressure overcame his reason. He could see it happening, but was not convinced about it. Something about it did not sit right.

Other than drifting off briefly at the noodle shop, Packer had not slept. Tiredness filled him.

Perry arrived first.

"You look terrible," she said, sitting on the other side of his desk, "How can you go without sleep?"

"Robust constitution," Packer said, dismissively, "Alicia Martin said DeSouza was only trying to get custody as a way of hurting Kasey."

"That's right," Perry agreed, "George said the counsellor at the women's shelter said something similar. Why?"

"It doesn't sit right."

"Why? He's vicious. Taking her daughter away is a good way to hurt her."

"It's too calculated. It's not a man who takes a golf club off someone and beats them with it."

"What about following your ex in your car and running them down? That's pretty calculated."

"Yeah, that's what doesn't sit right," Packer said, "It's not a man losing his temper when cornered. It's a man who lets anger burn away inside."

"So, what's the custody dispute about?"

"Maybe he's telling the truth about that," Packer said, "He's worried about his daughter. The woman at Family Services seemed to think he was genuine."

"She's the only one who does." Perry pointed at the CCTV image paused on Packer's computer screen. "And DeSouza doesn't look like a perfect father to me."

Packer nodded.

He stared out the window.

"Do you think he'll do an interview?" Perry asked.

"I doubt it," Packer said, "It's not his first rodeo. He knows how this works."

"So, we charge him with the attack on Bill Stewart?"

"Eventually. We've got him for another day and a half. Let him stew a bit longer."

Thompson arrived soon after and pottered around as he waited for his computer to power up.

Seoyoon arrived after that, looking immaculate and made tea before sitting at her desk.

Simmons walked into the room minutes later, and gave Seoyoon a cursory greeting before sitting at his own desk.

"Where's the jewellery case you found in Kasey's car?" Seoyoon asked.

"In the exhibits cupboard," Perry said, "Why?"

"I started checking with jewellers yesterday afternoon. I've just had an e-mail back from one of them. They said there should be a serial number under the lining for insurance reasons."

It took them a few minutes of fiddling with the case, but eventually Simmons discovered that the bottom of the black velvet lining was not secured. He peeled it back slightly and a tiny string of white digits was printed beneath.

"That should help narrow it down," Seoyoon said, "Well done, Mickey."

"No dramas," Simmons said, grinning

"How're you getting along with CCTV?" Thompson asked.

"What a complete waste of time," Simmons said, "Getting the prick at the Towers to give me his footage was like pulling teeth. I spent an hour on it yesterday and there's not a bloody thing in it. Wherever Kasey was going, it wasn't there."

"Were there cameras nearby?" Perry asked.

"Four," Simmons said, "And I'm still going through the stuff we got from up the road closer to where she was hit. It's taking ages to go through, though."

"Why?"

"It was raining really heavily, so the footage is really murky. You can see movement and lights in places, but it's hard to make out. It's like looking through smoke or something. It's really hard to see."

"To see or not to see," Thompson said, "That is the question."

"Oooh," Seoyoon groaned, "That's terrible."

Simmons through an eraser at Thompson.

He ducked aside, grinning, and it bounced off his computer screen.

"You philistines," Thompson said, "Have you no taste for the finer things? Shakespeare was the greatest writer in history."

"That wasn't Shakespeare," Simmons protested.

"It was," Thompson insisted, "It's one of his lesser-known works. '*Simmons - The Tragical History of a Useless Sod*'."

"Yeah?" Simmons asked Thompson, "Well, what have you found?"

"About the same as you," Thompson conceded, "Nine-tenths of sod-all."

Seoyoon's phone rang and she answered it, still grinning.

"Can you hold on a moment?" Seoyoon said into the phone, after a moment.

She looked up. "Sergeant Leyton from Drug Squad. He knows the number in Kasey's phone records. Can someone get the boss?"

Simmons went to fetch Packer and they gathered around Seoyoon's desk.

She put the phone on speaker.

"Okay, you're on speaker," she said, "Go ahead."

"Harry Leyton," Thompson said, "It's George Thompson. Do you owe me some money?"

"Thompson?" Leyton said, faking outrage, "You can't still be in the force. What the hell are Internal Affairs doing?"

"That's not answering the question, you tight bastard."

"That bet was rigged, George."

"Rigged, my arse. It was fair-and-square."

"You've never made a bet in your life that was fair-and-square."

"Okay," Packer said, interrupting, "Maybe you two can practice your stage act another time."

"Sorry," Leyton said, a smile in his voice, "Just don't lend the Irishman any money. How can I help?"

"I'm told you recognised a number that came up in our victim's phone records."

"William Scheuster?" Leyton said, "Better known as Richard Morton. Yeah, we know him."

"What can you tell us about him?"

"Low-level meth dealer, but pretty active," Leyton said, "He's been on our radar for a few months. He kept changing phones to make it harder to keep up with him. We're assuming someone smarter than him must have taught him that trick, because he always registered them under names of TV characters. Kind of defeats the purpose of using an alias if you pick a stupid one, right?"

"Any history of violence?" Packer asked.

"Stabbed someone in West Perth a few months ago," Leyton said, "That's why we first started looking at him. We couldn't find anything solid enough to charge him with the stabbing, but the word was that it was him. Anecdotally, there seem to be a few similar incidents."

"If someone ran up a debt, would he get violent?"

"Absolutely. We think that's what the stabbing was about. How has he come up in your job?"

"We're following up on a hit-and-run," Packer said, "Girl run down near the Bell Tower, which looks deliberate. She seems to have been in regular contact with this Morton."

"When did this happen?"

"Last Sunday morning."

"It's not Morton, then."

"How do you know?"

"We pulled him about three weeks ago," Leyton said, "He's on remand in Hakea."

"Right," Packer said, "That rules him out, then."

"Looks like it," Leyton said, "Sorry."

Something still nagged at Packer, though. There was a connection. He could feel it.

It lurked at the edge of his mind, just out of reach.

"What did you have on Morton when you arrested him?" he asked.

"We were monitoring his phones for a while," Leyton said, "There was a lot of TI."

TI stood for 'telephone intercept'. Police listened in on phone calls and text messages of suspects.

"How far did it go back?"

"We started at the beginning of November. We monitored him for about four or five weeks, then we had enough to pull him."

"Anything apart from the TI?"

"We ran surveillance on him for a while," Leyton said, "but it was limited. Couldn't get the budget approval to run it for long. We got a couple of things out of that, though. Footage of him doing a couple of transactions."

"Can you send over copies of all this?"

"Yeah. No dramas. I'll get someone to run it over."

"Did he have other associates?" Packer asked, "Standover men or anything?"

"He's pretty small fish, to be honest," Leyton said, "There a couple of hangers-on, but they weren't that involved."

"Who were they?"

"A big Māori bloke called Boonga who used to do a bit of debt-collecting and another bloke called Petey, who seemed to be on the sidelines."

"Tell me about them."

"There isn't that much to tell. There were a couple of calls where Morton was chasing up some outstanding money from someone, and told him he was going to send Boonga around for a 'chat' if he didn't get the money."

"Did he?"

"Nuh. The bloke paid up. Looked like the threat was enough."

"And Petey?"

"Seemed to be a courier of some kind."

"Have you got real names for Boonga and Petey?" Packer asked.

"We were focused on Morton, but I think one of the boys did manage to ID them. Why? What are you thinking?"

"I don't know," Packer said, "Just trying to find a connection with our victim."

"Okay. Look, I'll send over what we've got and you can have a look. Call me back if you want to talk about it more."

"Will do. Thanks."

Packer hung up.

"What are you thinking, boss?" Thompson asked.

Packer shook his head. "I don't know."

"This bloke, Morton, was on remand when Kasey was killed," Perry pointed out, "It can't be him."

"You reckon one of the hangers-on?" Thompson asked.

"She still had meth when you searched the house," Packer said, "so she was getting it from somewhere."

"There's a shitload of drug dealers in Perth," Simmons pointed out.

Packer nodded. Simmons was right, but it still felt like a connection. Morton had been Kasey's dealer until very recently. Something about this nagged at him, even though he couldn't work out what.

"Let's see what's in the stuff from the Drug Squad when it arrives," Packer said.

"I can go through it," Seoyoon said, "It's only about six weeks of calls, so it shouldn't take that long."

Packer nodded. "Alright. Claire, can you ring the hospital? See if there's any change with Bill Stewart."

"Will do."

"Mickey, you plug on with the CCTV."

"Yes, boss," Simmons said, resigned to his fate.

"You give him a hand, George," Packer said, "Should distract you from making any more crap Shakespeare jokes."

***

Packer stood in front of the whiteboard, trying to find a way to connect the pieces they had.

There was something that would unlock all of this. It was out of his grasp for now, but it was there, just beyond his reach.

"Boss," Perry said, hanging up the phone ten minutes later.

He turned and headed towards her desk.

"Bill Stewart's still in ICU," she said, "No change overnight. He's still being respirated, though, and they're not seeing any brain activity."

"Which means what?" Thompson asked.

"They're keeping him alive," Perry said, "but they doubt that he'll ever wake up."

"Sounds like DeSouza might have pulled off a hat-trick," Thompson said, "Two murders in two days."

Packer said nothing.

He turned back to the whiteboard.

He was surprised when the custody sergeant rang forty minutes later to tell him that Deon DeSouza had agreed to be interviewed.

Chapter 24

Packer closed the door of the interview room behind him.

Perry was sitting at the table, a large notebook open in front of her.

Deon DeSouza sat opposite them. His hands were cuffed in front of him.

"It's recording," Packer said, sitting beside Perry.

"The date is 14 December," Perry said, "and the time is 11:49am. I'm Detective Senior Constable Claire Perry and with me is Detective Senior Sergeant Tony Packer. We are at the East Perth Police Station. Can you tell us your full name, please?"

"Deon DeSouza."

"No middle name?"

"No."

"Date of birth?"

"3 November, 1996."

"Okay," Perry said, "Yesterday, you were arrested for assaulting Bill Stewart. You remain under arrest for that offence. Before we begin this interview, I need to explain your rights to you.

"Firstly, you have the right to remain silent. You do not have to answer any questions we ask. You may choose to answer some, all or none of our questions. If we ask you ten questions, how many do you have to answer?"

"None," DeSouza said. He sounded bored. He was clearly familiar with the standard caution.

Perry went through the rest anyway, and he agreed that he understood it all.

"Bill Stewart was your father-in-law until you were divorced," Perry said.

"Yep."

"How would you describe your relationship with him before yesterday?"

"Okay to start off with. Then it got difficult, so I stopped having anything to do with him."

"When did you first meet him?"

"Eight months ago, probably. Eight or nine."

"How did that come about?"

DeSouza thought about it for a moment. "Me and Kasey were together for about five years. Had Jessie together. We were thinking about having another one, too, but kids are expensive and money's a bit tight. We moved over here, 'cause I was planning to get a job on the mines, but that didn't pan out and a mate helped me get the workshop started, so I ended up doing that.

"Anyway, everything was going okay. We were a happy little family, right?

"And then one day, Kasey rang me up and asked me to come home. She was all upset on the phone. And I was saying to her, you know, 'What's wrong? What is it? Tell me what's going on,' but I couldn't get anything out of her. She just wanted me to come home.

"So, I left one of the boys in charge at the workshop and shot off home.

"When I got back to our place, she was acting really weird. Like kind of upset, but not upset at the same time. And I said to her, 'What's going on, babe?'.

"Took her a while to get it out of her, but she said she'd been to the shopping centre with Jessie, and she'd seen her father. Like, I thought her parents were dead. She'd told me that when we first met years ago, and as far as I knew it was true.

"But it turned out they were still alive. She just didn't want nothing to do with them. We were over in Sydney when we met. I'd been over there for years after I did my apprenticeship. Kasey said she'd over there to get away from her parents. This was all news to me, you know? And so I asked why she was trying to get away from them. She wouldn't tell me what had happened, just that she didn't want to see them no more.

"But then she'd run into her dad and he'd forced her to give him her phone number. And I said to her, 'Well, no stress. If you don't want to see them, don't see them. Get a new fuckin' phone or whatever.' I kind of calmed her down a bit, but she was still weirded out by the whole thing.

"That was it for a few weeks, but she was still acting weird. After a couple of weeks, she told me she'd been talking to her dad and wanted to meet up with him and her mum. I sort of said to her, 'Alright. Well, if that's what you want to do, we'll do it.' So, she made this arrangement to go to King's Park and see them.

"When we got there, her parents just seemed normal enough. Everything went okay at the park. I mean I don't know what I was expecting, but they were okay. Just like normal people."

DeSouza gave a slight snort. "That was what I thought then, anyway. Didn't take long to find out what they were really like."

"How was that?" Perry asked.

"Pair of shit-heads," DeSouza said, "Like her mum's always making these comments all the time. Putting down everything Kasey ever did. Nothing's ever right. The whole time, she'd doing it. Even when it was obvious Kasey was starting to get upset about it, she kept going. It even got worse then, like she saw blood in the water like a fuckin' shark.

"And her dad was weird, too. Treating her like a little kid, like holding her hand and putting his arm around her all the time. And he fuckin' hated me. He made that clear. He wasn't outright nasty about it, but he was always saying shit like he expected Kasey to end up with some rich dude. Making sure I knew I wasn't good enough for her. And he was always poking his nose into shit, too, like wanted to know all our business.

"In the end, I just said, 'Fuck this. Too much grief.' I stopped going to their place, and if they were coming over to ours, I went out before they arrived. Kasey didn't like that. We started having blues about me not being nice to her parents. And I said to her, 'Well, shit, babe. You moved to another fuckin' city so you didn't have to see them again. And I can see exactly why.' I mean, they were poison. They just made Kasey miserable, but she wouldn't stop seeing them. We couldn't move away, 'cause I've got the workshop, but I said to her, 'Look, just tell them you don't want to see them no more. I'll fuckin' tell them for you if you want,' but that started another round of arguments."

DeSouza gave a sigh. "I didn't know about the drugs for a while. I mean we weren't really talking to each other and I thought she was just miserable 'cause of her parents. Didn't know she was using drugs, though."

"How did you find out?"

"Alicia told me."

"Alicia Martin?"

"Yeah. Kasey's bestie."

"She was aware Kasey was using drugs?"

Desouza nodded. "Yeah. She'd known about it for a while. She figured I must have known, too. Felt pretty bad about it when she told me and found I didn't already know."

"How did you deal with that?"

"To start off with, I was worried for Kasey. I said to her, 'What are you fuckin' doing? You gotta stop this shit.' Of course, she denied it, said she wasn't using. But then, I started thinking, 'Shit. She'd been doing this when she was supposed to be looking after Jessie.' I mean I'm at work fuckin' sixty hours a week trying to pay all the bills, and she's at home shooting up with Jessie around. I mean, what kind of fuckin' mum does that? Whatever bullshit is going on with her parents or whatever, that's not on.

"So, I got out. And like I said to you yesterday, I wanted to take Jessie, but couldn't. So, I called Child Protection, thinking they'd sort shit out. But they didn't do nothing, and now I have to go through this Family Court bullshit to get Jessie away from her."

"What does this have to do with Kasey's parents, Mr De Souza?" Perry asked.

"She started using that shit 'cause she couldn't handle the grief they were causing her. I mean, she never needed it in the five years we were together. Then her parents turn up and make our lives a misery, and suddenly she's using drugs."

"There must have been other reasons."

"Fuckin' what? Look, you don't know what they were like. Her mum's always putting her down and her father's trying to run her life like she's little a kid. I'm telling you they were poison. They come back on the scene and a couple of months later, Kasey's a drug addict."

"Did that make you angry with Bill and Felicity?" Packer asked.

DeSouza looked at him. "Yeah, of course it fuckin' did. They ruined Kasey's life. They ruined our marriage."

"Did it make you angry with Kasey?" Packer asked.

"Yeah. I mean, it was fuckin' stupid. And when I realised she was doing it around Jessie, I just about hit the fuckin' roof. Jessie's our daughter. How can you do that shit?"

"Must make you angry that Kasey's still got custody of Jessie."

"Shit, yeah."

"Still using drugs around your daughter, too."
"Dad's have got no fuckin' rights. It's bullshit."
"Child Protection did nothing to help you."
"Nuh."
"Family Service did nothing either."
"Nuh."
"The Family Court's taking forever."
"Sure is."
"That's got be enough to fire up any man."
"Yeah, it is."
"Only choice left is to do something about it yourself."

DeSouza opened his mouth to speak.

He looked at Packer and stopped himself.

He shook his head.

"Look, I didn't fuckin' kill Kasey, right? There were times when I wanted to, I admit it. A lot of times. But I love Jessie. All I want is to get her back, so I can look after her. How could I be a good dad if I killed her mum? Didn't happen, right? It wasn't me. Some other cunt did it."

Packer stared at him for a moment.

Then he leaned back in his chair, signalling to Perry that he had finished for now.

Perry made some notes in her notebook.

DeSouza lifted his hands and ran them slowly over his shaved head. He leaned back in the chair and stared up at the ceiling.

"Okay," Perry said, "Now I wish to speak to you about what happened yesterday."

DeSouza sniffed and gave a slight grimace. He straightened up in the chair and nodded.

"Take us through what happened," Perry said, "One step at a time."

"I was sitting in the office, on the phone to a customer, when I heard shouting. I got up to look and see what was happening and Bill came in with the golf club and started smashing stuff up."

"Had Mr Stewart been to your workshop before today?" Perry asked.

DeSouza shook his head.

"Had you told him the address previously?"

DeSouza shook his head again. "Nah. But he knew the name and it's in the phone book. Wouldn't have been too hard to find it."

"Do you have any idea why he came there yesterday?"

DeSouza scoffed. "I can probably take a guess."

"Okay. Why then?"

DeSouza took a deep breath and let it out. He shrugged his shoulders.

"When youse came around yesterday, you said about how the Family Court stuff would be easier now that Kasey's been... well, now that Kasey's gone. And I started thinking that without Kasey there, Jessie was left with Bill and Felicity. I didn't want my daughter staying with that pair of fuckin' arseholes.

"So, I rang up to see if I could go and collect her. Felicity answered the phone. She was kind of pissed off when she realised it was me, saying 'How dare you phone me?' and all this shit. But when I told her I wanted to come and collect Jessie, she goes, 'Fine. Come and collect her'. Like, she was happy to get Jessie off her hands, you know? Which is exactly why I didn't want Jessie staying with them. I told her I'd come over to get Jessie and she told me to wait a minute while she spoke to Bill.

"Next thing I know, Bill's on the phone. He was screaming all this shit at me. I couldn't even understand most of it, he was that fuckin' wound up. Shouting that I was a thief and all this shit that didn't make no sense. He just kept saying he would make sure I never saw Jessie again. In the end I hung up on the prick.

"When I got off the phone, I rang me solicitor for help. She told me I had to wait, but she'd get in touch with Family Services and make some kind of application, an interim order or some shit. I asked how long that was gonna take and she said it could be weeks. I wasn't happy about it, especially when Jessie was left with Bill and Felicity until then, but the solicitor said it was better to wait until it was all legal, 'cause otherwise Bill and Felicity would have good grounds for getting Jessie taken off me again. I knew they didn't want her, but it's the kind of nasty shit they'd do just to cause trouble.

"So, I decided to wait and got back to work.

"Probably about an hour after that, Bill turns up at the workshop and goes apeshit smashing everything."

"What happened after he came into your office?" Perry asked.

"He smashed some stuff and tried to attack me. I managed to get the club off him while he was trying to hit me with it. There was a bit of a fight. He hit me, I hit him. He ended up on the ground - I think he tripped over the computer that he'd knocked onto the ground - and that was it."

"Stewart left in an ambulance," Packer pointed out, "We're told he's got a fractured skull, concussion and two broken bones. He's in a coma right now. You don't seem too badly injured."

"He fuckin' attacked me with a golf club, mate," DeSouza said, "What was I supposed to do? Stand there and let him put me in the fuckin' hospital? I was defending myself."

"We got some CCTV footage from the camera at your workshop," Packer said.

DeSouza gave a sudden start. Clearly, this had not occurred to him.

"Yeah?" he asked.

"It didn't look much like self-defence in the footage," Packer said.

"He was fuckin' crazy when he came in, shouting all this shit and smashing everything up. I had to get the club off him before he killed me."

"Yeah," Packer said, "I'm not sure you needed to hit him repeatedly in the head with the club after you got it off him. Or keep hitting him in the head after he was unconscious."

DeSouza looked down at the table.

"Fuck," he hissed.

He looked up after a moment. "I don't even really know what happened, man. Like, I was scared and the adrenaline was kicking in. He attacked me with the golf club. You must have seen that on the CCTV. Maybe I went a bit far, but it was all heat of the moment, mate. You weren't fucking there."

"Were you pissed off about him not letting you pick Jessie up?"

Deon shrugged. "Yeah. Of course, I was. I mean the only reason they were keeping her was to try to piss me off. They didn't want her. Even Felicity said that."

"And you didn't like Stewart much, even before this."

"Nuh."

"And he turns up and starts smashing your workshop up."

"Yeah, look, I told you, man. I was pissed off. I might have gone a bit far, but I was defending myself."

"Did you have to defend yourself against Kasey sometimes?"

"What?"

"You've got assault charges involving Kasey. She was using drugs. Drugs make you do crazy stuff. Did she attack you and you had to defend yourself."

Deon gave a snort of frustration.

"I know what you're trying to get me to say, but that's not what happened. She used to hurt herself and say it was me. I never touched her."

"Never?"

"No."

"Not even when she was keeping Jessie away from you to piss you off?"

"That was different. It wasn't like Bill and Felicity."

"Were you pissed off with Kasey on Saturday?"

DeSouza shook his head. "I wasn't fuckin' there, mate. I was nowhere near her when she got killed."

"Where were you?"

"In bed."

"On your own?

"No."

"No? Then who with?"

"With Alicia," Deon snapped, "Alright? I wasn't there when Kasey was killed, because I was fucking Alicia."

Chapter 25

"Deon's having an affair with Alicia Martin?" Seoyoon asked.

"I think 'affair' may be putting it too strongly," Packer said.

Seoyoon looked at Perry. "Is he good-looking, Deon?"

Perry nodded. "He is, actually. Bit of a bad boy."

Simmons put a finger in his mouth and mimicked vomiting.

"He's got a wicked double bogey with a nine iron, too," Thompson said, swinging an imaginary golf club through the air.

"Yes, alright," Packer said, impatiently, "That'll do."

They fell silent as they thought this through.

"Alicia Martin didn't tell you this when you spoke to her," Simmons said.

"Well, I can see why she might want to keep it quiet," Perry pointed out, "Can't you?"

"Yeah," Simmons said, defensively, "but it's a murder investigation. Surely she would have thought that was more important than keeping this secret."

"To be fair, she didn't actually have any reason to tell us," Perry said, "We were there asking about Kasey, not about Deon."

"We did ask about him," Packer pointed out, "She told us he was 'an okay bloke' at first, but turned into an arsehole trying to take Jessie away from Kasey. That doesn't sound much like someone she'd want to sleep with."

"You think Deon's lying?" Perry asked.

Packer shrugged. "It's a strange alibi it he knew Alicia Martin wasn't going to back him up."

"True," Perry said.

"She didn't mention Kasey's drug habit, either," Packer said, "and DeSouza told us she knew about that. I think we'll have another chat to her."

"Assuming she confirms that she was with Deon, though," Perry said, "That's him off the hook for Kasey's murder."

Packer nodded.

"What about Bill Stewart?" Thompson said, "Seems like a bit of an overreaction to go around there and try to attack DeSouza just because DeSouza rang up and asked to take Jessie."

"Agreed," Packer said, "but I don't think Bill Stewart's going to be explaining what happened any time soon."

***

Packer and Perry drove back to the Maylands apartment block and parked outside.

It took a few minutes for Alicia Martin to respond to the buzzer.

"Hello," she said, sounding clearly surprised.

Perry realised she could see them on the security camera. She looked up at the camera.

"Hello, Alicia," she said, "Just a few more questions we need to ask. Can we come in?"

"It's not really a good time."

"It won't take long, Alicia."

Again, there was another slight hesitation.

"Sure," Alicia said, buzzing them in.

As they walked into the foyer, Perry turned to look at Packer.

"Sounds like she's a bit reluctant to speak to us again," she said.

Packer nodded.

They made their way up to Alicia's apartment in the elevator. She was waiting for them at the door, holding Jake in her arms. The boy had food around his face and was holding a biscuit in one hand.

"I was just getting ready to go out," Alicia said, "Can this wait?"

"Sorry," Perry said, shaking her head, "It's important. It won't take long."

Alicia stood there a moment longer, then turned back into the apartment and went in. They followed behind her.

The place was still in disarray, toys and clothes strewn all over the place. The television was switched on in the corner, children's programs playing. Alicia put Jake down and he went over to sit in front of the TV, chewing his biscuit as he watched.

Perry moved some toys out of the way to make a space to sit down. Packer sat beside her. Alicia sat in the chair opposite.

"What's this about?" Alicia asked.

"Just a few more questions," Perry said.

"I told you everything last time."

"There's a few things we wanted to follow up."

"Like what?"

"Last time we were here, you said Kasey was 'dealing with a few issues,'" Perry said, "What sort of issues did you mean?"

Alicia swallowed slightly. She shrugged.

"Nothing in particular," she said, "I mean, you know. She's a single mum, like me. It's hard to manage. And she had the issues with the Family Court and everything."

"I thought you meant something else apart from that."

"Not really. No."

"Listen, Alicia," Perry said, "We believe Kasey was killed deliberately. We're trying to find out who did it. If there's anything you can tell us to help, you need to."

"I don't know anything else," Alicia said, "Like what?"

"Like drugs?" Packer suggested.

Alicia's eyes snapped up at him. She looked at him, but said nothing.

"It's okay, Alicia," Perry said, "We know she was using. You're not betraying any secrets."

Alicia looked down again. She took a deep breath and let it out. She rubbed at her eyes, shaking her head.

"It was so stupid," she said, "I had another friend after high school who started using meth, so I knew the signs. The stuff's everywhere in Perth. It's so easy to get hold of. But I never thought Kasey would start doing it. As soon as I worked it out, I said to her, 'You're an idiot. You've got Jessie. You need to put her first, not get yourself messed up on meth all the time.' But you can't talk to an addict."

"When did she start using?"

"Six months ago," Alicia said, "That's when I started noticing it, anyway."

"Did her parents know?"

Alicia shook her head adamantly. "No way. They never would have figured that out."

"What about Deon?"

Alicia took a breath and let out a slight sigh. "Yeah. He knew. Took him a while to figure it out, but he did eventually. He asked me one day if I knew.

I thought he'd be pissed off that I knew about it but hadn't told him, but he wasn't really. I think he'd kind of given up on Kasey by then. They split up soon after."

"He told you? Not the other one around?"

Alicia nodded. "Yeah. Not sure when he worked it out, but he didn't tell me straight away."

"Why didn't you tell us about the drugs when we spoke to you yesterday?"

Alicia let out a sigh and shrugged.

"Kasey's gone now," she said, rubbing one of her eyes, "She did stupid things, but she was my friend. I loved her. I don't want people thinking she was some stupid drug addict, because she wasn't like that."

Alicia's voice started to break down. "I mean, she was using, but she wasn't some loser, right? She was a beautiful person. She just had some stuff to work through, and she thought the drugs helped or something."

"What stuff did she have to work through?" Packer asked.

"I don't know," Alicia said, "I tried to talk to her about it, but she would just clam up. Wouldn't talk."

"You sure?" he asked.

"Yes. It's true," Alicia said, "I know I didn't tell you about the drugs, and I know I should have. But if I knew what was wrong with her, I'd tell you."

"What makes you think she had stuff to work through?"

"She kind of hinted at it sometimes. Like, we were talking about when we were at school once. And I said about how she got kind of distant and we lost touch. She said something like, 'It happened then,' or 'That's when it happened'. Something like that. But she wouldn't say what."

"Did you ask?"

"Of course I did. I tried a few times. Told her I could help, but she said, 'Nobody can help.'"

"Do you know where she was getting the drugs from?" Perry asked.

"It's not exactly hard in Perth, is it?" Alicia said, "I mean the stuff's everywhere here."

"No idea at all?"

"There was someone," Alicia said, "I don't know exactly. But she used to get text messages that she was secretive about. Jakey and I were around at her place once, and she was acting weird. Like, nervous or something. She kept checking her phone. When it chimed to say there was a message, she just about ran to check it. Then she said she had to go out for something. I knew what it was, but she denied it. It was so stupid."

"Do you remember when this was?"

Alicia thought for a moment. "Two weeks ago. It was Saturday. I remember that, because she was going to her parents' house for dinner. She didn't want to, but it was some big celebration Bill had organised for his birthday. I wondered if that was why she kept checking her messages. Until she got a reply and just about ran out of the house."

"How was she paying for the drugs?"

"I don't know. She was getting Child Support payments, but they're hardly anything. I don't think the cleaning work paid that much. I assumed she was getting money from her parents. They're loaded."

"Was she getting any money from Deon DeSouza?"

Alicia scoffed. "No. He never gave her anything. She wanted money from the Family Court, but there was some hearing about it, and she said afterwards that the court didn't order him to pay anything because he proved that he didn't have any money or something."

"You said a moment ago Kasey was a single mum, like you."

Alicia nodded.

"You don't have a boyfriend?"

Alicia shrugged. "No. I was seeing someone, but it didn't work out."

"You live here alone, then? Just you and Jakey?"

"Yeah."

"Must be difficult on your own."

Alicia shrugged. "Yeah. It's difficult to get stuff done. The place gets in a mess. But Jakey goes to daycare a couple of days a week, so I can catch up on things then."

She looked at Perry, obviously unsure where any of this was going.

"Does it get lonely here on your own?" Perry asked.

Alicia shrugged again. "Well, I've got Jakey, so I'm not on my own."

"No, of course not. I can't recall if we asked you last time, but you were home last Saturday night, were you?"

"Yeah, I was."

"So just you and Jakey home?"

Alicia nodded.

"Did you have any visitors?"

Alicia frowned slightly. "How do you mean?"

"Well, anyone come to the apartment at all on Saturday evening?"

"No."

"You're sure about that?"

"Yeah."

Perry looked at her for a moment.

"Deon DeSouza wasn't here, then?"

Alicia gave a slight start. Her eyes flickered from Perry to Packer and back again. "Deon? No."

"Definitely not?"

"No," Alicia said, "He definitely wasn't. We were here on our own."

"How would you describe your relationship with Deon?"

"I don't know," Alicia said, "Like, he's my best friend's ex. Former friend, I suppose."

"Former friend? Not a friend any more."

"Did he tell you we're still friends?"

Perry looked at her in silence for a moment. "Look, Alicia. As I said, we're investigating a murder. It's important that you tell us the truth."

Alicia looked down at her lap. Her arms were wrapped around her body, hugging herself. She took a deep breath, and shrugged.

"We were kind of seeing each other for a while."

"What does that mean exactly?" Perry asked.

"What do you think it means?" Alicia said, angrily. Tears began to form and she rubbed at her eyes.

"Are you saying it was a sexual relationship?"

Alicia nodded. "Yes." She looked at Perry, her eyes flaring. "We were having sex, okay?"

She rubbed tears from her cheeks, on the verge of crying, her face going red.

Perry nodded. "Okay. See, that surprises me a bit. Because last time, you said he was an arsehole."

"He is an arsehole!" Alicia said, loudly.

Jake turned his head to look and she calmed down, smiling at him.

He turned back to the television again.

"He is an arsehole," Alicia said, more quietly, "Trying to take Jessie away from Kasey. What kind of bastard wants to separate a mother from her own daughter?"

"And yet you slept with him?"

Alicia nodded. "It was a mistake. It shouldn't have happened."

"How did it happen?"

"I don't even know," she said, "We used to talk. I mean, he was a good friend for a lot of years when he still with Kasey. We kept in touch after they split."

She looked up at Perry.

"It wasn't like a regular thing or anything," she said, looking up, "We weren't having an affair or anything. There were just a few times when... I don't know, I just wanted some company, okay?"

"Okay," Perry said, "When did it start?"

"There's nothing to 'start', right?" Alicia said, a note of anger in her voice, "I told you, it's not an affair or anything."

"Okay. Sorry," Perry said, "What I meant was, when was the first time you slept with Deon?"

Alicia shrugged. "A while ago."

"Before he separated from Kasey?"

Alicia was silent for a moment.

She nodded.

"Yeah, but they were already finished by then. He hadn't told her yet, but it was over. He came around 'cause he was upset about it and wanted to talk. We just started... well, we were talking, and it just happened."

"Did Kasey know about you and Deon?"

"No," Alicia said, shaking her head.

She looked down. After a moment, she shrugged.

"Actually, I think she did," she said, quietly, "We were talking about Deon after the Family Court mediation and she said something about how she had no one to trust. I told her she could trust me, and she looked at me and said, 'I only wish I could'. I rang Deon after she left and said I couldn't see him again. He wanted to know why, but I told him it was over. I couldn't do it to Kasey any more."

"When was this?" Perry asked.

"Two months ago," Kasey said, "It was the same day as the mediation. Kasey was having such a shit time because of Deon and I was sleeping with him. It just felt so wrong, doing that to her. So, I stopped it right away."

"Have you had any contact with him since then?"

"None at all," Alicia said, shaking her head, "I told him after the mediation it was over. He texted and rang a few times after that, but I didn't answer."

"Okay," Perry said.

"Look, why are you asking this?" Alicia said, "I stopped it, right? What does it matter now."

"Deon told us he was with you on Saturday night. We wanted to know if it was true."

"No," she said, "He wasn't here. I told you. It was over months ago."

Chapter 26

"So was DeSouza there or not?" Thompson asked.

"Not according to Alicia," Perry said, "She was sleeping with Deon DeSouza, but it was definitely 'not a regular thing', and ended two months ago."

"Didn't she say last time that she hated Deon?" Seoyoon asked, "Called him an a-hole?"

"Yes," said Perry, "She did say that."

"'The lady doth protest too much,'" Thompson said.

"What?" Simmons asked.

"Shakespeare again," Thompson asked, "It's from *MacBeth*."

"I think it's from *Hamlet*," Seoyoon said.

"Is it?" Thompson said, "I thought it was *MacBeth*."

"*Hamlet*," Perry confirmed.

Simmon looked blankly between them. "What's it mean?"

"She said she hated DeSouza because she was secretly having a fling with him, and didn't want anyone to know," Thompson explained, an exasperated look on his face, "Just like in the play by Shakespeare. Oh, never mind."

"So where does it leave us?" Seoyoon asked.

Perry shrugged. "One of them's not telling the truth. My money's on him. Alicia Martin doesn't go around attacking people with golf clubs."

"She wasn't very forthcoming, though, was she?" Thompson said, "She neglected to mention any of this the first time you spoke to her."

"Why would she?" Perry asked, "She's hardly going to say, 'Sorry, I don't know anything about the murder. Oh, and by the way, I was having sex with my dead friend's ex while he tries to take her daughter away.'"

"Like the boss says, though," Thompson insisted, "DeSouza would have to be stupid to put this up as an alibi if it wasn't true."

"Maybe he panicked."

"What do you think, boss?" Thompson asked.

"I think DeSouza's till in the frame," Packer said.

He turned to Seoyoon. "How are you getting along with the stuff from the Drug Squad?"

"There's more than I thought," she said, "but I've been through a big chunk of it."

"And?"

"I can show you what I've found so far."

She turned back to her screen. The others stood around behind her.

"Drug Squad got a warrant to intercept three phones used by Morton on 4 November," Seoyoon said, "Every call and SMS he made after that was recorded and logged. I haven't been through two of the phones yet, but I've nearly finished on the one that he was using to contact Kasey."

She opened up a window on the screen which contained a spreadsheet. The Drug Squad used a standard template with columns for the date, time and phone number used. A column beside that recorded the name of the person was contacting, if that person could be identified, and a further column contained the notes made by the officer listening to the call.

Packer looked down the spreadsheet. The bulk of the calls seemed to be discussing drug deals.

"He was a busy man," Packer said.

"Yeah," Seoyoon agreed, "He was only selling very tiny amounts, a couple of points here and there, but he was selling a lot them. On some days, he was doing over forty sales, and he got up to sixty on one day."

"He's a flea," said Thompson.

"What does that mean?" asked Seoyoon, turning to face him.

"A flea on a dog's dick," Thompson explained, "Drug Squad slang, lass. He's a tiny flea jumping around on something bigger. It means he's a prolific, but low-level, street dealer."

"What about Kasey?" Packer asked.

Seoyoon turned back to the screen.

"She appears quite a lot. She seems to have been a fairly regular customer by the time the Drug Squad start monitoring Morton's phone."

She scrolled down the call log with the mouse pointer.

"She rings or texts Morton every day or two to buy meth. There are a couple of times when she rings him three days in a row and one day when she rings him in the morning to buy drugs and then again in the afternoon to buy more."

"Must have been a stressful day," Thompson said.

"What's the date of that call?" Packer asked.

"The ninth of November," Seoyoon said.

"See what's significant about that date when you have a chance," Packer said, "See if it lines up with a Family Court hearing or something."

"Okay, boss."

"Is there more?"

"There sure is," Seoyoon said.

She scrolled down further.

"Morton seems to have been supplying drugs to Kasey on tic. Some days, she paid, but other days she didn't have the money. There are a lot of calls where they're arguing about it."

Seoyoon scrolled down the log until she found the call she was looking for.

Then she moved the mouse pointer across to a file directory which contained audio files.

She selected one of the files and double-clicked to open it.

A window popped up with an audio player.

The tone of a phone ringing played through the speakers on Seoyoon's computer.

"*Yep,*" said a man's voice. There was a slight croak to the voice, the product of heavy nicotine use.

"*Hi, Rich. How are you?*" a woman's voice asked nervously.

Packer felt an odd sensation. It was eerie listening to the voice of a dead woman.

"*What do you want, Kase?*" asked the man.

"*Can I get some? Just a little bit.*"

"*You got me money?*"

"*Not right now.*"

"*Can't help you, then.*"

"*Please, Rich,*" Kasey begged, "*I just need a little bit.*"

"*I fuckin' told you, Kase. You ain't gettin' no more 'til you pay me back what you fuckin' owe me.*"

"*I can get it for you. I told you I can.*"

"*Then where is it?*"

"*I'll get it. I just can't get it today.*"

"Then call me back when you can."

"I just need some, Rich. Please."

The call continued in this vein for another few minutes. Kasey begged. Morton demanded payment. Eventually, Morton agreed to supply Kasey with drugs, but insisted that this was the last time.

"This seems to go on for another two weeks," Seoyoon said, "The calls are all pretty similar. It sounds like Kasey gave him some money on the tenth of November, but not all of it, because he keeps asking for the rest whenever she calls. He starts getting nastier and nastier, too.

"Then there's this call on the fifteenth. Morton rings Kasey this time."

Seoyoon clicked on another audio file.

They could hear the ringing tone again.

"Hi, Rich," said Kasey, her voice quivering.

"You got it?" Morton said.

"I can get it, Rich. I can-"

"Do you fuckin' think I'm jokin'?" Morton shouted, his voice so loud it was distorted over the computer's speakers.

"Rich, I can get it. All of it," Kasey pleaded.

"Fuckin' three grand, cunt. Where is it?"

"I'll get it, Rich-"

"I am gettin' sick and fuckin' tired of tellin' you the same fuckin' thing, Kase. I told you I wanted the fuckin' money and you're still fuckin' me around."

"I'm not, Rich."

"I am not fuckin' jokin' with you, Kase."

"I know-"

"Fuckin' listen, you dumb cunt. You owe me three grand. Give me the fuckin' money. Got it?"

"I will-"

"Have you fuckin' got it?"

"Yeah, Rich, I've-"

"You got one more day, you dumb cunt. Three grand tomorrow. If you don't give me the fuckin' money tomorrow, I am gonna come around to your place and feed that fuckin' retard kid of yours to me fuckin' dogs. You fuckin' got it?"

"Rich, I just-"

"Have you fuckin' got it?"

"Yeah, Rich-"
"One more day, cunt. One more day."
The phone clicked off before Kasey could speak again.
"What date is this?" Packer asked.
"The fifteenth of November," Seoyoon said.
"What happens after that."
"There's a gap of three days, and then Kasey calls him again for more meth. It's all very friendly again. That's as far as I've got."
"So, she got him the money?" Thompson said, surprised.
Seoyoon shrugged. "She must have. There's no more discussion about it in any of the calls, and he's supplying her again."
"Where did she find three thousand dollars?" Thompson asked.
"She must have been working as a prostitute like we thought," Simmon said.
"Three thousand's a lot of money," Perry said, "It would take one of those girls weeks to raise that."
"What about the surveillance material?" Packer said, "Anything in that?"
"Nothing involving Kasey."
"Is there footage where we can see Morton?"
"Yes, there's some," Seoyoon said, "but not much of it," Seoyoon said, "There were only a couple of days when they followed him."
"Leyton said he couldn't the budget approved for a proper surveillance team," Thompson said.
"Can you show us Morton?" Packer asked.
"Yeah," Seoyoon said.
She turned back to the screen and used the mouse to open up a window that had been minimised at the bottom of the screen. It showed a paused frame of a video. The screen showed the view out of a car window, looking across a carpark towards a row of shops.
"The day when he says he was going to feed Jessie to the dogs is the fifteenth of November," she said, "There are calls on the thirteenth and fourteenth arranging a transaction," she said, "They don't mention actual amounts in the calls, but the buyer keeps asking Morton if he is sure he can manage this. I'm guessing it was arranged on one of the other phones that I haven't been through yet, because there's nothing on this log about

it. Anyway, the buyer wasn't convinced that Morton could supply so much meth."

"He needed the money from Kasey so he could buy a bigger shipment from his supplier and sell it on to this buyer," Perry suggested.

Seoyoon nodded. "Could be."

"Makes sense," Thompson said, "He was getting pretty desperate in that last call."

"Anyway," Seoyoon went on, "because it looked out of the ordinary, Drug Squad followed him."

She clicked on the mouse and the video started playing.

The picture quality was poor and appeared to have been taken with a mobile phone. There were a couple of people walking past the shops wearing shorts and T-shirts.

A man appeared walking into view from the edge of the footpath. He was tall, but not heavily-built, although it was difficult to get any real idea of his size under his clothes.

"That's him," Seoyoon said, tapping the screen.

Morton was wearing a grey hoodie with the hood pulled up over his head and dark sunglasses.

"Look at the prick," scoffed a voice off-screen, "It must be forty degrees today and he's got the hood up."

"He's in disguise, mate," said another voice, "Trying not to draw any attention."

The two police officers filming the video both laughed.

Morton stopped in the middle of the footpath, then looked around him before walking quickly over to a parked car.

The image on the screen was zoomed in quickly, the picture shaking around jerkily and losing focus. After a moment, the blurry image snapped back into focus. Morton could be seen leaning down towards the driver's side of the car.

He spoke to the driver for a moment, then took something large out of his pocket and passed it through the window. The car began driving off and Morton hurriedly walked off in the other direction.

Seoyoon minimised the video again, then opened the window with the call logs.

"Morton then phones Kasey again on the next day, the sixteenth," she said.

Seoyoon moved the mouse pointer back to the audio files and clicked on one.

"Hello," came Kasey's voice from the speaker.

"You got it?" asked Morton, his voice harsh, clearing expecting to be fobbed off.

"Yeah, I've got it."

"All of it?" Morton asked, sounding surprised.

"Yeah, all of it. I can get you all of it today."

There was a slight pause. It was almost possible to feel how relieved Morton was.

"You better not be fucking me around."

"I'm not," Kasey said, urgently, *"I can get it to you."*

"Rightio. Outside the cinema at the Forum. Make it two o'clock."

"Okay," Kasey said, relief in her voice.

"Like I said, Kase, you better not be fucking me around."

"I'm not, Rich. I'm not. You'll get the money."

"'Cause you know what'll happen if you are."

"I'm not, Rich. I swear."

"Alright."

The call ended abruptly with a click.

"Drug Squad then waited for him at the cinema," Seoyoon said.

She moved the mouse pointer around and opened another window.

Another blurry image filled the screen, showing the carpark of a shopping centre. The entrance of the Hoyts cinema complex could be seen in the background, with people clustered around the entranceway.

Morton was standing by the entrance, hood up and dark glasses on again.

Seoyoon clicked with the mouse pointer and the footage began to move.

People walked in to the cinema or along the footpath.

After a moment, a silver-grey BMW sedan drove through the carpark and stopped outside the cinema.

Packer frowned.

For a moment nothing happened in the video.

Morton pushed himself away from the wall and walked over to the BMW. He stood there for a moment, talking to the driver.

The driver handed something to him and he pushed it into the pocket of his hoodie.

The car drove off and Morton stood there on the footpath for a moment watching, before walking away again.

Seoyoon paused the video.

"Did Drug Squad get an ID on the car," Packer asked.

"Um, I don't think so," Seoyoon said.

She opened the window with the surveillance log and began scrolling through it, reading the notes made by the Drug Squad officers who had filmed the transaction taking place.

"What is it, boss?" Simmons asked.

Packer ignored it, waiting for Seoyoon.

"No," she said, after a moment, "It was just the officers in the car filming the transaction and they prioritised following Morton instead of the other vehicle. They were too far away to get a licence plate."

"Why?" Simmons asked, "Does it matter?"

Packer nodded. "Yeah."

"Why?"

"Because that BMW was parked outside Kasey Stewart's house when Claire and I went to speak to her parents. It's Felicity Stewart's car."

Chapter 27

Packer and Perry drove south once again into Como.

They walked up the path and Perry rang the doorbell.

After a few minutes, Felicity Stewart came to the door. She looked exhausted, her eyes puffy with dark bags beneath them.

"Sorry to disturb you again, Mrs Stewart," Perry said, "but we need to ask some questions."

"Again?" Felicity said, weariness in her voice, "Alright. Well, I suppose you'd better come in then."

She walked back into the house, leaving them to follow behind her.

The television was on in the lounge room, with a children's program playing. A sheet had been spread on the floor, and Jessie was sitting on it. She was holding a large, stuffed rabbit that was almost as large as she was, and sucking on one of her thumbs. The pink backpack sat beside her.

Jessie did not acknowledge them or even look up. She remained staring at the television screen.

Felicity sat on one of the couches. Packer and Perry sat on another.

"We weren't sure if you'd be here," Perry said, "We thought you might be at the hospital."

"There's nothing there to occupy Jessie," Felicity replied, dully, "They told me they'd call if anything changed. Both of us sitting around there isn't going to make any difference."

"I suppose not."

"What is it you wanted to ask me?"

"Aside from the night cleaning, did Kasey have any other source of income?"

"She got a pension of some sort. A sole parenting allowance or whatever it's called."

"Is that all?"

"As far as I know."

"Did you and Mr Stewart help Kasey out at all with money?"

"We're paying the solicitor's fees for the Family Court."

"What about giving her money for other things?"

Felicity shook her head.

"Is there a reason for that?" Perry asked.

"You think we're mean-spirited, do you?"

"It just seems unusual," Perry said, "I mean, you and Mr Stewart seem quite well off and she was your only daughter."

Felicity let out a sigh. "Bill and I could never agree on this. If it was up to him, he would have paid for everything. He hated her working as a cleaner and living in that horrible house. He wanted to buy her a house somewhere nicer."

"You didn't agree with that?"

Felicity shook her head. "Kasey was twenty-six. A grown woman with a child of her own. We looked after when she was a child - not that she ever appreciated it, cutting us out of her life like that. We couldn't do it forever. She needed to stand on her own feet. I helped with baby-sitting Jessica and we paid for the solicitor. But there needed to be a line somewhere."

"You've never given her money for anything else?"

"There was a new television we paid for when the last one broke. Of course, it had to be the most expensive thing Bill could find. He loves grand gestures. Nothing less than the best for Kasey."

"Anything else."

"Nothing really."

"Large cash payments?"

"I don't think so."

Perry looked at her for a moment. "Mrs Stewart, we have reason to believe that you may have recently paid a sum of $3,000 on Kasey's behalf. Is that correct?"

Felicity's face remained unchanged, but she looked away.

She shook her head slightly in anger, before looking back at Perry again.

"You know about that, do you?" she asked.

"Is it true?"

"Yes, it's true."

"Can you tell us what the money was for?"

"Drugs," Felicity hissed in disgust, almost spitting the words out.

"You knew that Kasey was using drugs?"

"Yes, I knew."

"How did you find out?"

Felicity tutted. She looked away for a long moment, before replying.

"Kasey was so upset when her husband left her, although goodness knows why. She was well rid of the horrible man. But then he reported her to Child Protection to try to get Jessica away from Kasey, and they sent people around to the house to speak to Kasey. I was there when they arrived and told her they were looking for drugs.

"Kasey denied it all, told them it was Deon inventing things to hurt her. But I knew when she was lying. I saw it more than enough times when she was a child. It all came out after that. She was allowed to keep Jessica, but only on certain conditions and one of them was that she go to drug counselling sessions. She needed someone to look after Jessica while she was there, so she had to tell me about that."

"Did Mr Stewart know about the drugs?"

"No. He wasn't there when the Child Protection people first arrived and Kasey begged me to keep it a secret from him. He would have been so upset if he'd known about it."

"How did the payment for the drugs come about?" Perry asked.

"Kasey asked for it," Felicity said, "As simple as that. The counselling sessions and the testing didn't make any difference. She couldn't stop using drugs, and had run up a huge debt. She was being threatened. She told me if it wasn't paid, she and Jessie would be hurt. What else could I do?"

"How did you actually pay the money?"

"Kasey arranged it and told me what to do," Felicity said, "I had to drive to the shopping centre and stop near the cinema. I was told a man would be waiting for me, and he was. He walked over to the car. I gave him the money and left. That was it."

"Three thousand dollars is a lot of money," Perry said, "Didn't Mr Stewart notice?"

Felicity shook her head. "There's an equity account attached to the house in case we ever have an emergency. I took the money from there. We never used it."

"Was that your only involvement with the drugs?" Packer asked.

"Yes," Felicity said, firmly, "and I told Kasey that. I was never doing this again. She needed to sort her life out, for Jessie's sake, if not her own."

"And did she?" he asked.

Felicity sighed.

She shrugged her shoulders and shook her head.

"I don't know. I doubt it, to be frank. I didn't see any change in her, anyway."

"Why do you think she started using drugs?" Packer asked.

"Why do you think?" Felicity snapped, "That dreadful man. I mean, look at him. Tattoos all up his arms and a shaved head. He must have got her started on it."

"Alicia Martin seemed to think he left Kasey because of her drug habit."

"Maybe that's true," Felicity said, "Kasey was spending thousands on drugs. Perhaps she was costing him too much. I don't know. You've seen what kind of man he is."

"Do you have any idea why your husband went around to Mr DeSouza's workshop yesterday?" Perry asked.

"He was angry."

"Angry about what?"

"That man wanted to take Jessica. Bill was furious about it."

"How did that come about?" Perry asked.

"He phoned here during the day," Felicity said, "The nerve of the man ringing us directly. He knows he's not supposed to do that. All contact has to be through the solicitors."

"The situation has changed a bit, though," Perry said, gently, "and he told us that when he asked you, you agreed to let him have Jessie. Is that not true?"

Felicity gave her a glance of annoyance. "I did say that he might be able to take her, yes," she said, "but I wasn't happy about it."

"You wanted to keep Jessie?"

"It wasn't that so much. It was a question of doing things properly. He should have had the solicitors make the arrangement, so that we didn't have to deal with him directly. He knew that."

"In any event, you did agree that he could come to collect Jessie?"

"I said I thought it would be okay, but I wanted to speak to Bill first."

"And you did that?"

Felicity gave a small sigh. "I should have known exactly how Bill would react. He's devoted to that child. Like he was with Kasey. I knew he'd be reluctant to let her go to her father, but we can't be expected to look after her forever."

"Mr Stewart wasn't happy about Deon taking him?"

"He was furious. Started shouting and carrying on. He took the phone and started arguing about it. Then that man hung up on him. No respect at all for Bill or myself. No courtesy at all."

"What happened after the phone call?"

"I tried to calm Bill down. Tried to make him see that it might be best if Jessie went to her father, but he wouldn't have it. He wanted to ring Child Services and the solicitor to report it, in case he tried to take Jessie again. He wanted to ring you people to get him arrested."

"For wanting to collect Jessie?" Perry asked, frowning slightly.

Felicity looked at her. "No, it wasn't that."

"What then?"

Felicity let out a low sigh, but said nothing.

Perry and Packer said nothing, but waited.

Eventually, Felicity continued.

"Bill was convinced that Kasey was going to win her court case and get custody of Jessie. He believed that Jessie's father had realised that, too, and wanted Kasey out of the way so that he would get Jessie to himself, and killed Kasey to stop it happening.

"And after he phoned here this morning asking to take Jessie away, it just seemed to confirm this in Bill's mind. I had no idea he was going to do anything so stupid, though. No idea at all."

Felicity shook her head.

"Anyway, I suppose at least one good thing's come of all this."

"What's that?" Perry asked.

"Well, at least you've got the proof you need now, haven't you?"

Felicity looked at her expectantly.

"Sorry," Perry said, "I'm not sure I follow you."

Felicity frowned. "You can see what sort of man he is. He showed his true colours yesterday. He tried to kill Bill, and that proves he killed Kasey, too. What more do you need? Surely, you'll charge him with her murder now."

"We're still making enquiries," Perry said, gently, "but at this stage, we don't have any proof that Deon DeSouza killed Kasey."

"What?" Felicity said, her frown deepening, "but of course he did. He attacked Bill, just like he attacked Kasey. You must see that."

"I'm sorry, I can't discuss the investigation with you," Perry said, "but we don't have grounds to charge Mr DeSouza at this stage."

Felicity looked at her for a long moment, staring.

Then she shook her head in defeat.

"Very well, then," she said, "but it's ridiculous that you people haven't joined the dots yourself. There's a violent thug going around attacking members of this family and you don't seem to be able to put two and two together."

"Thank you for your help, Mrs Stewart," Perry said, standing up, "We'll be in touch if we need anything else."

"I'm not sure what else you could possibly need," Felicity muttered, "A signed confession from him?"

She got up and showed them to the door.

They walked down the path and back to the car.

"I suppose that explains why Felicity's car is in the surveillance footage," Perry said.

Packer nodded, but said nothing.

She looked at him. "You're not convinced?"

"Something odd about it."

"In what way?"

"I don't know," Packer said, "It just seems out of character. Bill's devoted to Kasey. It's him buying her a new TV and wanting to buy her a house, him wanting to sort out her life. I can see him paying off drug dealers. Felicity wants Kasey to 'stand on her own two feet' and sort her life out on her own. Helping her out seems odd."

"She obviously wasn't happy about doing it," Perry pointed out, "and she didn't have much choice. She knew Kasey and Jessie had been threatened."

Packer nodded.

He started the engine.

"It seems odd, though, that she didn't try to stop Bill yesterday or phone us," Perry said, as they drove, "She knew where he was going and she knew Bill was upset. She must have known it wasn't going to end well."

"Yeah," Packer said, "She must."

Chapter 28

It was so momentary that Simmons almost missed it. There was brief flash on the screen, making him pause, and he felt a slight twinge of excitement.

He had been watching the CCTV footage at double-speed, convinced the exercise was pointless and trying to get through it faster. Moving the mouse across his desk, he slowed the footage to normal speed, then moved the bar back a minute to watch the footage again.

It was there.

"Look at this," he said, raising his voice, "I think I've found her."

Seoyoon slid her chair across the floor towards his desk. Perry and Thompson walked across to stand behind him, and Packer emerged from his office.

They were looking at a view of the front of the Towers apartment buildings and the Ritz-Carlton Hotel beside them. In the foreground was a road and a row of bollards. It was dark, the heavy clouds blocking out the moonlight and the only lighting coming from a streetlight at either end of the footage.

"Where is this from?" Perry asked.

"There's a camera behind the bus stop near the river," Simmons said, "It's pointing back towards the Bell Tower, which is here."

He touched the left side of the screen.

"Okay. Watch here," he said, touching the right-hand edge of the screen with his finger.

Simmons moved the footage back a minute and slowed it to half-speed, then clicked on play again.

On the right of the screen, they could see a row of wide pillars beside the road. On the other side of them was the entrance to the Ritz-Carlton and a narrow strip of bitumen used for cars to pull up directly outside the entranceway. The pillars obscured the view, but there was a dim corridor of light beyond them cast by the lighting in the hotel's lobby.

"Here," Simmons said, touching the screen.

As they watched, they could see a tiny figure move behind the first and second of the pillars. The lights were behind her, reducing the figure to little more than a dark shadow. It disappeared behind the second pillar, then emerged into the open again.

The figure was closer to the lights now, so more visible.

Simmons paused the image.

It was difficult to make out, but the figure was wearing a tiny dress and very high heels.

"It's her," Thompson said.

"Yep," Simmons said.

He clicked play again. In slow motion, Kasey walked between the pillars and up the front steps of the hotel to the entrance.

The twin glass doors slid open and she disappeared inside the hotel.

"She was going to the Ritz-Carlton," Thompson said, "That's why she was down that way."

Perry looked down at the time code at the bottom of the screen.

"10:17pm," she said, "She left home at 9:00."

"And she was found at 3:45am," said Packer, "Six and half hours later."

"So, what was she doing in the hotel for six and a half hours?" Simmons asked.

"What do you think she was doing, lad?" Thompson asked, "Dressed like that."

"Prostitutes don't take that long.

Thompson raised an eyebrow. "Oh? Got some first-hand experience, have you?"

"No, he's right," Seoyoon said, "She was in there for six hours and forty-five minutes. If she is charging, that's a very expensive night for the client."

Thompson considered this for a moment. "More than one client maybe?" he suggested, "Maybe she arranged to meet a few."

"Plus a night at the Ritz-Carlton isn't cheap," Seoyoon said, "What kind of clients did she have?"

"It's not unheard of," Thompson insisted.

"It's not really the sort of place, though, is it?" Perry added, "Cheap hotels don't ask any questions. The Ritz-Carlton is a bit more upmarket than that."

"Alright, fine," Thompson said, "So if she wasn't there for a home call, what was she there for?"

"We thought she was meeting someone," Perry said, "Maybe she was meeting them at the Ritz-Carlton."

"Someone with plenty of money," Simmons said.

"Play the footage again, Mickey," Packer said, impatiently, interrupting the chatter.

Simmons used the mouse to move the CCTV footage back a minute, then pressed play again.

In silence, they all watched the hazy video of the front of the hotel while Kasey Stewart walked into view, moved along the roadway behind the pillars and up the steps into the lobby.

"Go back a bit," Packer said, "and slow it down again."

Simmons replayed the same footage at half speed.

"Stop there," Packer said, as Kasey walked out from behind one of the pillars, "Go back just a little bit. Pause as soon as she comes out."

It took Simmons a few goes to find the right place in the footage.

"The necklace?" Perry asked.

Packer nodded. "I think so."

"There's something shining, alright," Thompson agreed.

It was difficult to make out in the hazy footage, but for a few frames as Kasey emerged into the gap between the pillars, a shape could be made out on her chest and it flashed slightly as it caught the light.

"There's no one else around," Thompson said, "She arrived on her own. So, if she's meeting someone, they arrived later."

"Or they were already there," Simmons said.

"Aye, that could be right. Does the footage show anyone else arriving earlier or later?"

"Well, I haven't been through it all," Simmons said, "but there's heaps of people arriving before she does. Doesn't really help us, though, does it? We don't know who they are or if they were there to meet Kasey."

"No," Thompson conceded, "It doesn't."

"What about when she leaves?" Perry said, "Is that in the footage?"

"I haven't found it," Simmons said, "but I suppose it must be."

"Her death was reported at 3:45am, so find that."

They all watched while Simmons scrolled the footage forward. The front of the hotel looked the same, but the quality was noticeably poorer. The heavy downpour of rain created a thick fog between the CCTV camera and the front of the building, reducing the image to a blurry sludge.

"You can hardly see anything," Thompson mumbled.

"It's the rain," Simmons said.

He clicked play on the footage and they all watched.

At this time in the early hours, there was little movement on the road or outside the hotel. They watched the footage for long minutes, but could see no movement at all.

"That's too far," Perry said, looking at the time code on the screen, "It's after 4:00am now. Uniform would have arrived."

"Alright, I'll go back then," Simmons said.

Using the mouse, he moved the footage to 3:05am and clicked play again.

They watched in silence, looking for any sign of movement at the front of the hotel. Long minutes went by.

Just as it appeared hopeless, there was a shift on the screen. The light between two of the pillars was blocked by a dark shape.

"There," Thompson said.

"Yep," Simmons said, already rewinding the footage slightly.

He reduced the speed to half and clicked play again.

It was difficult to make out now with the haze of rainfall obscuring the vision, but a figure could be seen moving down the steps at the front of the hotel. With the light behind, the figure was little more than a shadow, but as the glass doors first opened and the figure emerged from the lobby, the light was stronger. Naked arms and legs and the small dress could be made out. The dark shape on her chest of the necklace was visible.

So was the second figure walking behind her.

"There is someone else there," Perry said, "Behind her."

"A man?" Seoyoon said.

"Looks like it," Perry agreed.

"Can you get it clearer?" Thompson asked.

Simmons spent a long time moving the footage back and forward, slowing it down as much as he could, and rapidly alternating between 'play' and 'pause' to move the image forward fractionally. After ten painful minutes of playing with the footage, he finally managed to get an image of the second figure in the hotel doorway.

"Well, it's definitely a man," Perry said, "but that's all you can tell."

From the height and build, the figure paused in the doorway appeared male. But it was impossible to make out much more detail in the grey haze created by the camera's distance from the hotel and from the haze of rain in front of it.

"Play it forward," Packer said.

Simmons clicked on play and they watched. Kasey walked to the bottom of the steps and stopped at the bottom. She was beside one of the pillars, but just visible.

The man walked down the stairs and stood behind her.

For a long time, there was no movement at all. They simply stood there.

Then the man moved closer to Kasey.

"Is he kissing her?" Seoyoon asked.

"Maybe," Perry said.

They watched as the man moved forward slightly and stood there again.

After a moment, he moved quickly behind the pillar, then hurried through the gap beside it and disappeared off the edge of the screen.

A few moments later, Kasey did the same.

"3:22am," Simmons said, reading out the time code, "Say two minutes to get from the hotel to where she was killed, so she must have been lying on the road for about half an hour before the drunk bloke reported it."

"What was he waiting for?" Seoyoon asked, "Why not just call '000' straightaway?"

"If he actually saw her being run down," Thompson said, darkly, "instead of just finding the body half an hour later. Frankly, I don't believe much of what that bastard told us."

"Well, we know now that she was definitely meeting someone at the hotel," Simmons said, "It wasn't a house call."

"No, we don't know that," Thompson said, "The bloke with her might have been a client."

"They looked very friendly," Seoyoon said, "He kissed her goodbye. Would a client do that?"

"Depends on the client," Thompson said, "The kind who's prepared to pay for a night at the Ritz-Carlton might."

"Either way, it rules him out as the killer," Perry said, "He'd hardly have kissed her, then run her down two minutes later. Wouldn't have had time to get to a car, either."

"So, if the killer's not the person she was meeting," Simmons said, "who is it? Can't be someone she knows. If they didn't arrange to meet Kasey there, what are the chances of them driving along and just seeing her there by chance?"

"It can't have been by chance," Perry said, "They must have known she was there at the hotel."

"Maybe," said Packer, quietly, "or else they followed her there and waited for her to come out."

Chapter 29

"Is there better footage of this?" Thompson asked, "Did we get the CCTV from the Ritz-Carlton?"

"They don't have any," Simmons said.

"Really?"

"That was the manager told me," Simmons said, "She said they have a reputation for valuing their client's privacy."

"Seems odd."

"I thought so, too," Simmons said, "I wondered if they had it and just didn't want to give it to me, because of privacy issues or whatever."

"Even if they've got it," Perry said, "They're not actually obliged to hand it over if they don't want to. We'd have to get a warrant to force them to, and I don't think we'd get one on the strength of this."

"Okay," said Thompson, "So leaving that aside. We know Kasey was at the Ritz-Carlton overnight with a gentleman 'friend'. Someone ran her down minutes later. Presumably, they weren't happy about her seeing this 'friend'."

"Deon DeSouza?" Seoyoon suggested, "He didn't like Kasey using drugs around his daughter. If he found out she was working as a prostitute, he'd be angry about that, too. Killed her to get custody of Jessie, or at least thought that was what would happen."

"Aye" Thompson said, "I like DeSouza as a choice. Motive and opportunity. Penchant for beating people with golf clubs."

"Alicia Martin?" Simmons suggested, "Wanted Kasey out of the way so that she could pick things up with DeSouza again."

"Why kill her there at the hotel?" Thompson asked.

"Followed her, looking for an opportunity and that was the first one that came up."

"The hotel's just a coincidence then?"

Simmons shrugged. "Maybe it is."

Thompson looked at Packer, who was staring at the frozen image on the screen.

"What do you think, boss?" Thompson asked.

Packer was silent, staring at the screen.

"Can you pull up Kasey's phone records again?" Packer asked Seoyoon.

She nodded, and turned to the computer.

"What are you thinking?" Perry asked.

"When we asked Alicia Martin about the drugs, she said she knew Kasey was using. She was at Kasey's place on Saturday two weeks ago and kept checking her messages."

"Looking for a fix?" Thompson asked.

"That was what Alicia thought," Packer said,

He turned to Seoyoon. "Who'd she get in touch with on that day?"

Seoyoon pulled the records up on her screen and scrolled through them until she found the right day.

"There's a phone call to Alicia Martin just after nine o'clock," Seoyoon said, "and a couple of text messages between them half an hour later. A couple of texts between Kasey and Miriam Todd after that. Then a few texts between Alicia and Kasey in the afternoon. That's it."

"No one else?" Perry asked.

"No," Seoyoon confirmed, "That's it."

"Could she be wrong about the day?" Thompson asked.

"I don't think so," Perry said, "She remembered it because it was some special celebration dinner Bill Stewart had organised for his birthday."

Packer nodded, staring at the phone records on the screen in silence.

"What do we know about Miriam Todd?"

"She was a bit evasive, but she seemed alright to me," Simmons said, "You're not saying you think Kasey got drugs from her?"

"I can't see it, boss," Thompson agreed, "Didn't seem the type."

"See if she's got a record," Packer said to Seoyoon.

Seoyoon moved the mouse and clicked on the edge of her screen. She tapped away at the keyboard for a moment, entering the details.

"A couple of traffic offences, some drunk and disorderlies," she read on the screen, "but that's it. No drugs."

"Do you want us to go and talk to her again?" Thompson asked.

Packer looked at the screen a moment longer, trying to connect the dots. He shook his head. "I think I'll go this time. You come with me, Mickey."

***

Simmons and Packer headed out to Sunrise. Simmons knew the way, so drove.

He pulled up in the parking space at the end of the narrow row, and they walked along to the unit.

There were two women with babies sitting on the rug at the front. One of them looked like she was about fifteen, with acne across her face. The other looked a little older, but not by much.

Miriam Todd was sitting cross-legged on the floor with them, talking animatedly.

As Packer and Simmons walked in, the bell on the back of the door gave a slight tinkle and Miriam looked up.

Recognising Simmons, she told the two women she had to go and pushed herself up off the floor.

She walked quickly across to them.

"Hello, again," she said to Simmons, taking his arm, and drawing him across the room to her desk at the back.

"Hello," Simmons said, "This is my boss, Senior Sergeant Packer."

"Okay," Miriam said, "Just keep it down a bit, eh? Don't want to give anyone a fright."

She looked meaningfully back at the two women on the rug.

"Oh, right," Simmons said, "Sorry."

"It's okay," Miriam said, "But just keep it down a bit."

She reached out a hand to Packer. "Hi. I'm Miriam."

He nodded and shook her hand. Her skin felt moist and clammy in his hand.

They sat down around Miriam's desk.

"How can I help?" she asked.

"Just a few more questions about Kasey," Simmons said, "We've been talking to some of her friends, trying to follow up on a few things."

"Right."

"We think she might have come two weeks ago on Saturday. Do you remember?"

Miriam nodded. "Yeah, she was here."

"You're sure."

"Yeah, I remember it." She gave a slight sigh. "Her father had organised a dinner to celebrate his birthday. Kasey wasn't at all keen on going."

"Why's that?" Simmons asked.

Miriam looked at him for a long moment, before replying.

"Kasey had issues with her parents," she said, "You know that. She didn't get back in touch with them. They got in touch with her - well, her father did. Kasey didn't really want to rebuild the relationship with them. She would have been happy not to see them. But her father was really pushing her. Like, pretending they'd never been apart, wanting to see her all the time. Apparently, he kept saying this dinner was going to be something really special, to make up for all the birthdays they'd missed. That kind of thing. It was pretty full-on, and Kasey really didn't want to face it."

"She told you all this on the day?"

"We talked about it before then. Then on the day, she came here in the morning for a while and we talked about it some more."

"You managed to calm her down?" Packer asked.

Miriam looked at him. "We talked. I told her that if she didn't want to go, she could call them up and say she was sick. She said she couldn't. It wouldn't be fair to her father. And even if she did, they'd just insist on coming to her place, so she had to go. We discussed coping strategies."

"What sort of coping strategies?" Packer asked.

"Finding you own space," Miriam said, "Looking for anxiety cues. Emotional deflection strategies."

"Did you discuss any ways to deal with the issue other than coping strategies?"

Miriam frowned at him. "I don't understand you."

"You sure?"

"Is there something you're trying to ask me?" she said, her voice hardening.

"Did you know Kasey was using drugs?"

Miriam looked at him for a moment. "What makes you think she was?"

"We found them at her house," Packer said.

Miriam looked away. She watched the two women on the rugs, who were playing with the babies and laughing.

"Yes, I knew," Miriam said, quietly, "A lot of the girls who come in here are using. You get to recognise to the signs pretty quickly. I was surprised, though, to be honest. I knew she was stressed about it, but it still surprised me."

"Stressed about what?" Packer asked.

"The thing with her parents," Miriam said.

"I think you've lost me."

Miriam looked at me for a moment. "There was some history between Kasey and her parents. I couldn't disclose it to you even if I knew, but I don't know. It was something that I told Kasey would we could explore together, but we didn't get that far before... well, before she passed. There was an issue there, though. Resuming her relationship with them seemed to be triggering her. She started using drugs a few weeks after seeing them again, so I assume that was why. As I said, though, it surprised me. I didn't think she would."

"Any idea where she was getting the drugs?" Packer asked.

"Maybe. But I'm afraid I can't tell you that?"

"It's important."

"I won't betray a confidence, Sergeant," Miriam said, "Some people might call that old-fashioned."

"Some people might call it obstructing a murder investigation."

Miriam eyes widened slightly. She swallowed.

She looked at Packer for a long moment

"I don't know for sure," she said, "but I've got a pretty good idea."

Packer said nothing, but waited.

"I run this place on a volunteer basis," Miriam said, "and there's never enough money. There're always problems with this place. Air conditioning doesn't work, the plumbing has problems, whatever. One of the girls had a friend named Olly who was a bit of a handyman. He offered to do a bit of work, and I thought it was a good idea. Helps to have a man around who's friendly, too. Shows the girls and their kids that now all men are bad, right? He comes in a bit and helps out. He painted the walls, fixed up the room out the back.

"I found out after a while he uses meth, too. Some of the girls who come in here are users. I don't judge, and I try to help them stop. Olly was sharing, though, which wasn't helping."

"Dealing?" Packer asked.

"Not really dealing," Miriam said, "From what I heard from the girls, it was more of a mutual arrangement. If he had it, he'd share it, and if they had it, they'd share it with him in return. Anyway, as soon as I found out, I had a talk with him. Told him the drugs had to stay away from here."

"Why didn't you stop him coming in?" Simmons asked, "Tell him not to come back?"

"I don't judge people," Miriam said, "A lot of the girls who come here are in trouble and they need help. I don't ask questions and they know they can trust me. I don't like Olly using drugs, but it's his choice. So long as it stays out of here."

"Did you see this Olly giving drugs to Kasey?" Packer asked.

Miriam shook her head. "No. But I know they're friends. They see each other sometimes."

"Did Kasey tell you that?"

"I heard them talking about it. They arrange things sometimes when they're here."

"Was Olly here two weeks ago on the Saturday?"

She nodded. "Yeah, he was still painting. Kasey texted me in the morning to ask if he was coming in that day."

"Do you know Olly's last name?"

"Jameson. Oliver Jameson."

"Have you got a phone number?"

"An old one. He lost the phone, I think."

Miriam moved around to the back if the desk and pulled out the drawer. She took out a cardboard box and lifted out a mountain of paper. There were dozens of pieces of paper of various sizes and colours. She began to check through them, looking at each, then putting them back in the box.

"Here," she said, eventually, passing a scrap of paper across the desk. It was a receipt from Coles with the name, 'Olly J' and a phone number written on the back.

"Thanks for your help," Packer said.

"Is that it?" Miriam asked.

"For now."

"Okay. Listen, can you do me a favour? I'm happy to talk to you. I want to help you get the mongrel what did this to Kasey, you know? But it's not good to have cops turning up here. Can you phone up next time?"

Packer nodded.

"Thanks. Appreciate it."

Packer and Simmons left the unit and returned to the car.

"Ring Seoyoon," Packer said, "Get an address for Olly Jameson."

Chapter 30

Oliver Jameson lived a few suburbs away from Sunrise in Redcliffe.

Redcliffe was the suburb adjoining Perth's airport, with the freeway running through it and regular air traffic passing overhead. There were nice parts of Perth out this way, but where Jameson lived was not one of them.

They found his house down a side street lined with old weatherboard houses that had last looked presentable some time in the sixties. There was no front fence, but a concrete path led through the overgrown grass to the front door.

A battered Toyota ute was parked at the front with rust holes around the back wheels.

Simmons parked on the street at the front, and they began to walk to the house.

As they drew closer, a furious barking began. There was a screen door at the front of the house and it began to bulge outwards as a large brown pit bull began pushing against it.

"Ginge," yelled a voice from within, "Get down. Get down."

Before they got to the door, a man had appeared behind it. He was approaching sixty and wearing faded stubbie shorts and a black Harley Davidson T-shirt. His long, grey hair was pulled into a loose tail at the back and he was holding a cigarette in one hand.

He looked up as Packer and Simmons approached the house.

Holding the dog's collar with one hand, he pushed the screen door open. "It's alright," he said, "He's fine."

Simmons held up his police badge.

"Detectives Simmons and Packer," he said, "Are you Oliver Jameson?"

The man gave a slight sigh of frustration.

Then he nodded. "Yeah. That's right."

"We need to ask you a few questions. Can we come in?"

Jameson looked at him a moment longer. The dog pulled at his hand, trying to get free.

"Yeah," Jameson said, "No worries. Just give me a moment. I'll put him in the bedroom."

They waited while Jameson dragged the dog through the house and into a room. He shut the door behind him and the dog barked a few times before falling silent. Clearly, this was not a new routine when visitors arrived.

Jameson returned to the door.

"What did you say name your name was?" he asked.

"Detective Simmons," Simmons said, "and this is Detective Packer. Alright if we come in?"

"Yeah, no worries."

Jameson walked back into the kitchen. There was a lino-topped table with a few mismatched chairs around it and a couple of newspapers on the top. A full ashtray sat in the middle next to a packet of tobacco and papers, with an open can of beer beside it.

"Do you want a drink?" Jameson asked.

"No, that's fine," Simmons said.

Jameson sat down on one side of the table. Simmons sat on the other. Packer remained standing.

"We understand you do some volunteer work at Sunrise?" Simmons said, "The women's centre."

Jameson nodded. "I do a few odd jobs for the sheila there."

"Did you know Kasey Stewart? She goes in to the centre sometimes."

Jameson nodded again. "Yeah. I know Kasey."

"How long ago did you last see her?"

"Dunno. The weekend maybe."

"Last weekend?"

"Yeah. I think so. Could have been on the Friday."

"How would you describe your relationship with Kasey?"

"Oh, there's no relationship, mate. She's just a friend of mine."

"What does 'friend' mean?" Packer asked.

Jameson looked at him.

He shrugged. "We talk a bit. I go around for a beer sometimes. Do a few jobs around the house sometimes if she needs it."

"How long have you known her?"

"Not that long. Couple of months, I suppose. Something like that."

"How often do you see her for a beer?"

"Dunno. Most weeks."

"Anything other than a beer."

Jameson shrugged. "If I'm holding, I give her some."

"Holding what?"

"Speed."

Packer looked at him in silence.

"Well, fuck, mate," Jameson said, "Youse obviously know or you wouldn't be here, would youse? Kasey told you I give her some, did she?"

"What's the arrangement there?" Packer asked, "You just give meth to her, or get something in exchange?"

"I'm not a fuckin' dealer," Jameson said, "If I have it, I share it. If she has it, she shares with me. Look, sometimes you need it, but you don't have the money right? If someone helps you out when you need it, then you help them out down the track. Everybody wins."

"Do you charge each other?"

He shook his head. "It balances out."

"And that was the arrangement with Kasey?" Packer asked.

"Yeah," Jameson said, "If I shared some with her, she shared some with me next time. Gave me a blowie sometimes."

"That was very generous of her," Packer said.

"Oh, fuck you, mate," Jameson said, "Are youse cunts gonna bust me for sharing a couple of points with someone? Haven't you got nothing better to do? What's Kasey saying? She telling you I'm some big-time fucking dealer or something?"

"Kasey's not saying anything any more."

"What's that supposed to mean?"

"We're investigating her murder."

It took Jameson a moment to react. He looked at Packer, the annoyance disappearing from his face and the colour draining away.

He looked at Simmons, then back at Packer again.

"Murder," he said, "What? Like, she's dead?"

Packer nodded.

"Oh, fuck," Jameson said, "Fuck, mate. No."

He leaned back in the chair, staring across the room, his eyes unfocussed.

"That's fucked," he muttered after a while, his voice shaking, "What happened to her?"

"She got hit by a car."

"What, like a fuckin' drunk-driver or something?"

"We think it was deliberate."

"Oh, shit," Jameson said. He shook his head, and sighed. "Do you know who done it?"

Packer shook his head.

"Who the fuck'd want to hurt her?" Jameson said, still shaking his head, "What a fucked thing to do."

Packer gave him a moment to come to grips with the news of Kasey's death.

"How did you first meet, Kasey?" he asked.

Jameson looked up at him. "At the women's place. You know, fuckin'... Sunrise or whatever."

"How did that happen?"

"I was there doing some work for the big sheila that runs the place. Painting or whatever. Kasey comes in a bit with her kid. I just started talking to her one day."

"About what?"

"I dunno, mate. The weather or some shit. Whatever. She told me she was having some trouble with the doors at her place and I told her I could fix them. So, she gave me her address and I went around there one day.

"Anyway, while I was there, she got a phone call from her lawyer. Her ex is trying to take her kid away from her and there was some problem in court or whatever. So, she got upset and I tried to calm her down. She started talking to me about it, and I listened. That was it, I suppose. I went around to fix something else and we used to just talk."

"Just talk?"

"Yeah." Jameson looked at him. Realisation dawned. "Yeah. Alright. And I offered her some shit. Shared a bit with her after that sometimes. It helps you talk, you know. Helps you open up."

"How often did you talk to her?"

"Most weeks. Used to go around there a fair bit. We'd have a smoke and a talk."

"What did you talk about?"

"The shit with her ex, mostly. She had some family problems, too. Something to do with her parents and that."

"Did she tell you what problems?"

"Not really," Jameson said, "I didn't push her or nothing. And she didn't really say that much. I think she got raped when she was a kid."

Packer frowned. "Why do you think that?"

Jameson shrugged. "Dunno, really. Just something she kind of hinted at. She never come out and actually said it, but we were talking about her kid once and she said something about how she was watching the kid all the time. Like an eagle. 'Cause she never wanted her kid to go through what she gone through when she was a kid herself."

"She said she was raped?"

"Nah, she never actually said that, but what else could it be? I mean, from the way she was talking about protecting her kid."

Jameson shook his head. "Fuck, mate. I can't believe she's dead. That's fucked."

"You said there was something to do with her parents, too."

"Hey?" Jameson looked up at him. "Oh, yeah. She hadn't seen them in years. She moved away to Sydney to get away from them. There was some kind of problem between them. Then just recently they got back in touch again. Kasey didn't really want to see them, but her father was really pushing her. He used to stress Kasey out."

"Did she tell you what the problem between her and her parents was?"

"Nah, mate. It was the same thing again, like with her getting raped. She never really said nothing. I just kind of read between the lines, you know."

"What about the ex?"

Jameson looked at him and nodded. "Yeah. She fucking told me about that cunt, alright. He used to beat the shit out of her. He's a savage beast, that prick. I don't know how blokes beat up on women. Especially someone like Kasey, someone with such a gentle soul. Guess it makes them feel strong or whatever.

"But, yeah. She told me he used to kick the shit out of her. He was trying to take her kid away, too. Just to make her life even more miserable, I reckon."

"Was she still with the ex when you first started talking to her?"

"Don't think so. They'd only just split, though. She was still pretty upset about it."

"What was Kasey doing for money?" Packer asked.

Jameson shrugged. "She was on the pension, I think. Single mother or whatever."

"Did she ever mention a job?"

"Nah. Don't think so."

"She had enough to pay for the meth, though?"

"Yeah, it was never a problem," Jameson said, "She always had the money. Got it from her parents, I suppose."

"Did she tell you they gave her money?"

"Yeah, I think so. Can't remember exactly what she said, but they were paying for her lawyer, I think. Gave her money sometimes. They're fucking loaded, apparently."

Packer looked at him a moment longer.

"Okay," he said, "Thanks for your help."

"Is that it?" Jameson asked, looking up at him, a slight look of surprise on his face.

Packer nodded. "This time."

He and Simmons left the house. As the door closed, the dog began barking furiously in the other room.

"I feel a bit sorry for him," Simmons said, as they headed back towards the car, "Sounds like he was actually pretty good friends with her."

"I'm sure that's why she was blowing him."

"Yeah, alright. I mean, she was getting drugs off him, but he seemed pretty upset when he found out she was dead. He was almost in tears."

"Maybe it was her round," Packer said.

Chapter 31

"So, Kasey was getting drugs from this Olly guy?" Seoyoon asked, "Not from Morton?"

"Probably both," Simmons said, "Morton was her regular supplier until he got arrested. Olly Jameson was more like a drug-buddy who she used to trade with. It's not that unusual with addicts."

"Did he get her started?"

Simmons shrugged. "Maybe."

"I don't think so," Packer said, "The timing's wrong. Alicia Martin said DeSouza left after he found out Kasey was using drugs. Jameson said he started sharing with her after the split. She must have started before then."

"What about Miriam Todd?" asked Perry, "Is she involved?"

Packer shook his head. "She knew about it, though."

"She says she doesn't judge people," Simmons said, "What they do is their business so long as it doesn't cause problems for her place."

Perry snorted. "Right."

"What about Kasey getting raped?" Thompson asked, "Do you believe that?"

"No, Olly's imagining that," Simmons said, dismissively, "Kasey never told him that. He just guessed that."

"It makes some kind of sense, though," Perry said, "and it fits with what Alicia Martin said about when they were teenagers. She said Kasey became withdrawn and closed off. Rape victims do."

"But she would have reported it," Simmons said, "and it would show up in our records. Nobody else knew anything about it."

"Her parents would have told us," Seoyoon said.

"Not necessarily," Perry said, "If it was ten or twelve years ago, they wouldn't see why it was relevant now."

"I don't either, to be frank," said Thompson, "Even if she was raped, what's it got to do with her being murdered? It's ancient history now, surely."

"Not if she was using meth to deal with it," Perry said.

"*If* that's why she was using," Simmons pointed out, "and she only started doing that six months ago."

"Rape victims don't get over it straightaway," Perry said, "Some of them never do."

"Alright," Simmons said, "but she had other stuff going on that was stressing her. The divorce and the custody battle, for instance."

"That started after the drugs, though," Seoyoon pointed out, "According to Alicia Martin, the drugs were the cause of that."

"Aye, well, Alicia Martin wasn't exactly straight with us about everything, was she?" Thompson pointed out, "The first-"

His voice trailed off as the door of the incident room opened.

Inspector Base walked in, his face grim.

"A word, Tony," he said, striding past them and into Packer's office.

Packer watched him go for a moment, before following behind.

"I think the inspector's good mood may have come to an end," Simmons said quietly.

Packer walked around his desk and sat down on the other side, facing Base.

"What the bloody hell's going on?" Base hissed.

"We're following some leads," Packer said.

"Following some leads?" Base spat, "I'm told there's been another attack. The woman's husband is in custody for attacking her father."

"Ex-husband," Packer said, "and the father attacked him. Bit off more than he could chew, though."

"Why wasn't I kept informed about this?"

"There's not much to tell you at the moment. The ex-husband's in custody. The father's in hospital."

"Did the ex-husband kill the woman?"

"I don't know yet," Packer said.

"The attack on the father must be connected."

"Yeah," Packer agreed, "I'm not sure how, though."

"What does that mean?"

"There are other things involved," Packer said.

He briefly outlined what they learned since he had last spoken to Base.

Base listened in silence, his anger slowly dropping back below boiling point.

When Packer finished, Base sat there for a moment.

"Never bloody simple with you, is it, Tony?" Base asked, "Are we any closer to an arrest?"

Packer shrugged. "There are pieces that still don't fit."

"Well, find out how they fit. Or make them fit. I don't want to hear about another attack while you're still thinking things through."

Packer nodded, but said nothing.

"We've had enough cock-ups recently, Tony," Base said, "I don't want any more. Clear?"

Packer nodded again.

"Right. Get on with it then," Base said, standing up and collecting his cap, "and keep me posted this time."

Without waiting for an answer, Base turned and left.

He walked back across the incident room and closed the door behind him.

"Enough cock-ups recently?" Thompson said, incensed, "Has he forgotten who was making those cock-ups?"

"Maybe you should have reminded him," Perry said, "Still not too late. You can catch him before he gets to the lift."

"Aye, well, maybe next time," Thompson said, "The inspector didn't seem to be in great spirits right now."

"I think an announcement's about to be made about Superintendent Canning's replacement," Seoyoon said.

"Not Inspector Base?" Thompson asked, eyebrows raised in mock surprise.

"Not Inspector Base," Seoyoon confirmed.

Packer ignored them.

Chandra had e-mailed her preliminary report to him the day before. It was brief and told him little more than she had outlined at the hospital. He opened it on his computer and began reading over it once more.

Something was still missing.

He closed the report and returned to the forensic photos from the scene yet again.

There was a knock at his door.

He looked up to find Seoyoon standing there.

"I've been checking with the jewellers," she said, "I think you should see this."

Packer stood up.

He followed Seoyoon back to her desk. The others were already gathered around. Clearly, she had already told them she had made a discovery before fetching Packer.

Seoyoon sat down and moved the mouse forward.

"Once we knew about the serial number inside the necklace case, I started phoning all the jewellers in the area. Greentree and Stone have an office in the city. It's pretty exclusive.

"They checked the serial number and confirmed its one of theirs. They keep photos and details of the weights and things, in case they're ever needed for claims on the insurance or something later on."

Seoyoon moved the mouse and clicked it.

A window opened on the screen showing a photograph. A black velvet cloth was laid out flat on a tabletop. Sitting on top of it was a gold necklace. Fine chain links at the back grew wider as they got closer to the front, and thin metal panels hung down in a wide arc, alternating between pale gold and blue plating. The centre of the necklace held a large blue stone, surrounded by a stylised image of a bird.

"It's Egyptian-inspired," Seoyoon said, "Handmade. There's only one."

"That's the one in the CCTV," Simmons said, "There was something shining when she was out the front of the hotel. It's that big jewel in the middle there."

"It's beautiful," Perry said.

"Expensive, too," Seoyoon added, "They charged $42,000 to make it."

"What?" Thompson said, sputtering, "Forty grand for a bloody necklace?"

"Yes," Seoyoon confirmed.

"Who the hell pays forty thousand dollars for a necklace?" Simmons asked.

Seoyoon closed the image. She moved the mouse pointer over the e-mail and scrolled down further.

"Bill Stewart did," she said.

They all looked at the details on the screen.

"Yeah, I suppose that makes sense," Simmons said, disappointedly, "I mean where else would she have got it from, right? A rich dad buying her expensive gifts."

"But he didn't say that when Claire and the boss asked him," Seoyoon pointed out.

"No," Perry said, "He didn't. In fact, he said he didn't know anything about a necklace at all. Told us he didn't recognise the case."

Simmons frowned. "So, what does that mean? I don't get it. He didn't want us to know that he bought her a $40,000 necklace?"

"He didn't want Felicity to know," Packer said, "She was sitting there at the time."

"Why wouldn't he want her to know?" Simmons said, "I mean it doesn't really matter any more, once Kasey's dead, does it?"

"It does," Packer said, "because Kasey put the necklace on to go to the hotel."

"So?" Simmons said.

Packer looked at him.

"Kasey put the necklace on because she was meeting Bill Stewart," he said, "She spent the night in the hotel having sex with her father."

Chapter 32

She felt his hands on her body, his mouth against hers.

He leaned back, smiling at her. She looked at his face, in the dim lights from the hotel.

He looked so old now, his hair thinning and his face hanging at the sides. He had developed a slight stoop now, his back hunching over.

He had been so handsome when she was a child, like the prince from all the stories he had read to her at bedtime. When he began to touch her and tell her it was what all girls did, it had seemed so exciting. He was sharing something special with her, something that was just for her.

Part of her still enjoyed his touch. It was comforting to know that he wanted her, even after all these years and all the hurt she had caused him. He desired her so much he still bought her expensive gifts, and brought her here to a luxury hotel to be with her.

Another part of her understood how wrong this was.

He was her father.

She was nauseated, sickened by his touch. In the hotel room, she needed to use the lubricant before they started. She could feel no arousal for him, no matter how hard she tried.

He smiled at her, his mouth moving as he said words she could not understand.

She smiled back, wanting to please him.

She wanted this over, wanted him to go.

Finally, he turned, hurrying into the rain and quickly disappearing in the haze.

She looked out through the gloom.

She felt a vague feeling of unease, something she could not identify.

Her eyes searched the night, seeking danger, but finding nothing.

She touched the necklace with her fingers. The gold felt cold against her skin, alien, invasive.

The rain fell harder.

With no choice, she clutched her handbag against her side with her hand and stepped out from under the overhanging roof.

The shock was immediate as the rain beat down against her body. Ice needling her naked skin, wind hammering against her, threatening to knock her down.

The rain stung her eyes and she squinted, her head down as she ran.

Behind her, an engine hummed into life, its headlights moving slowly through the gloom.

Her ankle turned as she ran, the heel sliding sharply on the ground.

Pain shot through her ankles as she struggled to remain on her feet. The ground was slippery, the water cascading along the footpath dangerous beneath her.

She stumbled forward, feeling her feet sliding away beneath her again.

With an effort, she managed to right herself and pushed forward into the gale.

It was so cold, the rain buffeting against her, trying to tear the skin from her arms.

She hurried on, forcing herself forward.

A corner loomed ahead of her and she felt a slight surge of relief.

It was one step closer, a tiny step, but closer nonetheless.

She turned the corner.

It was like walking into a tornado.

The wind smashed her back, and she stumbled, taking a step backwards.

She whimpered at the cold.

Forcing herself on, she staggered forward.

One foot in front. Now the other. Don't stop. Keep moving.

Without even realising it, she staggered under the overhanging lip of the building.

The wind still hammered against her, trying to knock her over, but it was weaker here. The building offered little protection, but it was something.

She staggered on.

Closer now.

The lights flared up behind her, lighting up the ground in front of her. Her shadow stood out starkly against the ground, growing longer as the lights rushed towards her.

The sound of the engine cut through the storm, screaming at her.

She was knocked forward, her legs folding beneath her.

Agony flared up her body as the bones shattered, stabbing through her skin, and her back folded around the car.
She screamed.
Packer jumped slightly, his eyes snapping open.
The room was in darkness, lit only by the dull haze of the moon outside and the reflected glow of the street below, glistening against the glass of the bedroom window.
Chandra lay beside him, her face against the pillow and her brown eyes focused on his.
She watched him, as he breathed hard, needing a moment to reorientate himself.
"Are you okay?" she asked, gently.
"Yeah," he said, "Sorry."
He rubbed a hand across his face, and found it was bathed in sweat.
Chandra put one hand on his chest, her skin soft against his, and leaned over. She pushed her lips against his, kissing him softly, her breath warm in his mouth.
She lay back, watching him.
"A nightmare?" she asked.
"Kind of," he said, looking away.
"It's not the first time," she said, "How often does this happen?"
He shrugged. "Sometimes."
"A lot?"
"Maybe."
She rubbed her hand slowly across his chest, her fingertips running gently over the hard muscle beneath the skin.
"What is it you see when you close your eyes, Tony?"
He shook his head slightly. "I don't know."
Chandra breathed in and out slowly.
"Talk to me about this, Tony," she said, "Help me to understand what is happening with you."
For a long moment, he lay on his back looking upwards. The ceiling was bathed in shadow, the fan turning slowly in the darkness. He watched its slow rotations through the night.
"I... see things," he said, eventually.

"What things?"

"The dead."

"People you know?"

"The people whose deaths I'm investigating."

"Like a psychic?"

Packer snorted, frowning. "No. Not like a psychic."

He let out a slow breath and turned on the pillow to face her. "I can't sleep. I go days without sleeping. It's worse when I'm working on a job. When I do close my eyes, sometimes I see it happen. The murder."

She watched him silently, her face completely emotionless.

"Look, I know how this sounds," he said, "but I'm not crazy. The best explanation I can come up with is that my subconscious is somehow filtering all the information. I absorb it all, and then my brain shifts it around somehow. Helps me see the things I can't see when I try to think it through consciously."

"Does it work? I mean, do you see how these murders actually happened?"

"Not exactly. But it... I don't know. It makes things clearer. Steers me in the right direction. Helps me to focus on what's important."

He looked at her, watching her face in the dark, as she looked back at him.

He had never spoken to anyone about this before and didn't know why he was telling her this. He had never even tried to articulate it to himself, and saying it out loud now made it seem nonsensical.

"Does that make me sound crazy?" he asked quietly.

She stared at him for a long moment.

She blinked slowly, long eyelashes closing over her dark eyes, as she watched him.

"Yes, Tony," she said, gently, "I'm afraid it does. I think you're suffering delusions. I'm going to have you checked in to the mental health ward at the hospital as an involuntary patient."

Chandra looked back at him in the darkness, her eyes full of sympathy.

Packer breathed harder, feeling the tension rising up through his stomach.

Then the corners of her mouth twitched slightly. Despite her efforts to keep her face straight, she grinned, white teeth appearing between her full lips.

"Oh, you bitch," Packer said, feeling the smile spreading over his own face.

He tried to sit up, but she put her hands on his chest and pushed him down, squealing.

He grabbed her wrists and pulled them away, shoving her onto the bed beside him as he sat up.

Before he could get any further, she tugged his shoulders back.

"I'm sorry," she said, giggling loudly, "Oh, Tony."

She swung one long, thin leg over his lap, straddling him. Pushing against his shoulders, she shoved him onto his back and sat on top of him. He gripped her narrow waist, trying to lift her off, but she hooked her ankles behind his knees and pulled her legs tight around his sides to stop him.

Still laughing, she gripped his head in her hands and pulled his face against hers as she leaned down to kiss him.

He tried to turn his head, but her tongue slipped between his lips, and he felt his resistance rapidly disappearing.

He held her waist while they kissed, tasting her in his mouth. Her long, brown hair fell around his face, her breasts pushing against his chest.

After a moment, she began to move her hips slowly back and forth, rubbing against him.

He felt himself harden beneath her and pulled her closer.

Wednesday

Chapter 33

Packer watched Chandra sleeping. Her mouth was open slightly, glossy brown hair hanging down across her cheeks.

Moving carefully, he rolled to the side of the bed and sat up.

Chandra shifted slightly and let out a breath, but didn't wake up.

Packer collected his clothes from the floor and closed the bedroom door behind him.

It was still dark, but light filtered in from outside. There was enough for him to dress silently in the kitchen of the apartment.

He thought briefly about leaving a note, but left without doing so.

The police station was eight blocks from where he lived. He sprinted the whole distance, using the sudden exertion to force his heart to pump and fight off the numbing tiredness he felt.

He was sweating and panting hard when he arrived at the darkened building and let himself in.

He took the elevator up to his level and walked down to the bathroom at the end. He showered and shaved, then changed into fresh clothes from his locker.

It was just after 4:00am when he arrived in the incident room.

He switched on his computer, then walked out to the coffee machine and made coffee while the computer powered up.

An e-mail message was waiting for him. He read it and made a phone call.

All interviews with suspects were video-recorded for later use as evidence in court, and were also saved on the police computer network. Packer found the video recording of the interview with Deon DeSouza and began watching it as he drank the coffee.

He had been through the interview twice and was watching the CCTV footage of DeSouza's attack in slow motion when his phone chimed. Frowning, he paused the footage so he could check the message.

I know you're working so I'm making allowances.
This time.
You owe me breakfast when it's over, crazy man.

- Lonely N.

Packer pressed 'reply' and held the phone for a moment. When he could think of nothing to type, he pressed 'cancel' and returned to the CCTV footage.

Perry arrived just before seven o'clock.

She sat down opposite his desk, and looked at him.

"Couldn't sleep, huh?" she asked.

Packer shook his head without taking his eyes off the screen.

"Me neither," Perry said, "I only got about three or four hours. Which still looks like more than you got."

"DeSouza told us that he rang and spoke to Felicity about taking Jessie," Packer said, "She agreed, but then Bill got on the phone and started accusing him of being a thief."

"Did he?"

"Yeah. I didn't understand what it meant at the time. I think Bill was talking about the necklace."

"You think Deon killed Kasey and took the necklace?"

"I think Bill Stewart believed that."

"That's why Bill tried to attack Deon?"

Packer shrugged. "Partly. He tried to attack him because he thought DeSouza killed Kasey. The missing necklace, followed by the phone call asking to take Jessie made him think DeSouza killed her."

"Do you think DeSouza did kill Kasey?"

"Maybe."

"So, what now?" Perry asked.

"We talk to DeSouza again," Packer said, standing up, "I'll lead."

***

"The recording is on," Perry said, entering the interview room and closing the door behind her.

"The date is 15 December," Packer said, "The time is 7:47am. I'm Detective Senior Sergeant Tony Packer. With me is Detective Senior Constable Claire Perry. Can you state your full name?"

"Deon DeSouza."

"We spoke to you two days ago, Mr DeSouza, and informed you that you had certain rights. I'm going to remind you of those rights again."

Packer went through the standard caution once more.

"Last time we spoke, Mr DeSouza, you told us that you were with Alicia Martin last Saturday night."

"That's right," DeSouza said, nodding.

"Were you at her home?"

"Yeah."

"Where does she live?"

"An apartment in Maylands, near the Chinese restaurant up on the hill. I can't remember the address, but I know the building. I've been there heaps of times."

"What time did you get there?"

"Dunno. Nine thirty? Ten? The little fella was in bed asleep anyway."

"You mean her son?"

"Yep."

"Had you arranged to meet Alicia?"

DeSouza frowned. "How do you mean?"

"Did you contact her before going to her home or simply turn up at the door?"

"Oh, nah," DeSouza said, "I rang her first. We spoke for a bit and I said, 'How abouts I come over for a while?'"

"She agreed to that?"

DeSouza gave a slight scoff. "Not straight away. She said, 'no,' at first, but she always does that. Likes to think she's makin' me work for it, you know? But she always comes across in the end."

"And she did on Saturday evening?"

DeSouza grinned. "Yep."

"Which phone did you use to contact her?"

"What?"

"Which phone?"

"Me own phone."

"How many do you have?"

"Just one."

"You told us previously that you had sex with Alicia on Saturday night."

DeSouza nodded. "Had a couple of drinks in the loungeroom when I got there. Then I gave it to her on the lounge. She's a noisy root, Alicia, screams a lot, you know? She kept sayin' she wanted to go to the bedroom in case it woke the little fella up, but I told her we weren't movin' 'til I finished. Had to put me hand over her mouth.

"After that, we went into the bedroom. Gave it to her again in there. Fell asleep after that."

"You were at her home for some hours, then?"

"Yep," DeSouza said, "Stayed all night."

"What time did you leave?"

"Dunno. Probably seven? The little bloke was still in bed anyway."

"Did you have any contact with Alicia after you left?"

DeSouza grinned and gave a snort. "You could say that, yeah."

"What sort of contact?"

"She sent me some text messages."

"Saying what?"

"Nothin' worth repeating, mate, eh?"

"Abusive?"

DeSouza nodded. "Yep."

"Why would she do that?"

DeSouza snorted again. He shook his head.

"See, the thing with Alicia is, she gets a bit carried away, right? I started seein' her months ago after I split with Kasey, 'cause I just wanted a root. And Alicia's an easy root. You show her a bit of interest and her fuckin' panties hit the ground. So, I went around there a couple of times to give it to her. That was it. No strings, right?

"But then she starts givin' me this."

DeSouza held his hand in the air and flapped his fingers up and down, imitating a mouth speaking rapidly.

"She was talkin' about moving in together and all this shit. And I had to say to her, 'Whoa, girl, settle down'. It was just a bit of fun, right? I mean, I was still sorting shit out with Kasey. The last thing I was gonna do was fuckin' move in with Alicia. But she got all shitty about that, sayin' I was just using her for sex. It took her a couple of weeks to settle down after that. Then we went back to just the usual routine again."

"What happened last Saturday?"

DeSouza shook his head again. "On Saturday, when I first got there, she started sayin' she didn't want to be on her own any more. And I just kind of went, 'yeah, sure, of course you don't'. I mean, whatever. You say whatever they want to hear, right? Anything to get their legs open.

"Then in the morning, she started all the same shit again. So, I had to set her straight. I said to her, 'Look, we've been through this. I told you I need to sort out the shit with Kasey and get Jessie back. I'm not interested in any of that shit'. And that set her off again."

DeSouza raised his hand and flapped it in the air again. "'You're just using me'," he said, imitating Alicia Martin in a high-pitched squeak, "'You're just using me for sex. You don't care about me.' I couldn't get out of there fast enough, you know? I hadn't even left the street before she was texting me, sending me all these bullshit messages."

"And this was Sunday morning, was it?" Packer asked.

"Yeah."

"Three days ago?"

"Yeah."

"You're sure about that?"

"Yeah," DeSouza said, frowning, "Of course, I'm fuckin' sure."

"And she sent these messages to your phone?"

"Yeah. Where else?"

"The same phone you used to phone her on Saturday evening?"

"Yeah. Of course."

Packer nodded.

"We spoke to Alicia Martin," Packer said, "and she told us she had had a sexual relationship with you, but she broke it off two months ago after the Family Court mediation."

DeSouza looked across the room for a moment, thinking about that.

"Yeah," he said, "We did talk in the evening after the mediation. She said she didn't want to see me again. Felt bad for Kasey or some shit. I remember that."

He shrugged. "Didn't fuckin' last long, though. I texted her about a week later and it was business as usual. Went around that night and gave it to her again."

"Alicia says she had no contact with you after she told you it was over on the day of the mediation."

"Then she's full of shit," DeSouza said, "'Cause I've been round there four or five times since then."

"Including last Saturday night?"

"That's right."

"Three days ago?"

"Yeah. Look, why do you keep fuckin' askin' me this? We're just goin' around in circles."

"I'm just making sure we're clear, Mr DeSouza, so there's no confusion."

"Right. Well, we're fuckin' clear, right? I was with Alicia on Saturday."

Packer nodded.

"When you were arrested, Mr DeSouza, your pockets were searched and the contents were seized. You remember that?"

"Yeah. Of course I do."

"A mobile phone was found in your pocket and seized."

"Yep."

"Is that the same phone you used to contact Alicia Martin on Saturday evening?"

"Yeah. I've only got one."

"And the same phone she sent text messages to on Sunday morning?"

"Yeah."

Packer reached below the table. He retrieved a brown paper evidence bag, and placed it on the desk in front of them.

"This bag contains the items seized from you after your arrest, Mr DeSouza," Packer said, "It has been sealed with tamper-proof tape."

Packer read the barcode from the tamper-proof tape aloud for the video-recording, then tore it across and opened the bag.

He reached inside the bag and retrieved a silver mobile phone.

He placed it on the table in front of DeSouza.

"Can you unlock the phone, Mr DeSouza?"

"Alright," DeSouza said.

He reached forward and pressed his index finger against the button below the screen. The phone read his fingerprint, then the screen lit up.

"For the recording," said Packer aloud, "I am now checking the recent call history on Mr DeSouza's phone."

He thumbed through it.

"Outgoing call to 'Alicia M' at 8:17 pm on Saturday, 11 December," he said aloud, "A duration of nineteen minutes and eighteen seconds."

He moved his finger across the screen again.

"I am now checking the text messages. There is a message chain with 'Alicia M' on Sunday, 12 December. First message from 'Alicia M' to Mr Desouza at 6:53am, reading, 'Get fucked, arsehole.' A second message at 6:57am on the same date, reading, 'Next time you want a fuck go fuck yourself'. Seven more messages over the next half hour, all of similar content."

Packer locked the phone and returned it to the exhibits bag.

"See?" DeSouza said, "Told ya. Alicia's fuckin' nuts. And now youse know she's a liar, too."

Packer looked at his watch.

"Interview terminated at 8:18am."

He stood up and lifted up the brown paper exhibits bag.

"Is that it?" DeSouza asked.

"For now," Packer said.

"What's that supposed to fuckin' mean?"

"It means we'll be back to charge you before your forty-eight hours are up?"

"Charge me?" DeSouza said, incredulously, "You know I couldn't have killed Kasey."

"Not Kasey," Packer said, "I spoke to the hospital this morning. Bill Stewart died last night."

Chapter 34

Packer's tiredness had gone when they left the interview room.

It was close.

He could feel it.

There was something moving just out of his sight.

"You didn't tell me about Bill Stewart," Perry said, as they walked back along the corridor.

"They e-mailed me overnight. I rang them when I got in."

"Yeah, but you didn't tell me."

"I was thinking about DeSouza."

"This isn't good enough, boss," Perry said, frustrated, "We're supposed to be a team."

They reached the incident room and went inside.

Packer stood in front of the whiteboard.

"Deon DeSouza's alibi checks out," Perry told the others, "There are messages on his phone that confirm he was with Alicia Martin on Saturday night."

The others looked at her a moment.

"So, she was lying?" Simmons said.

Perry nodded. "And Bill Stewart died last night."

"Jesus," Thompson said, "So we're charging DeSouza with his murder?"

"Yeah," Perry said.

"Do you think DeSouza knew about Bill Stewart and Kasey?" Seoyoon asked.

"He didn't say anything about it," Perry said, "Why?"

"It might explain why he was so angry with Bill," Seoyoon said.

"Maybe," Perry said, "but he didn't anything sooner."

"There's no sound on the CCTV from the workshop," Simmons said, "We don't know what Bill said to Deon when he first arrived."

"No," Perry said.

She looked at Packer.

He was staring at the whiteboard in silence.

"Well, whatever happened with Bill Stewart," Thompson said, "DeSouza didn't kill Kasey. Shame. I liked him as a choice."

"You sure did," Simmons said, "You wanted to bet me a hundred bucks it was him."

"Just as well you didn't take me up on it, lad," Thompson said, "I'd be a hundred down right now."

"Yeah, and I'd be a hundred up," said Simmons, "I should have taken it."

"Aye, well," Thompson said, grinning, "Luck of the Irish, eh?"

"I still don't understand why Alicia Martin lied about Deon DeSouza, though," Seoyoon said, "Why tell you he wasn't at her place on Saturday night?"

"She was pissed off at him," Perry said, "Telling her what she wanted to hear to get her into bed, then telling her in the morning it was all lies. It wasn't the first time he'd done it, either. She wanted to get back at him through us."

"Yeah, but she knew this was a murder investigation," Seoyoon said.

"She was pretty angry," Perry said, "You should have read the messages she sent him."

"And it's not the only thing she lied about, is it?" Simmons said, "I mean, if she was lying to Kasey about sleeping with her husband, why wouldn't she lie to us, too?"

"I'm sure she would have come clean if we'd actually charged Deon with Kasey's murder," Perry said, "She wouldn't have let him go down for it. She just wanted to see him squirm for a while first."

"Even so," Seoyoon insisted, "What a nasty thing to do to him."

"Aye, well, as the line says," agreed Thompson, "Hell hath no fury."

Something twisted at the edge of Packer's thoughts.

He reached for it, but it squirmed away, avoiding his grasp.

It was there.

So close now.

"I don't get it," Simmons said, "What's that mean?"

"The full line's 'Hell hath no fury like a woman scorned,'" Thompson said.

"Is that Shakespeare again?" Perry asked.

"Aye, I think so," Thompson said, "Don't ask me which play, though, because I haven't the foggiest."

So close.

"I'm not sure it is Shakespeare, actually," Seoyoon said, "It's Blake or Tennyson or someone, isn't it?"

"Forget about who said it," said Simmons, "What does it mean?"

"It means nobody gets as pissed off as a girl who's been rejected," Perry said.

"You should be writing this down, lad," Thompson said to Simmons, "Make a note of it."

"Why?" Simmons asked.

"Because you never know what's going on behind those baby blue eyes," Thompson said, avoiding eye contact with Seoyoon, "or brown ones."

It was like a hammer blow, the realisation slamming into his stomach with an intensity that was almost physical.

"Oh, Christ," Packer hissed.

He took a step back from the whiteboard.

How had he missed it?

It was so obvious.

He breathed hard, the writing on the board blurring before his eyes.

"Boss?" said Thompson, "I said, 'are you okay, boss?'."

Packer stared dully at him.

"She knew," he said.

"What?"

"When Kasey was a child. She knew then."

"You're not making any sense, boss."

Packer looked at Perry. "Get Prior to find us some uniforms. Female officers."

"What for?" she asked, confused.

"To look after Jessie."

"Why?"

"It was Felicity Stewart," he said, "She killed Kasey."

***

Packer used the light on his mobile phone to examine the BMW's front.

It had been through a car wash, probably several times, which had left milky grey spots of soap residue across the paintwork and destroyed any forensic traces.

The grill had a crack across the bottom, though, and part of the fibreglass moulding below it had been broken off.

The tyres were shiny and black, the Bridgestone logo on the side walls standing out crisply against the rubber.

He straightened up, turning off the light on the phone and pushing it back into his pocket.

He stood by the side of the car to wait.

They hadn't put handcuffs on her, but one of the female officers was holding Felicity Stewart's arm. They walked down the steps together, Perry a couple of paces behind them.

Felicity looked oddly calm, no hint of emotion at all, as she was walked down the path towards the front gates.

As they drew closer, she realised Packer was standing there.

Her eyes focused on his.

She stopped beside him, staring silently at him, the faintest hint of a challenge in her eyes.

"You were her mother," he said, quietly.

"Yes."

"You should have stopped it."

"Stopped it?" Felicity asked, a frown appearing on her face.

"You should have protected her."

The frowned deepened.

She glared furiously at Packer, then shook her head in anger.

"Men," she spat, "You understand nothing. Nothing at all."

Packer felt the tension in his fists.

He looked at the female officer holding Felicity's arm and jerked his head towards the waiting police car.

"Come on," she said, hurrying Felicity along the path.

She looked back over her shoulder at Packer, then quickly back to the street.

Perry stopped beside Packer and watched them go.

"Are you okay, boss?" she asked.

"Wait in the car," Packer said, quietly, "I need a minute."
Perry walked down the path and out through the gate to the waiting car. She heard the loud crack as Packer smashed his fist into the fence.
Followed by another.
And another.

Chapter 35

Packer closed the door of the interview room behind him and walked across to the table.

Felicity Stewart was sitting on one side, her hands on her lap. She was looking calmly at Packer.

Perry sat opposite Felicity, a notebook open and a pen ready.

"It's recording," Packer said, as he sat down.

"The date is 15 December," Perry said, "and the time is 12:25pm. I'm Detective Senior Constable Claire Perry and with me is Detective Senior Sergeant Tony Packer. We are at the East Perth Police Station. This interview is being recorded. Can you please state your full name?"

Felicity looked at her. "You know my name."

"It's for the recording," Perry explained, "Can you say it, please?"

"Oh, alright, then," Felicity said, vaguely irritated, "Felicity Anne Stewart."

"Date of birth."

Felicity gave a slight hiss of frustration. "25 January, 1964."

"Before we begin," Perry said, "I need to explain to you that you have certain rights."

"I know about that," Felicity said, "You went through all that before at the house."

"Yes, but I have to explain them again," Perry said, "You have the right to remain silent. During this interview either Detective Packer or myself may ask you questions. You do not have to answer any of those questions if you do not wish to do so. You may choose to answer some, all or none of those questions. Do you understand?"

Felicity gave another hiss of annoyance and nodded.

"You need to answer verbally," Perry explained, "Do you understand?"

"Yes," Felicity said, "I understand."

"If I ask you ten questions, how many do you have to answer?"

"None of them if I don't want to," Felicity said.

"You have the right to legal advice. You have said you do not want to see a solicitor. Is that correct?"

"I've seen enough solicitors lately with the Family Court rubbish, thank you."

"You have the right to medical treatment. You have told us that you do-"

"No, I don't need medical treatment."

"You have the right to speak to-"

"I don't want to speak to a friend or family member."

"Alright," Perry said, calmly.

She made some notes on her notebook.

"Now," Perry said, looking up, "We want to speak to you about your daughter, Kasey."

Felicity looked at Packer, her eyes emotionless.

"It was an accident," Felicity said.

Packer stared back at her.

"We'll come to that in a moment," Perry said, "but first I want to ask you about some background details."

"What's the point?" Felicity asked.

"It's just the procedure," Perry said.

Felicity gave a sigh and waved a hand in the air in defeat. "Alright, then. Whatever has to be done."

"What's Kasey's date of birth?"

"4 February, 1997."

"And who is Kasey's father?"

"My husband, Bill."

"So, you were how old when you had Kasey?"

"Thirty-three. I had a good career as an accountant. Had to give that up, of course."

"How did you feel about that?"

"Well, I wasn't happy. I'd spent eight years of hard work to get to be an associate principal at the firm I worked for. I would have been partner in a few more years if not for Kasey. Do you have any idea how hard it is for a woman to get ahead in a world dominated by men?"

Perry gave a wry smile. "Yes, I do. The police service isn't any different, believe me."

Felicity looked at her for a moment. Her annoyance dropped a notch.

"Yes, well. That was all lost when Kasey was born."

"Did you take maternity leave?" Perry asked.

Felicity shook her head. "No. It was a small firm and it was made clear to me that they couldn't bear the expense. Or didn't want to, anyway."

"I don't think it's optional. Even in 1997. They were required to provide it, weren't they?"

"Yes, and I could have insisted, but what would have been the point? If I had, I would never have been promoted after that. Either way, my career was destroyed."

"Why the decision to have Kasey, then?"

"Bill wanted children. I didn't." Felicity looked up at her, staring defiance. "When I found out I was pregnant, I booked in for a termination. Bill found out, though, and that was the end of that."

She shook her head. "So much trouble could have been avoided if he hadn't found out. We both would have been so much better off."

Perry looked down at her notepad and jotted a few pointless notes, letting the silence hang. Felicity waited.

"What was Kasey like as a child?" Perry asked after a moment, looking up again.

"Demanding," Felicity said, "Always demanding. Even as a baby, she was always difficult. Wouldn't sleep, wouldn't settle, wouldn't drink the formula. The second I sat down to do something on my own, she'd be yelling again."

Felicity gave a slight snort. "She always settled for Bill, of course. He would always say she was an easy baby, but he had no idea what she was like when he was out of the house.

"It got worse when she got older. Once she was old enough to talk, she was always demanding something. At least I got some peace when she was in daycare, but whenever she was at home, she was causing problems."

"What sort of problems?" Perry asked.

"Always looking for attention. Always wanted me to stop whatever I was doing to entertain her. If I left her on her own, she'd start crying and complaining."

"Didn't she have friends to play with?"

"Once she started school, she did. Alicia was always at our house. There was another girl before that, too. I can't remember her name. Lisa? Or Linda?

She had dark hair. I still couldn't get any peace, though. She was always running around with whichever one it was, yelling and causing a ruckus.

"It all stopped when Bill came home from work. She behaved perfectly for him."

Felicity's voice took on a note of anger. "Of course, I didn't know what she was up to, then. Not until much later."

Perry felt a surge of anger at that, but let it go. There would be time to draw that out later.

She made some more notes to create a pause.

"So, when Kasey was still a child, still at school, it was a difficult relationship between she and you?"

"Yes."

"But a much closer relationship between Kasey and Bill?"

"Yes, it was. He gave her anything she wanted."

"Did that bother you? That Kasey was closer to Bill than to you?"

"Yes, of course, it did. He should have been spending his time with me, not with her. But all he wanted to do was waste time with her. I was at home all day on my own, and as soon as he got home, he was playing silly games with her. Even if we went out for dinner or somewhere, he spent the whole time with her. Ignored me completely."

"Did this cause problems between you and Kasey?"

"She was the problem. She took away my career and then she took away my husband."

"Took him away in what sense?" Perry asked.

"She seduced him," Felicity said, almost spitting the words out, "Not satisfied with taking away his attention, she took that from me, too."

Felicity sat there, breathing harder. Her anger was almost physical.

"To be clear," Packer said, quietly, "What do you mean be 'seduced'?"

Felicity's eyes snapped around to him.

"She was sleeping with him."

"She was having sex with him?"

"Well, that is what 'sleeping with him,' means," Felicity said, as though talking to a child.

Packer kept his face blank.

He said nothing, waiting for Perry to resume.

"How old was Kasey when you first became aware that was happening?" Perry asked, after a moment.

Felicity let out a breath as she thought about it.

"Fourteen," she said, "There had been some sort of function at the school. An award night, or some rubbish. It was meaningless, of course. They give awards to all the students now, regardless of whether they've actually done anything to earn them. I was going to a friend's house for dinner, so Bill took Kasey along to the school.

"There was an argument at dinner, and I couldn't be bothered putting up with my friend's nonsense, so I left early. Bill and Kasey were already back from the school when I got home. They hadn't heard me come home. I was walking up the stairs towards the bedroom, when I heard them. They were in the bedroom together - in my bed - laughing and giggling. Making a fool of me. I was so angry, I went to the bathroom to clean off my makeup.

"When I returned after a few minutes, the laughing had stopped. They were making other noises now."

She fell silent, a look of fury on her face at the memory.

"What sort of noises?" Packer asked.

Felicity glared at him. "Do I have to spell it out, you idiot?"

"Yes, you do."

"They were having sex. In my bed. In my own bed!"

"Did that surprise you?" Packer asked.

"Not really. I'd suspected it was happening for a while before then. It just confirmed I already knew."

"What did you do when you heard them in the bedroom?" Packer asked.

"I went downstairs. Got myself a drink and watched television."

"You didn't confront them?"

Felicity shook her head angrily. "What would be the point? I knew what they were doing. And they knew I was aware of it."

"Did you see them that night?"

"Kasey went to bed. Hid from me. Maybe she felt some guilt, although I doubt it. Bill came down eventually. He asked how dinner was, attempted to make some idle conversation as though nothing had happened."

"Did anything change after that night?"

Felicity shrugged. "I was angry with them both for weeks afterwards. I went and stayed in a hotel for a time and thought about leaving. But it was my home. What right did they have to push me out? If Kasey wanted to take my place, then fine. Let her have Bill. She was welcome to him."

"Kasey was fourteen when this happened?" Packer asked.

"Aren't you paying attention? I told you that."

"You didn't think Bill might have been responsible for what happened, rather than Kasey?"

Felicity rolled her eyes. "Bill's a weak fool. He always has been. She'd had him on a leash since she was a small child. Once she got old enough to start developing *desires*, she simply took what she wanted. He was too weak to stand up to her."

"Did you confront either of them about this at a later time?"

"Why give them the satisfaction? I moved into the spare room. They made this pretence that everything was normal and waited until I was out of the house to carry on with this disgusting affair of theirs. They always made this pathetic attempt to hide it from me, as though I didn't know what they were doing."

"How long did this go on for?"

"It went on for years," Felicity said, spitting the words out, "Eventually, Kasey left. She finished high school and got a job somewhere in Sydney, so moved away. That's what she told Bill anyway. I never believed it."

"Did you keep in touch with Kasey after she left?"

"Bill tried. I never bothered. Why would I? After what she'd done to me. Bill was phoning her for a time, but eventually she stopped answering the phone and changed the number. Bill went looking for her, went all the way over to Sydney to find her, but the address she'd given him was false. She wasn't living there at all. She'd got what she wanted from him and moved on, washed her hands of him. Serves him right, useless fool that he is."

"Kasey eventually got in contact again, though?"

Felicity tutted and shook her head. "Yes. She turned up again. About a year ago, Bill came home one day, jumping with excitement. He'd been out somewhere and run into her, purely by chance. That was what he thought, anyway.

"She had a husband and a daughter now. She told Bill she'd started a new life and was happy."

Felicity gave a low hiss.

"But of course, it was just Kasey up to her old tricks again. She wanted something. She wanted money and a free babysitter. And something else."

Felicity looked up at them.

"She wanted my husband back again."

Chapter 36

"It was the most ridiculous thing," Felicity said, "We'd had some work done on the swimming pool and the repairman had dropped the motor from the pool filter on the edge, which had smashed one of the tiles. The pool had been put in twenty years ago, so they no longer made tiles that matched, but Bill hunted around everywhere for them. He finally found them at a tile supplier all the way down in Belmont. On the way back from the tile shop, he stopped in at the shopping centre to buy lunch.

"While he was there, Kasey walked past.

"She was pushing a stroller. Jessie was three years old. Our own granddaughter and Kasey hadn't even bothered to tell us. She was as selfish as always."

Felicity shook her head. "Anyway, Bill called out and chased after her. He told me she'd been wary at first, polite, but making this big show of not being sure if she wanted to get back in contact again. It was all an act, of course. She was just reeling Bill in.

"He wouldn't let her leave without sending her phone number to him and promising to get in touch. Then she strung him along for weeks, ignoring his calls until he was desperate to see her.

"Finally, she spoke to him and agreed to meet us.

"I should have put a stop to it right away. But I didn't."

Felicity fell silent again.

"So, you met?" Perry asked.

Felicity nodded. "They made an arrangement to meet at King's Park. When we turned up, there was no sign of Kasey. Bill wanted to phone her, but I told him he was being stupid. It was just Kasey playing games again. We were going to leave, but then they turned up. She and Jessie, and that pathetic creature she was married to."

"How did that meeting go?"

"It was disgusting. Bill was trying to act like everything was back to normal, saying they must come to our house for dinner one night and saying Jessie would love the pool. Kasey kept saying she'd think about it and saying she wanted to take things slowly. She was so good at it that I even half-believed it myself. But the whole thing was a big act to lure Bill back again. I know that now, of course."

"You did meet her again?"

"Not straight away. Another few weeks went by. Then we went to a restaurant for dinner. Bill insisted on paying for everything, and Deon certainly didn't put up a fight. Pathetic man.

"We did that a few more times, and then they came to our home. Eventually, we went to their house."

"You became more comfortable with each other again?"

"Bill did. He was acting like the past six years had never happened. I did my best to put the past behind us, but part of me knew it was a mistake. I couldn't stand Deon. He was like some tradesman who'd come to do the yard and wouldn't leave afterwards. I've no idea how Kasey ended up with someone so disgusting. I suppose it was just so that she could have Jessie. She certainly lost interest in him quickly enough once she realised she could have Bill again."

"You said you tried to put the past behind you. Were you happy about Kasey coming back into your lives?"

Felicity shrugged. "Obviously, there was still the hurt there. I knew what Kasey had done to me and nothing was ever going to change that. But it had been six years and I'd come to terms with it. There was Jessie, too, now. My granddaughter. So, I had to make allowances."

She raised a finger in the air.

"I told Bill, though, told him clearly. There could be no repeat of what had happened before. If I got even the faintest hint of anything happening between them, that was it. It was all over. I made it clear to him that if I had even the slightest hint of something starting again, I would leave him and take half the house and the money. He made this show of not knowing what I was talking about, but he said he'd go along with whatever he wanted because he just wanted Kasey to be part of our lives again."

She shook her head. "And that was fine for a few months. Deon had enough sense to stay away and then eventually, he left all together. It was a relief when he went. I couldn't stand the sight of him and I was glad he was gone.

"But then he started trying to take away my granddaughter. He must have known what Kasey was doing with Bill. The humiliation of being cuckolded. Trying to take Jessie away must have been his idea of revenge."

She gave a sigh. "And, of course, it fell to Bill and I to sort out the problems. Yet again, it was just take, take, take with Kasey. I made it clear that we were not going to give her money. She was an adult, and had to stand on her own two feet. So, then she started taking in other ways. We wouldn't give her money, so she got a job and it was left to me to babysit while she was away. She had been such a demanding child and now she was a demanding adult."

"Did you and Bill both baby-sit Jessie?" Perry asked.

"No," Felicity said, shaking her head, "It had to be me. Bill always wanted to. He loved Jessie, couldn't spend enough time with her. But Kasey insisted that it was me. Insisted that it had to be me, not Bill. It was her playing her games again.

"So, it fell into a pattern. I would go to Kasey's house after dinner and she would go to work. She would put Jessie to bed before she left and I'd sleep at the house overnight. Kasey would come home in the early hours and in the morning, I'd go home."

"How did Bill feel about that arrangement?"

Felicity gave a humourless grin. "Well, he said he wasn't happy about it. He said he wanted to baby-sit sometimes, but Kasey wouldn't agree.

"It turned out that was just part of the show, didn't it? Kasey wanted me to look after Jessie because it left her free to start things up with Bill again."

"How did you find out about that?"

"I didn't know for a long time. Fool that I was, I thought Bill would listen to me when I warned him."

She sighed. "And then Kasey got into trouble with the drugs. She needed thousands of dollars to pay off the drug dealer, or he would harm her and Jessie. So yet again, Kasey came with her hand out, wanting to take more from me. But she had put Jessie at risk, so what choice did I have?

"Bill and I had an equity account attached to the house for emergencies. It was there just in case. We didn't use it - or so I thought anyway. I thought if I drew the three thousand from that account, Bill would never know.

"But then, when I went to the account, there were thousands gone. Thousands and thousands. Bill had been giving all this money to Kasey, thinking I would never check the account. She was using it all for drugs, of course, although Bill would never have known that."

Felicity shook her head angrily. "I knew then. She was doing it again. Sleeping with him behind my back. Filthy harlot that she was, she couldn't keep her hands off him."

Felicity lapsed into silence.

"You didn't confront them?" Perry prompted.

"I thought about confronting Bill, daring him to deny it. But I didn't. A part of me still wanted to believe it wasn't happening. So, I went to Kasey's house as usual. She put Jessie to bed and told me she was going to work.

"I followed her. I had to wait until she left before going to the car, so she wouldn't see me, but I managed to catch up with her at the traffic lights. It was dark and it was raining hard, so she didn't see me driving behind her.

"I followed her all the way across the city to Elizabeth Quay. I watched her park at the Convention Centre, then walk down towards the river. She'd changed her clothes, put on a tiny dress and high heels for him. Slut. As soon as I saw her, I knew what she was doing.

"She went into Ritz-Carlton. The Ritz-Carlton. Bill had never taken me to the Ritz-Carlton, but she was making him take her there, and only for them to rut like rabbits. It was disgusting.

"I parked on the other side to wait. Sat there and waited. Then it began raining. It was so hard I was worried I wouldn't be able to see her come out. But I did."

"She was inside all night. All night with my husband.

"When she came out, she was with Bill. Hand-in-hand. They stood on the steps and kissed, then he left.

"And Kasey began running through the rain, back towards the Convention Centre.

"I wanted to talk to her. Demand to know what she was doing, how she thought she could take Bill away from me again.

"But it was raining so heavily and it was growing worse. I tried to pull over beside her, to tell her to get in, out of the rain. But the car skidded on the wet road and slid onto the footpath. I didn't even realise I had hit her until it was too late.

"I panicked after that and drove away. I managed to get a hold of myself a few blocks away and went back to help her, but by the time I got back there, the police were already there and I knew there was nothing more that I could do to help."

Felicity looked up at them. "It was terrible. Such a terrible accident."

Packer looked silently at Felicity. Beside him, he could feel the tension in Perry as she struggled to remain silent. Her pen was pushed against the page.

"Tell us about the point when the car slid up onto the footpath," Packer said, after a moment, "How was it facing?"

"The same direction as the road," Felicity said, "but it skidded. The rain was so heavy, you see."

"How did you get back onto the road again?"

"I simply drove forward and turned away from the footpath. I know I should have stopped, but I wasn't thinking clearly. Accidents do that to you, I'm told. The shock of it."

"You just drove forward?"

"Yes, I did."

"Didn't reverse?"

"No, of course not. Why would I?"

"Didn't the bollards get in the way?"

"Are there bollards there? I didn't notice them. It was very hard to see in the rain. I must have slipped between them when the car skidded."

"When you saw Kasey coming out of the hotel, was she wearing any jewellery?"

There was a slight twitch in Felicity's left eye. It was barely noticeable, but it was there.

"It's so hard to remember. No, I don't think so. I don't think she was."

"A necklace?"

The flare in her eye was much stronger now. Her jaw clenched visibly.

She shook her head.

"The Egyptian necklace that cost $42,000?" Packer asked, "One of his grand gestures. One that Bill paid for using the equity account. Behind your back."

Felicity glared at him, her fury written across her face.

"The necklace that Bill bought for Kasey," Packer asked, "and not for you."

Felicity's face was beginning to colour. A flush of red spread out across her cheeks, as she fought to keep her anger under control.

Silently, she glared at Packer.

"Did it make you jealous seeing her wearing it?" Packer asked, "Angry? Is that why you killed her? Why you stood beside her body and took the necklace?"

Felicity twitched slightly, the raw anger making her muscles spasm slightly.

For a long moment, her eyes were locked on Packer's.

He could feel it below the surface, so close.

But he knew it would never come.

The colour began to fade from Felicity's cheeks. She took a breath and let it out slowly.

"Is there some evidence of that, Mr Packer?" she asked, "No? Then you must be mistaken about that. I didn't see any necklace. Or her handbag. Someone else must have taken them."

She looked at Packer. "It was an accident. I lost control in the rain, as I said."

Packer looked at her a moment longer, holding her eyes with his.

Eventually, he nodded.

"Interview terminated at 1:45pm," he said.

Chapter 37

Perry stood inside the entranceway of Bill and Felicity Stewart's house.

Two uniformed officers were in the lounge room, with Jessie Stewart, a man and a woman. The male officer was hiding behind the couch on the other side, popping his head up and making a silly face.

Jessie laughed as she watched.

The officer ducked down below the couch again and the female officer asked, "Where's Matty gone? Matty, where are you?"

Matty crawled across to the other side of the couch and stuck his head around the side, making Jessie laugh again.

"Felicity's going to get away with it," Perry said, "There's no way to prove it was deliberate."

Packer was silent.

"There's circumstantial evidence," Perry went on, "but not enough. The FME will say she had two sets of tyre marks, but that doesn't prove it wasn't an accident. The handbag and the necklace were missing, but they could have been stolen by someone else in the half hour before police arrived."

Packer nodded.

"All she confessed to is failing to stop after an accident," Perry said, "I don't know that she'd even get jail time for that."

Packer watched in silence, as Abigail Moore from Family Services entered from the other end of the lounge room. The man with her was carrying a pink backpack, and had a well-worn pink rabbit under his arm.

"Just your bag and the rabbit, Jessie," Moore said, "Is that all your gran brought from your place, love?"

Jessie looked up at her, her smile disappearing.

She nodded mutely.

"Okay, good," Moore said, "We've got those, so we're ready to go."

Jessie turned her head to look at the female police officer.

She nodded at Jessie. "It'll be okay, Jess. Abigail's gonna find you somewhere nice to stay."

Jessie shook her head, tears appearing in her eyes.

She leaned forward, rubbing against the female officer.

"Oh, it's okay, Jess," the officer said, trying not to cry herself, "It'll work out alright. You'll see."

She hugged Jessie for a long moment, while Jessie cried against her chest.

Eventually, she unwrapped her arms from around Jessie and put her hands on her tiny shoulders. Gently, she moved Jessie away from her.

Moore reached out to take Jessie's hand.

Jessie let her hold it, but sat on the couch, looking down at the floor.

"Come on, love," said Moore, "It's time to go."

She pulled a little harder, firmly pulling Jessie up into a standing position. Clearly, this was not the first time she had done this.

Packer and Perry watched in silence as Jessie was led out of the room to the front door.

The two uniformed officers followed behind, offering encouragement.

Perry watched through the curtains, as Jessie walked down the path, holding Moore's hand. She and the man put Jessie in the back of a car and drove away.

"All done," Perry said to the two uniformed officers, "Have you got the key? I'll give it to the owner when she's released from custody."

"How come she's not taking Jessie?" the male officer asked.

"She doesn't want her," Perry said.

"Really? Her own granddaughter."

"Believe it or not," Perry said, "It's probably best she doesn't."

They left the house and pulled the door closed behind them.

The two uniformed officers returned to their own car.

Packer and Perry walked out to their car. Packer got into the driver's seat.

"Poor girl," Perry said, putting on her seatbelt, "Losing her mother and being brought up by strangers in foster homes. How's she going to live a normal life after that? It'd ruin anyone's chances."

Packer started the engine.

"There are worse things," he said.

***

The boy placed a long, white sachet of sugar on top of another, then a third on top of that.

His small face crinkling in a frown of concentration, he reached for a fourth and slowly placed it on top of the pile.

He held it in place for a moment, then gently began to open his fingers, carefully releasing the edges of the long, flat packet.

The sachet rested there without moving.

The boy reached for another sachet.

As he did so, the pile toppled over, collapsing into a heap beside his mother's coffee cup.

He gave a small sigh of frustration, unnoticed by his mother, who was still talking animatedly to the other woman sitting at the table.

The boy looked up and glanced around the room.

He discovered Packer watching him from the next table and gave a guilty grin.

Packer gave him a half-smile in return, then nodded towards the packets of sugar.

The boy grinned and picked up the first packet again.

Packer looked at his watch, then around the coffee shop.

He took in a breath and let it out slowly.

He was struggling to stay awake now. It had been four days since he had slept and he was exhausted.

His wall was behind his chair and he leaned back against it, feeling the cool wood against the back of his head.

He closed his eyes.

Just for a moment.

He felt her lips on his and inhaled the scent of jasmine.

Chandra sat down beside him, as he opened his eyes.

The next table was empty. The boy and his mother were gone.

"You're a really lousy date, you know that?" Chandra asked, "I arrive and you're fast asleep."

"You were late," Packer said.

"I was busy. Other people appreciate my time more than you do."

"I appreciate your time," Packer protested, "I could be home in bed right now."

"You could," Chandra agreed, "but I'm on call until five. You'll have to wait until then."

He felt himself grin.

"And I don't have a lot of time for lunch," Chandra said, picking up a menu, "so let's eat."

Packer reached out and took the menu from her hands. He turned it over to the back, where it read, 'All Day Breakfast'.

"Ohh," Chandra said, fluttering her eyelids at him, "You're such a romantic."

She pushed her chair back to stand up.

"I'll order," he said.

"No, you stay here," Chandra said, "I'm not confident you can stay awake long enough to make it to the counter."

She walked across the coffee shop towards the counter to stand behind another woman placing an order. He watched her narrow hips sway as she walked.

Still feeling tired, he leaned back in the chair.

The lunchtime crowd had moved on now, and there were only a few people left in the shop. It wasn't the most luxurious place in Perth, but it was halfway between the police station and the hospital.

Something caught Packer's eye.

A newspaper had been left on one of the nearby tables beside a dirty plate and a coffee cup, waiting for the waitress to clear it away. The front of the newspaper had a headline reading, 'New Development Approved,' above a photo of a man holding one hand in the air, waving to the crowd.

Packer got up and walked across to the table to collect the newspaper.

He returned to his own table and skimmed over the article.

The government had just approved the development of six tower blocks, containing 230 apartments, on the former site of a railway holding yard. The article outlined how the development would 'provide luxury housing for the rapidly-growing population of Western Australia and represent a significant investment for the city of Rockingham'.

Packer began to frown, as he continued reading the article.

'The development is a joint project,' the article read, 'bringing together funding from the state government's Urban Renewal Committee and private enterprise. Now that funding has been approved by parliament, the project will commence construction by its joint-financier, P&R Developments'.

Packer felt his stomach clench, as he read the name.

He looked at the photo above the article.

Raising his hand and waving to the crowd was Jim Chalmers, the member for Rockingham and the man who appeared in the videos on Frank McCain's USB drive.

Chalmers grinned as he proudly announced the project he was constructing with P&R Developments, the shelf company that acted as a front for Jeffrey Frazier, the man who had recently gotten away with the murder of Emily Mtuba.

***

PACKER RETURNS IN
WEAVING SORROW

***

If you enjoyed this book, please leave me a rating and/or a review on Amazon and Goodreads. I really appreciate your support.

To join my mailing list and receive news on work-in-progress and new releases, please e-mail me at james.viner.author@gmail.com. I will never provide your e-mail address to any third party.

About the Author

JT Viner was a prosecutor for the *Office of the Director of Public Prosecutions* in Perth, Western Australia, for over fifteen years.

During that time, he conducted criminal trials for murder, rape, abduction, child sex offending, armed robbery and other serious offences.

He spent fifteen years learning the investigative methods of the police force and the inner workings of the criminal mind.

His books are inspired by real crimes.

Printed in Great Britain
by Amazon